Jane
AND THE Year
Without
a Summer

BEING A
JANE AUSTEN
MYSTERY

Jane
AND THE Year
Without
a Summer

STEPHANIE
BARRON

SOHO
CRIME

Published by
Soho Press, Inc.
227 W 17th Street
New York, NY 10011

Library of Congress Cataloging-in-Publication Data

Names: Barron, Stephanie, author.
Title: Jane and the year without a summer / Stephanie Barron.
Description: New York : Soho Crime, [2022]
Series: Being a Jane Austen mystery ; 14
Identifiers: LCCN 2021029618

ISBN 978-1-64129-409-6
eISBN 978-1-64129-248-1

Subjects: LCSH: Austen, Jane, 1775-1817—Fiction.
LCGFT: Biographical fiction. | Detective and mystery fiction.
Historical fiction. | Novels.
Classification: LCC PS3563.A8357 J43 2022 | DDC 813/.54—dc23
LC record available at https://lccn.loc.gov/2021029618

Interior art and title design: Jim Tierney
Interior design by Janine Agro, Soho Press, Inc.

Printed in the United States of America

10 9 8 7 6 5 4 3 2 1

Item 71: Have Mom dedicate one of her books to me.
Item 72: Learn to read.

#StridersBucketList

This latest Jane is dedicated to Strider, the Very Good Boy who helped me write it, but was forced to leave us before it was published. We love you, Strides. Give Jane a big wet sloppy kiss for me, wherever you both are.

Jane AND THE Year Without a Summer

1

CONSULTING THE APOTHECARY

Monday, 20th May, 1816
Chawton

"**A**unt Jane!"

I closed the door of Mr. Curtis's apothecary shop behind me and glanced along the Alton High Street in search of my niece Cassie's slight figure. I found her instantly, gloved hand swinging from Fanny's elegant one, as the two picked their way through the fresh puddles that dotted the paving. Cassie, at seven years the eldest of my brother Charles's three motherless girls, gloried in the undivided attention of her fashionable and much-older cousin, and her cheeks were flushed with pleasure. The young woman by her side appeared unconscious of the child's admiration—having such a number of younger brothers and sisters, Fanny is well accustomed to adoration. At three-and-twenty, she retains her freshness of countenance, aligned with a genius for millinery, that must beguile every eye. A number of heads turned to follow the two bright countenances along the country-town street; but even in London, I suspect, Fanny would not pass unnoticed.

"She has been spoiling the child again," my sister Cassandra observed indulgently; and indeed, Cassie clutched in her free hand a twisted bit of brown paper fresh from the local confectioner's. A few boiled sweets, perhaps, purchased with the pennies Fanny had pressed into her palm while The Aunts, as both girls call us, conducted our business with Mr. Curtis. Harmless enough; the Lord knows that treats come only rarely in poor Cassie's way. With my brother Charles presently at sea, his daughters have been consigned to the care of his late wife's sister in London. I am sure that Miss Palmer is a very good sort of woman, who loves Charles's children as her own; but her serviceable charms cannot equal in Cassie's estimation the superior claims of Miss Fanny Austen Knight, of Godmersham Park in Kent—handsome, clever, and rich—who saunters with such ease down Alton's modest streets, a frivolous silk parasol dangling from her hand.

Fanny and her father, my brother Edward, have been visiting us at Chawton Cottage this past fortnight, and Cassie this past month; a happy coincidence that provided both my nieces with interest and amusement, despite the fifteen years' difference in their ages.

"You have been prompt in your consultation," Fanny observed, as she came up with us on the High. "I did not think to meet you for another quarter-hour at least."

"Mr. Curtis's opinions were succinct," I replied. "He looked at me—and *into* me, by way of a lanthorn beam directed down my throat—and pronounced me in want only of a period of rest and refreshment."

I spoke with determined cheerfulness, for in all truth I

have not been very stout of late, and at my sister Cassandra's urging had at last sought the advice of the Alton apothecary. Lassitude, a want of spirits, and a persistent pain in my back dogged me throughout the winter months. The spring has been wretched and stillborn, with incessant rain, but we look forward to a June of warmth and sun—and with the summer months, an improvement in my animation and health. Mr. Curtis has a yet more active recommendation; but of this, I said nothing to my nieces. My intelligence would keep until we achieved our home in Chawton.

"Rest and refreshment!" Fanny exclaimed darkly. "And how are you likely to obtain either, pray, with all the world pulling up at your door? I shall inform Papa that we may certainly not delay our departure beyond Wednesday."

"Wednesday!" Cassie cried out in disappointment. "When we were to walk to the fair on Alton Green to meet Cousin Caroline! She was to have shown me her doll, and permitted me to change its clothes. It is too *bad*, Fanny!"

"Hush, child," Cassandra said in mild reproof. "You would not be wishing Fanny to think that the unhappiness of a treat denied, is heavier than the pain of parting with her!"

Cassie flushed, looked all her mortification, and hung her head.

Fanny squeezed the little girl's hand. "The fair begins tomorrow. I shall certainly find occasion to walk with you in the morning, instead of Wednesday." Then, glancing at me, she continued, "It is scandalous how all your brothers presume upon the good nature of Chawton Cottage, Aunt. One might suppose you were running a boardinghouse explicitly for the

4 · STEPHANIE BARRON

care of elderly gentlemen, tossed and wracked by sudden ill-fortune!"

I smiled, for Fanny spoke with a cajoling good humour; but in truth her jest was not far off the mark. Since the first of the year, my brothers have met with so many crushing blows that the Austen family appears set apart by Providence for a collective trial of faith.

First, Henry's banks in London and Hampshire were ruined—the result of a plunge in receipts following the defeat of Buonaparte at Waterloo. With the Peace has come a bitter decline in the Kingdom's economy, and the bankruptcies of the Great are strewn everywhere in the newspapers. Henry was obliged to give up his offices in Henrietta Street, near Covent Garden, and his home at Hans Place—his worldly goods sold at auction—the proceeds being turned over to his creditors.

The month of March saw Henry arrived at our cottage door, with no home or coin to his name; and having welcomed all of us so generously over the years in each of his houses, he could expect nothing less in return. At the advanced age of four-and-forty, he determined to take Divine Orders—and worked up a fair proficiency in schoolboy Greek against the event. Having travelled in April to Winchester to present his catechism, however, my brother was disappointed to pass through the archbishop's hands without the slightest inter-rogation. It seems the archbishop's Greek is even worse than Henry's.

This will be the fourth or fifth career our quicksilver brother has chosen; I cannot pretend to number his many roles over the course of his life; but a clergyman's lot bids fair to be as happy a choice as any. It must be disinterested, at least. Henry means to fill the office of *curate* here in Chawton—a post in Edward's gift. He will earn a mere fifty-two guineas per annum. How far my brother has strayed from his days among the Great at White's Club and Carlton House!

"Will your papa be ready to journey into Kent so soon as Wednesday?" I enquired of Fanny as our small party turned back along the High in the direction of the post office. This was always our final errand before the mile of exertion that lay between Alton and Chawton village.

"I believe he will." Fanny lent me the support of her arm, and I was grateful to accept. "His business was concluded some days since."

Her papa's business, as she called it, had been tiresome, complex, and unremittingly lowering, being financial in nature. Edward is come into Hampshire to meet with his solicitor, young Mr. Trimmer. One could hardly discover from Fanny's clear-eyed looks that the Austen Knights had been burdened with acute anxiety these several months; tho' I am certain she is wholly aware of her father's obligations and cares. It must be Fanny's concern to show an unruffled front to the world.

My Uncle Leigh-Perrot and my brother Edward together had pledged some thirty thousand pounds (!) in surety against the loans made by Henry's bank—an enormous sum, now irrevocably lost. My brothers Frank and James were similarly stripped of lesser investments, equally vital to each. Even *I* was so unfortunate as to lose £13.*7s.0d.* of my earnings from

Mansfield Park—entrusted to my account in the Henrietta Street branch. My sick horror at the extent of our collective misfortune is compounded by the fact that Frank, James, and Henry are obliged now to retrench and economise. They must therefore suspend their annual monetary gifts to my mother's household. Each was in the habit of contributing fifty pounds per annum for the Austen ladies' maintenance, and the want of funds must be felt by all four of us who live so simply beneath the cottage roof.

Edward has assured us his support shall be unchanged; but as if all this were not enough, the detestable Hintons— our neighbours at Chawton Lodge—persist in their lawsuit against my brother's Hampshire estates.[1] They have wearied Edward two years already with their dark hints, writs, and indignation—and the affair does not appear any closer to settlement.

As though my mental powers had conjured him, a rough-hewn fellow in brown serge leggings swung through the broad door of the brewery as we came abreast of its odorous yard. A

---

1 John Knight-Hinton (1774–1851) and his nephew, James Hinton-Baverstock, were lateral descendants of the Knight family of Chawton, which owned considerable estates in Hampshire and Kent. In 1814 the two men sued Jane's brother, Edward Austen Knight, contesting his right to inherit from his adoptive father, Thomas Knight II (1735–94). Knight's primary residence was Godmersham Park, Kent, where he was active as a member of Parliament for two decades. He and his wife, Catherine Knatchbull, were childless. In 1783 Thomas Knight adopted Edward Austen, a distant maternal cousin, as his heir when Edward was sixteen years of age. In 1812, by then the widowed father of eleven children, Edward took the surname Knight. The Hinton lawsuit dragged on until 1818, when the case settled for £15,000.—*Editor's note.*

carved pipe stem was clenched between his teeth. Removing this with one hand and doffing his cap with the other, he inclined his head.

"Miss Austen," he said to Cassandra. His small dark eyes ignored me to rove instead over Fanny's neat figure. "And Miss Fanny Austen."

"It is Miss *Knight*, sir," Fanny said quietly—the name she adopted four years ago.

He grinned with cheeky insolence. "Not for much longer, I daresay."

We passed on without another word, but I am sure I was not the only one of our party to feel Mr. James Hinton-Baverstock's gaze boring into my back. The brewer is a clever and rather scampish fellow, nephew to the very Hintons whose desire for ill-got wealth plagues my brother. They, along with their cousins the Dusautoys—respectable tradesmen who own the upholsterers' shop further up the High—claim descent from the Knights of Chawton; and together they allege that poor Edward has conspired to rob them of their rightful inheritance. They beg the courts to turn over all Edward's Hampshire holdings, including Chawton Cottage, to themselves. This must be mere groundless Devilry, to be sure, as Edward's adoptive patron, Sir Thomas Knight, long ago broke his family entail in my brother's favour. But the Law may yet strike a whimsical justice, and strip Edward of two-thirds of his fortune, leaving only his estate in Kent—an unspeakable loss after Henry's bankruptcy. Needless to say, the prospect of giving up our cottage to the Hintons—or worse yet, being obliged to pay them rent—must make us uneasy, tho' we would not speak of it before Fanny for the world.

"May I fetch the mail?" Cassie begged, her hands clasped, "by myself? While the rest of you wait here?"

"If you promise faithfully not to read any of it before us." Cassandra attempted to look severe.

"Upon my honour, Aunt, I should not dream of doing so."

Fanny opened her reticule. "Pray, Cassie, place these letters in the outgoing bag." She handed three folded and sealed sheets of hot-pressed paper to her young cousin. "And here are some coins, against the postage, for any letters you receive from the postmistress."

"You cannot be franking our mail, Fanny," I scolded, as Cassie hurried off on her errand.

"Why not? I derive so much amusement from it; your correspondents are invariably droll."

We were in the habit of reading our letters aloud by the fire after supper. The missives from Edward's boys at Winchester were particularly delightful; those from brother James's wife, Mary, amusing in their self-absorption.

Cassie thrust herself back through the post office door in an excess of excitement. "Fanny! Aunts! Only think—there are *two* letters from Papa! I knew his fist as soon as ever I saw it!"

"His *handwriting*, Cassie," my sister corrected, but I was already sorting the letters in search of Charles's. These would not keep until we reached the cottage; poor Cassie was hopping on one foot to know what her papa had written—whether he was well—if he should be granted leave to be at home before the summer was ended . . .

From the multiple directions scribbled and marked out on the cover of Charles's first letter, it had passed through the hands of too many captains on the Mediterranean Station before reaching England. The second bore a more recent date, and had been sent out from Gibraltar. It was not uncommon for correspondence to be held in suspense, only to arrive in a heap; such are the vagaries of the Royal Navy. I broke the seal of the older missive and glanced at the date.

"But he wrote this in February!" I quickly skimmed the page, which was covered and then crossed again in Charles's fine, flowing script. "Your papa is very well, Cassie. He has been so far as Egypt! And quit his ship in Alexandria to see the ancient city, where he purchased some views of the port in watercolours, which he means to show you once he is come home. Here is something exciting . . . Papa has chased a party of desperate pirates along the coast of North Africa . . . Only think if they should have a chest filled with treasure aboard!"

I continued my perusal silently, absorbed in my particular little brother's words. Then of a sudden I gasped, and placed my fingers to my lips.

"Jane?" Cassandra touched my arm.

"Aunt?" Fanny murmured.

I glanced down at Cassie's small face, which had flushed red, then paled. Wordlessly, I opened Charles's second letter and devoured the intelligence. Then I drew breath and attempted a smile. "It is nothing, truly—only what might happen to any captain in the Royal Navy! Your papa's ship, Cassie, was wrecked off the coast of Smyrna—nearly two months ago."

The child gave a sharp cry. Fanny gathered her close.

"But Papa and his crew are safe and well in Gibraltar," I assured them. "Indeed, Charles is even now en route to London. If we are *very* fortunate, we may have him with us in a matter of weeks!"

2

SHIPWRECKED HOPES

Monday, 20th May, 1816
Chawton, cont'd.

"What do you consider the most likely result of Charles's misfortune?" I asked my brother quietly. Edward was warming his hands at the fire in the dining parlour. We had just risen from the table, having enjoyed a repast of fresh lamb brought especially from Godmersham, his Kentish estate. My mother's vegetable garden had provided new peas, and the cellar some of last year's potatoes. In the presence of Cassie and my mother—each likely to be overset with anxiety, according to their respective ages—we had avoided canvassing poor Charles's news. But now I lingered after the others had removed to the sitting-room, from a desire to know my elder brother's mind.

"From his account, Charles ought not to be blamed," Edward replied, knitting his brows as he gazed into the glowing coals. "He states precisely that the *Phoenix* foundered in a hurricane—and due to the carelessness of the native pilots, who drove her onto the rocks."

Phoenix was the name of my brother's frigate; he had been

in command of her some years. "He cannot be blamed, to be sure," I agreed, "but as captain, can he not be held *responsible*?"

A faint and somewhat grim smiled flickered over Edward's lips. "How like you, Jane, to cast the dilemma in words of dueling precision! Yes, Charles will certainly be held responsible—and accountable—for the wreck of the *Phoenix*, blameless tho' he be. Indeed, he may never get another ship."

I sighed in vexation. "That is unjust!"

"Charles advises us he must appear before an Admiralty Board of Review. When His Majesty's vessels go to the bottom, with or without their crews, such authority is empaneled to mete out guilt—as well as punishment. Being unable to flog, demote, or demand restitution of the native pilots long since set down in Smyrna, the Admiralty may find satisfaction in ordering the frigate captain—in this case, Charles—permanently ashore."

I shivered, and joined Edward on the hearth; despite the advanced date in May, the evening was drawing in with a chill, and the blight of further rain. "I suppose now the Monster is at St. Helena and the war over, Charles is unlikely to win further prizes or advancement in any case. But, oh, Edward—that his career should founder with his ship! If he should be stripped of rank—struck from the Navy List and the pay that comes with it—what is to become of his little girls?"

My brother laid his arm about my shoulders and drew me close. "We must hope for better, my dear. Do not be entirely cast down. Think how Charles is everywhere admired by his fellows! How otherwise unblemished has been his decade of service. How much praise was heaped upon him for his blockade of Marshal Murat, at Naples, two years since, commanding this very same *Phoenix*! And Charles is an excellent witness on his own behalf—so clear in his histories, so meticulous in his ordering of events. Only consider the case he makes for himself in this letter."

Edward wished to persuade me out of my fears, but I could not shake off worry. Our whole family has suffered too much ill-fortune this winter for optimism to seem advisable. "But will this panel of admirals credit his account?"

"If they possess either conscience or understanding."

"Let there be one man among them who regards Charles as his enemy," I mused, "—from pettiness, jealousy, or excessive regard for a rival in the Service—and the temptation to see our brother ruined must be great."

"Do not borrow trouble, Jane." Edward met my gaze, his own sombre. "It cannot improve Charles's chances, and will only disorder your sleep. You must endeavour to divert your mind, my dear—and await the outcome as our sister Cassandra does: with cheerfulness and sanguine hope."

"What is this, Edward?" I rallied him. "Enjoining me to imitate *Cassandra*—who performs every duty in life with a grace that is truly Angelic—when you know me constitutionally incapable? I shall never have her goodness!"

But my brother did not smile; instead, he searched my countenance. "You take too much upon yourself, Jane—the cares of the whole family. I confess I have wished I might spare you even a part of it. Will you consider returning into Kent with Fanny and me, so soon as Wednesday? Let us cosset you for a little. I am sure a month at Godmersham would do you good. You might even *write*, without interruption!"

I hesitated, then glanced over my shoulder towards the sitting-room. The sound of Fanny's gentle murmur drifted along the passage. "That is very kind in you, Edward, but as it happens, I have a different scheme in hand, and mean to act upon it immediately."

His eyes narrowed in speculation. "What sort of scheme?"

"One of heedless dissipation and stolen freedom," I confided. "Do but think, Edward! I mean to spend *an entire fortnight* away from home, with only Cassandra for company!"

He looked bewildered, as well he might; we Austen ladies rarely quit Chawton unless it is to visit one of our brothers. "But where are you going, Jane?"

"Cheltenham Spa!" I told him triumphantly. "We mean to take lodgings, and stroll with the *ton* about the Arcade, and eat ices and drink French wine, and be above vulgar economy! For *two whole* weeks, Edward. And you are not to be worrying that we will be a charge upon Mamma's purse, or hanging on your sleeve. I mean to treat Cassandra. A small part of my profits from *Emma* should meet the expence handsomely."

"Cheltenham," he repeated. "Do you mean to take the waters, then?"

"Perhaps." I shrugged, as tho' the thought had only just come to me. "Cassandra may wish to do so, to be sure, and I shall be happy to indulge her whims. Perhaps by the time we return from our journey into Gloucestershire, Charles's Board of Review will have declared him blameless!"

"You consulted Curtis today in Alton, did you not?" Edward persisted. "—The apothecary?"

"I did." Now it was my turn to stare at him. "I wished to procure a trifling sleeping draught."

"And what did Curtis advise—regarding your trifling draught?"

"He was warm in his praise of an infusion of chamomile before bed."

"You pecked like a bird at dinner," Edward observed. "Indeed, this past fortnight you have eaten too sparingly."

"Pooh." I turned away. "Go and join the others; I shall just fetch the herb for my tea. Cassandra is sure to have chamomile put by in her stillroom."

"The waters at Cheltenham are chalybeate," Edward said. "Rich in iron. Ideal for those who suffer, Jane, from disorders of the bowels. Is this why Curtis would send you there?"

I waggled my fingers dismissively at him. "Perhaps! But if we persist in gossiping here all night, your tea shall be cold. Do leave off your questions, Edward, and join the others in the sitting-room—before I am out of all patience with you!"

3

THE WAGES OF SIN

Thursday, 23rd May, 1816
Steventon Rectory

Wednesday morning, wet and grey, saw us collected in the cottage doorway, bidding *adieu* to Edward and Fanny, whose progress towards Kent would be tediously encumbered by the mire and mud of country lanes. Fanny is an excellent traveller, however, and had her sketchbook, her needlework, and a small chess board at hand. My brother meant to ride his gelding alongside the travelling-coach, regardless of the driving rain. They would change horses in Basingstoke and rest this night at the Bear in Reading.

When the last bandbox had been strapped on behind and the last handkerchief waved, Cassandra and I hurried inside to attend to our own packing. We meant to quit Chawton for Cheltenham the next morning, and were prepared to break our journey twice—first at brother James's in Steventon, where we would set down Cassie for a visit with her cousin Caroline; and again Friday night in Swindon, where we had written ahead to bespeak a room at the Crown.

Saturday should see us arrived in Cheltenham—and though

the miles we must travel that day are long, we should not be too late, I hope, for dinner.

"I AM SURE I should benefit immeasurably from a fortnight at Cheltenham," Mary observed, from her position on the rectory sopha. "It has been an age since I was last there—full three years!—and I am sure the waters set me up remarkably when I took them. Indeed, I should profit as much from the change of Society and relief of boredom as anything else. You might have considered *me*, Jane, when you contemplated your scheme. I might have borne you company as easily as Cassandra, and my health been improved beyond recognition, if only you had thought of someone other than yourselves. But it is always the way, I find; others may run madcap about the country, in search of dissipation and pleasure, while I am expected to remain confined and quiet at home."

I had anticipated a variation on this speech from Mary, who generally met the happiness of her friends with indignation. "We made our plans in haste, my dear, but perhaps on another occasion—"

"Have you been unwell?" Cassandra enquired with an expression of sympathy.

"These three months and more," Mary replied, and closed her eyes with a sigh. "My strength ebbing—my chest wracked with pains—my nerves worn to a thread . . . and James so unfeeling for all I suffer! He shall be sorry, I suppose, when I am cold in my grave."

Cassandra managed a soothing noise and untied the strings

of her bonnet. It was quite wet. James keeping no carriage, we had travelled the seven miles from Basingstoke to Steventon in a hired open cart, and a shower of rain.

I studied my brother's wife an instant—Mary was swathed in a variety of shawls drawn close about her person, and I suspected her of wearing a quantity of flannel next to her skin, beneath the faded muslin dress that late May demanded. I cannot, in truth, blame her—Cassandra and I were chilled through, and I feared Cassie might have been so unfortunate as to have taken a cold in the head. There was no fire, however, in the rectory grate; and my boots were uncomfortably damp. How like James's wife to languish in misery in a cold parlour, like an heroine in a Gothic novel, in the hope her husband should discover her in a swoon, and exclaim all his remorse romantickly over her insensible head!

"Drusilla!" I called down the passage to the maid-of-all-work. "Some kindling and a supply of wood, if you please!"

Mary's head rose abruptly from her couch. "We never have fires in the rooms after April, Jane. The economies of a country parsonage do not run to extravagance."

Having been raised myself in this very parsonage, when my far more harassed father had stretched his living to feal eight children and numerous pupils lodged in the atticks, I had only one word for this.

"Nonsense," I said briskly. "We are perishing of cold. I shall press a few shillings upon James in recompense if that will make you easy, Mary."

"I suppose you have any amount of funds to waste," my brother's voice said drily from the doorway, "now that your shocking novels have gained the notice of the Prince Regent."

I turned and smiled at him. He could only be referring to my spoiled child *Emma*, which had been published so recently as January and dedicated, much against my wishes, to the odious Prince. "James! You are looking very well!"

He crossed the room and kissed Cassandra's cheek, but only inclined his head to me. "That any female of my acquaintance should find her name bandied about among the *Carlton House Set*! And for a work of such sustained frivolity as *Emma*! This is the result of too much indulgence, Jane. Too much licence, indeed, long accorded to a feverish imagination. I blame my father—may he rest in peace, poor soul. He ought never to have encouraged your writing; the female mind is too weak to support the rigors of composition, and must necessarily fall into vice."

"I apprehend you have been composing your sermon, James." I beamed at him with unruffled serenity. "How unfortunate that we shall not be with you this Sunday to hear it! We might have benefited so much; I am sure you are everything that is earnest and forthright on the subject of women's weakness."

My brother looked startled. "Are you quitting us so soon? And leaving the *child* completely to our care?"

"Only the deepest anxiety for Jane's welfare would drive us from the door," Cassandra attempted. "She has been most unwell of late, James, and Mr. Curtis is insistent on the benefits of Cheltenham."

"I had thought it solely a pleasure-party." A pucker of

disapproval on my brother's brow was swiftly smoothed away. "You will wish to consult with Jenner. There is no trained physician—no natural philosopher, indeed—whom I regard more highly. I allowed him to try his methods on my own dear child, when last we were in Cheltenham."

"Do you speak of Edward Jenner? The smallpox man?" I asked. The physician is of such dubious brilliance that some regard him as the Devil, and others as a god. He is an advocate for what he calls *vaccination*—a word he coined years since, from the Latin *vacca*, or cow. Observing that dairy maids, being exposed to cowpox in the course of their work, rarely contracted the far deadlier disease of smallpox, Jenner theorized that the one illness might offer protection against the other. He tested his notion on a serving boy in his household, and happily for the child, was proved correct. By cutting the skin of a healthy person, and smearing the blood of the resultant wound with pus taken from cowpox, Jenner preserves his healthy patients from ever contracting the kindred disease of smallpox.

"Whatever the cause of my present indisposition, James, it is hardly the pox. Recollect that I, too, was vaccinated some fifteen years ago, by my dear Madame Lefroy."

Anne Lefroy, once our neighbour at Ashe Lodge and the mother of James's son-in-law, Ben, was my dearest friend before her untimely death. She was a woman of considerable learning, possessed of significant understanding, and one of the earliest to adopt Edward Jenner's philosophy. She was used to read his pamphlet aloud, when first it was published, and as the vicar's wife, determined to cut and smear every resident of Ashe against the smallpox disease. The local inhabitants being less knowledgeable of Jenner and frequently unable to read, Anne Lefroy implored the ladies among her acquaintance to set an example in her home, so that word of the practise might spread and become acceptable. Naturally, as a member of her younger set of friends, I had sacrificed my arm to her knife.

Madame Lefroy died on my birthday in 1804, after a fall from her horse.

"Impossible to accept that she has been gone already so long," Cassandra mourned.

At that moment, the maid appeared, all the essentials of a hearty fire clutched in her arms.

"Drusilla!" James cried, instantly diverted. "What are you about?"

"You may blame me," I interposed smoothly. "There is no end to the luxuries an authoress celebrated by the Carlton House Set may require."

I untied the strings of my reticule and drew forth a pound note, pressing it into my brother's hand. A fraction of the sum should have sufficed, but I confess my pride encouraged a flaunting of wealth. "Pray accept this trifling gift against coals, James. And kindling. And Cassie's dinners for the next fortnight. While you are about it, Drusilla—be so good as to lay a fire in our bedroom, and Mistress Cassie's as well. Be sure to cosset her until we return to retrieve her."

"The *children's* room!" James sputtered. "You shall be giving them ideas dangerously far above their station!"

I patted his sleeve, my temper unstirred. "Resign yourself,

my dear. I daresay if you are *very* saving, a pound may run to a fire for your own chamber. Only consider! A warm wife beneath the bedclothes! What a change that shall be, indeed!"

4

SEEKING HEALTH AT THE BOTTOM OF A WELL

Saturday, 25th May, 1816
Cheltenham Spa

The intelligent reader of gossip-sheets and scandal-rags will be wondering, I am sure, why Cheltenham, and not the far more celebrated watering hole of Bath, has been our object. Were Cassandra and I as determinedly bent on pleasure as I took pains to suggest to my brothers, the concerts and card-parties of the far more ancient town, as well as the delights of the Abbey and the Pump Room, the shops of Pulteney and the paths of Sydney Gardens, must have been unrivaled by any attractions Cheltenham Spa may offer. The latter is to Bath what a heedless country maid is to a dowager; lacking in refinement and dignity, and prone to a good deal of untempered noise.

And indeed, as we achieved the outskirts of the town late on Saturday, our carriage side-windows streaming with wet, Cassandra remarked on the differences from Bath: the crescents of new houses, girded with stone paving not yet mellowed by time; the raw mud splashed on foundations and walls; the fresh roadways branching from the High Street, where a once-modest village has in recent decades swelled to something greater. So many saplings, where there ought to have been trees! But neither my sister nor I have any deep love for Bath, where we resided for some years, at James's succeeding to our father's living. Bath must be forever associated in our minds with the loss of our home—and of Papa, too, as he passed from this life in our lodgings at Green Park Buildings. But I have another reason, one of considerable delicacy, for wishing to avoid the place; there is a widowed gentleman of my acquaintance presently residing there, in the company of his daughter, whom I hesitate to meet.

Mr. Raphael West—who claims as parent the celebrated artist, Mr. Benjamin West—is a valued acquaintance, tho' our friendship is of recent formation. Possessed alike of an excellent understanding and a distinguished countenance, he is fully capable of engaging any woman's heart. At the mere thought of him now, I felt a warmth steal over my frame and my pulse quicken—a sharp longing for his gaze that felt as deep as hunger. But it would not do; I closed my eyes and resolved that *it would not do*.

When I was last in his company, at Henry's home in Hans Place, it was to resolve the puzzle of a curious map, discovered near a dying soldier in the Prince Regent's library. That was six months ago; and at parting, Mr. West earnestly informed me of his intent to visit Bath, and his hope that I might do the same. There was *that* in his looks and manner that suggested I was dear to him—that our friendship was viewed on his side, at least, as capable of something more. But the sad events of this winter, the collective misfortunes of my brothers, and my dubious health, for a period of months put travel beyond my power.

Moreover, the lowering weeks of relentless rain, confining me within-doors, and the oppression of my own thoughts, urged me to confront certain truths: I am over forty years of age. My mother, my beloved sister, and our companion Martha Lloyd look to me for support in our collective household, where the modest earnings of my pen contribute greatly to the comforts of each. With every financial calamity gathering over Chawton Cottage and its defenceless inhabitants this year, the mite of income I supply is surety against future want. Could I be so selfish as to run away to Bath and the attractions of Mr. West's society, abandoning duty and the claims of those who rely upon me?

I cannot.

And a glance in the mirror confirms what my flagging energy and vanished appetite already apprehend: the few charms remaining to my person are swiftly waning under the influence of ill-health. My countenance is sallow and dull, my eyes shadowed, my cheeks gaunt. I feel the jut of my hip bones with gloved fingers through the cambric of my travelling gown.

I should be ashamed for Raphael West to see me as I now am. Indeed, my lips compress with mortification when I consider the picture: a hag-ridden spinster descending upon Bath, to parade the Pump Room in hope of a chance encounter with the darkly handsome Mr. West. The gentleman, at first surprized and distressed, recovering to lift his hat and offer an introduction to his daughter—only to move on in a matter of moments, with the words, "Poor creature! She is sadly altered since I saw her last!"

Cheltenham would do very well for escape, I thought as our carriage rattled along the Gloucester Road and crossed the stone bridge over the narrow river. The silhouettes of buildings that line the Lower Turnpike loomed ahead; the highway gradually became the High, where our lodgings must be—and further to the south, all the pleasure-grounds and incidental buildings of the different wells stretched in tree-lined avenues before us. The High Street ran on for perhaps a mile, dotted with lodgings, the theatre, the Assembly Rooms and libraries; but beyond this brave front and the various spas, Cheltenham offered little more. In such a town as this, I might pass unremarked. I would drink the waters, think nothing of brothers or their cares, and perhaps recover a little of my health. I would endeavour to grow stout, and on occasion set down a few words of the story presently taking shape in my mind.

The Elliots is a fable of another aging woman, her bloom quite gone off, whose family is too dependent on her compliant spirit. I had sketched the initial scenes of an interesting dilemma—an heroine confronted with the return of a man she once loved and refused—earlier this winter. But the demands of family and ill-health had limited my time at the small, twelve-sided table in the dining parlour where I prefer to write. Now, however, with a full two weeks of leisure before me, matters were otherwise. While I sought refuge in Cheltenham, Anne Elliot might enjoy a renewal of youth and good fortune . . . in Mr. West's streets in Bath. In writing of *her*, I might even think of *him*, in the familiar beauties of that city. Tho' I dare not set foot among them myself.

Our conveyance pulled to a halt in the yard of the Bell Inn. The lodgings we sought—Mrs. Potter's, on the north side of the High—were but a few steps further. I reached for my reticule and the handbox that held my second-best bonnet, and followed my sister out into the rain.

⌒❧

Monday, 27th May, 1816

"Good God, Jane!"

Cassandra's lips were pursed as tightly as a blighted rose. Her eyes swam with tears. As I studied her in trepidation, her throat convulsed and her countenance was suffused with disgust.

"It cannot be so dreadful, surely?" I attempted.

"Worse than your worst imaginings." She set down her glass. "How can such a peculiar draught be everywhere proclaimed as an aid to health? The most blatant poison could not taste more vile!"

"Perhaps one grows accustomed to the flavour?"

"Only if one were to sample it repeatedly," she retorted. "And nothing could prevail upon me to do so—not even my most earnest wishes for your welfare."

I studied my own glass doubtfully. The water it contained was as brown as the bottom of a horse's trough. Cassandra and I had taken our doses quite meekly from the hands of Hannah Forty, a pumper who had ruled the Royal Well for as many years as her name suggested; but neither that woman's challenging look nor the crowd of genteel patrons surrounding us had quelled my sister's revulsion.

"This particular pump is said to be saline," I observed. "It cannot be worse than a mouthful of sea water, surely?"

"It is as sulphurous as a clutch of rotten eggs." Cass turned briskly away from Mrs. Forty. "I must bespeak a cup of tea if I am not to retch this instant."

I tossed the contents of my glass into a waste bowl and followed my sister further into the Long Room, the elegant saloon that housed the Royal Well's pumps. Tho' it was only half-past eight o'clock in the morning, a crowd of fashionable patrons strolled its length while the musicians ranged on the balcony overhead played a concerto by Beethoven. From the Long Room's crush this morning, I concluded that half the Kingdom was come to the spa town determined to banish the humours from their blood, tho' the end of May is still considered early in Cheltenham's Season.

"We may discover the waters at Lord Sherborne's Well or the Montpellier to be more to our taste," I called after Cassandra. "We might remove to either immediately. Neither is at a very great distance; I am persuaded neither is beyond our powers."

"But what adventure, then, may we hope for tomorrow? Or the day after that?" my sister answered with a pitiable groan. "Surely *some* of these delights may be put off to a later hour!"

IF ONE IS NOT to take the waters at a spa built for the purpose, one may at least enjoy the parade of those who do: elderly gentlemen bent over their canes, attempting to appear sprightly; groupings of young ladies newly come upon the town, and determined to go in white regardless of the mud everywhere in the streets; harassed mothers of unruly off-spring, scandalising their neighbours with excessive spirits and noise. And then there are the invalids: propelled by compan-ions or family, intent upon the salvation of lives overburdened merely with *living*. In Bath, these are legion; in Cheltenham, more common still. Novelty will always draw those hopeful of cure. Had I not travelled three days in pursuit of it myself?

"Do observe, Jane," Cassandra whispered as she slipped her hand through my arm and drew me away from the teacups we had drained at one side of the Long Room. "Such a pretty creature, and so young, too, to be wheeled in a Bath chair!"

She was attempting not to stare openly at an interesting young lady, whose sweetness of countenance and modest air must draw every eye. Flawless skin, tho' too wan and pallid; shadowed eyes of cornflower blue; guinea-gold curls trailing from a deliciously upturned poke bonnet, a frail figure hand-somely gowned—and yet all confined to the basket-chair of an invalid's conveyance. There was a thinness, a languor, that spoke of suffering gallantly borne. Such a picture, eloquent of Divine gifts and burdens equally bestowed, must inspire the most sympathetic concern! Little ripples of notice followed the lady's progress down the room. Heads turned, and were as swiftly averted.

I guessed her to be in the middle-twenties. Her companion, a dark-haired, sober lady in dull grey, propelled the chair with devoted attention, indifferent to the impertinences of strangers. An elder relation, perhaps?

"How distressing, if she should be in a decline," Cassandra murmured. "If she should be consumptive, perhaps! Do you suppose it is her nurse who accompanies her?"

"A relative, surely. There seems an intimacy between them that argues against mere paid employment."

"I cannot think any indisposition of mine more than trifling," Cassandra sighed, "when I reflect that I have enjoyed twice that young life's span already, and yet command the use of my limbs. How happy I am that *you* are my companion, Jane! That I am not thrown upon strangers, while indisposed!"

I forbore to point out that it was *my* indifferent health that had driven us to Cheltenham. I owed Cassandra too much; where she loves, she is unflagging in her support. "To be sure. We have much for which we must be thankful."

"Such elegance in her aspect! Such refinement in her features, despite the toll of ill-health! I am sure she is well-born, Jane. Every quality in her looks declares delicacy and breeding. She is likely the daughter of a baronet. —Or of even an earl, perhaps!"

I stifled a sigh. Although I am commonly supposed to study my fellow creatures on the sly, so as to invent amusing histories for them, my sister is no less avid a student of human nature. Indeed, I sometimes suspect she lives for gossip.

"Surely not," I whispered. "However refined her looks, the Fair Unknown cannot be greater than the daughter of a viscount, or she should certainly be at Tunbridge Wells, and attended by two footmen at least."

The intriguing pair had outpaced us, and were drawn up before the Patron's Book, a large, gilt-edged volume in which the Long Room's subscribers were meant to sign their names.

Though it must be judged relatively small and rustic compared to Bath, Cheltenham apes the grander spa town in this respect, as in many others: sharing the same Master of Ceremonies, Mr. King, to preside over its publick Assemblies on Mondays and Fridays, while reserving certain evenings for card-parties (Wednesdays) and others for the theatre (Tuesdays, Thursdays, and Saturdays). Indeed, so great is its ambition to empty the purses of the Select, that Cheltenham is embarked upon the construction of far larger Assembly Rooms than it presently claims. The new rooms will accommodate more dancers to its balls—some six hundred!—than is possible at present, and offer billiards and backgammon in addition to whist. His Grace, the Duke of Wellington, is to open the new Assembly in July.

Cassandra is excessively disappointed that we shall have quitted Cheltenham before the Duke's arrival. To cheer the Hero of Waterloo in publick, and perhaps observe him to waltz (for the Duke is reputed an excellent dancer), in rooms that cost upward of fifty thousand pounds to construct, should be something to report to Mary, indeed!

"We are not the interesting invalid's only admirers," I murmured. A gentleman in the blue coat of a Naval officer had just approached the two ladies and offered a scrupulous bow to both. I judged him not much above thirty, yet he bore the rank of captain on his coat—which announced a history of some daring and valor in the recent wars. Then, too, he suffered from a slight lameness in his left leg—had he come to Cheltenham for a rest cure, and once turned upon shore, discovered a fervent desire for a lady's conversation?

"It is a charming grouping," Cassandra said.

The sailor, frank and open of countenance, supporting himself on an ebony stick; the girl, her piquant face upturned confidingly to his own; the companion, with a faint look of consciousness, as tho' embarrassed by the gallant figure's notice—

I might invent stories all the day long, when supplied with sufficient matter. "Ought we to inscribe our names in the Patron's Book?"

"If any of our acquaintance are presently in Cheltenham, they might then be apprised of our arrival," Cassandra suggested.

We should certainly have known if even one of our friends had travelled out of Hampshire in parallel to ourselves, but I did not quibble with my sister. Any acquaintance might enliven our stay in the town. And Cassandra meant to learn the identity of the Beauty in the Bath chair. Wild horses could not prevent her.

We waited until the intriguing ladies progressed onward, the officer still in attendance, with a pleasantry on his lips— then we approached the book with a suitable air of unconcern.

"Miss Williams," Cassandra read, "and Miss Fox. I wonder, Jane, which is which?"

Not an *Honourable* between them, I noted; not even a viscount could they claim as parent. Cassandra must suffer a disappointment.

The name scrawled beneath theirs, I observed, was equally democratic. *Captain H. Pellew.* Such a man might be anyone— but for his surname! There was an Admiral Sir Edward

Pellew, familiar throughout the Kingdom, if one cared for the Royal Navy. My brother Frank had recounted the daring fellow's exploits—how he had been taken prisoner in the Colonial wars, where his brother was killed; how he escaped being sunk in sea-battles against superior French firepower; how he swam out to the rescue of some five hundred souls grounded at Plymouth Hoe, with a rope clenched between his teeth—by which lifeline, most were saved. But the name must rivet my attention from a nearer concern—for the same Baron Pellew had been Commander-in-Chief, the Mediterranean Station, these past several years, and as such, must have one *Charles Austen* and his ill-fated *Phoenix* under his command.

Was this *H. Pellew* a near relation of the famous admiral? A son, a nephew, a cousin, perhaps? The Pellews were certainly an extensive Naval family, originating in Plymouth, I believed. Was the captain who limped slowly away from me at all acquainted with my Naval brothers—and could his famous relations bring any influence to bear on Charles's Admiralty Board?

Some of these questions might be answered in a perusal of the Navy List, but the remainder must await a proper introduction to the unknown officer himself—unlikely, alas, to fall in my way. We possessed no acquaintance in Cheltenham capable of enlarging our circle.

With a sigh, I took up the pen set neatly by the Patron's Book, and dipped it in the silver standish. *Miss Jane Austen*, I wrote. It looked very well on the page, however undistinguished by titles or honorifics.

5

RUMOURS OF CALAMITY

Monday, 27th May, 1816
Cheltenham, cont'd.

"And what is your opinion of our famous waters, ma'am?" our landlady enquired as I mounted the stairs an hour later. "They do say as there's nothing to equal 'em for restoring health."

"I cannot undertake to say," I replied, "as I have tried only one pump, and that only briefly. Perhaps in a week's time I may give a truer report."

"That would be the Royal Well," Mrs. Potter guessed shrewdly. "I can always tell from the way a patron's mouth turns down at the corners when they speaks of it. Powerful sulphurous it is. I thank the Lord I've never had cause to go near."

The wife of a local draper, Mrs. Potter is round, rubicund, and red-haired. Her person is always adorned with a starched apron and her freckled arms folded over her broad stomach. Although her neat rooms came highly recommended by James's Mary, and are situated directly next to the handsome York Hotel, where any number of elegant Sprigs of Fashion put up for an interval of dissipation, Cassandra and I have discovered Potter's prices to be exorbitant, at three guineas per week for a shared bedchamber! Our purses, you must understand, do not stretch to the hiring of a *private parlour.* But the town is so full, despite the earliness of the Season, that a removal to cheaper lodgings is not to be thought of; and so we have determined to be sanguine in the face of expence.

Mrs. Potter's cooking is unobjectionable, however; her household clean; and the common sitting-room genteel enough for the little time we expect to spend in it. We mean to be chiefly upon the town, strolling the extensive avenue of elms known as the Well Walk, viewing the pictures in Mr. Fasana's exhibition room, and patronising the numerous libraries at our disposal.

The tedious society of fellow-lodgers had not entered into our calculations at all. Taking dinner the first evening in our bedchamber, we naturally encountered no strangers; Sunday being given over to devotions at the handsome medieval parish church of St. Mary's, the reading of Scripture, and retirement, we were similarly undisturbed; but within hours of visiting the Royal Well this morning, peace was at an end.

As ever this frigid spring, inclement weather proved inescapable as Cassandra and I hurried back along the Walk from Hannah Forty's pump. Rain spattered the fresh leaves and dripped in sheets from the edges of our silk umbrellas, drenching the hems of our wool gowns. We had both worn stout boots, but the leathers were sadly marred by the puddles that spanned the Well Walk's gravel. Once we achieved the High, we found it crowded with others hastening towards home, shoulders hunched and eyes bent upon the paving. Neither Cassandra nor I spared a thought for the wares displayed so lavishly in the shop-windows at either hand, no matter how sumptuous the bolts of cloth or bonnet-trimmings. Even Fashion has no power to beguile, when one risks an inflammation of the lung.

We discovered breakfast had been laid on our return—complete with kidneys and rashers of streaky bacon—tho' I contented myself with tea and fingers of buttered toast. We were left in solitary command of the table, our fellow-lodgers being either too indolent or too busy to join us. After breakfast, Cassandra repaired to our shared bedchamber to read her daily sermon; but finding the atmosphere distressingly suffused with attar of roses, Mrs. Potter's preferred weapon against the general fug of damp wool, woodsmoke, and roast mutton, I swiftly changed my soaked stockings for dry, my wet boots for soft velvet house slippers; and anticipated a cosy interval with a novel by the fire. I had barely settled myself in a comfortable chair when the world obtruded painfully on my notice.

"Such inclement weather!" a woman exclaimed.

I glanced up from the second volume of Miss Edgeworth's *Belinda*, which I had discovered lying without its companions on one of Mrs. Potter's parlour shelves, and inclined my head to the lady who stood in the doorway, a furled and dripping umbrella suspended from her gloved hand. In the other she held a leather dog lead. A fawn-coloured pug with a black mask and glistening eyes panted at her ankle, his pink tongue rakishly lolling. Both dog and lady, I judged, were accustomed to indulging their appetites more freely than they ought, and wet through from the storm. The pug shook himself roundly; unperturbed by the shower of drops, the lady bent to loose his lead.

"Ah," came a gentleman's voice from the passageway. "A fellow-lodger. To be sure. When one *particularly* wishes for a position near the hearth—"

He was two feet taller than his companion, grizzle-haired and mournful, as gaunt as she was stout, stooped where she was round. Bony fingers brushed ineffectually at the sopping shoulder of his black cape, then travelled tentatively to the round brim of his hat, which he removed with apparent distaste. His gaze bent accusingly upon me, his narrow mouth turned down. Clearly, I had occupied his preferred armchair, and was expected to remove myself on the instant.

I turned a page of my book instead.

"I am sure, Richard," the lady said in an authoritative accent, "that this person will take herself off when she perceives how necessary the coals are to ourselves, and how selfish she must appear, in reserving the *best place*. Never mind that we have claimed the spot already a se'ennight in this house—I am sure she will apprehend how very ill-natured and presumptuous her behaviour is, as one only newly-acquainted with our dear Mrs. Potter."

At that moment, the pug, being freed of restraint, rose on his hind legs and placed his forepaws in my book, his squashed nose and earnest gaze lifted to my own. Startled, I pulled *Belinda* clear of the damp pawprints and gently set the little dog back on his haunches.

"Thucydides!" his owner commanded. "Come away at once! I trust he has not dirtied your gown?"

"Not in the slightest," I assured the lady, rising from my place and setting my book upon a table. The pug sniffed noisily at my skirts, but I bent to stroke his head regardless; I have an easy affection for dogs, and this one reminded me of just such another, a pet of my brother Edward's late wife, Lizzie.

"Aren't you a cunning fellow," I murmured, caressing the damp, silky fur of the dog's domed skull. He emitted the strangled gurgle common to such creatures, and a wet snuffle of satisfaction.

"I suppose you have had bacon to your breakfast. Thucydides adores it beyond everything great." The lady snapped her fingers, but the dog paid no heed and threw himself down upon the hearthrug at my feet, back legs extended.

"If you have marred your gown with bacon grease, you will wish to apply a paste of vinegar and ash as soon as may be. The odour is penetrating."

"I took no bacon this morning, I assure you."

"Then perhaps the gown is worn too often, and the odour permanent. I am Miss Garthwaite," the pug's mistress said abruptly, "and that is my brother, Mr. Garthwaite. Richard, you may claim the chair by the fire now, as Miss . . ."

"Austen," I supplied.

"Miss Austen has at last surrendered it."

I glanced about the parlour. It was a good-sized room, with a sopha against one wall; a round oak table suitable for needlework or a nuncheon; several straight-backed chairs drawn up to the same; a neat writing desk; and three arm-chairs arranged comfortably within reach of the fire. Mr. Garthwaite must derive peculiar benefit from the one I had chosen, for he hastened to shed his cloak and lay his claim. Neither word nor gesture of politeness did he offer me as he folded his frame into the cushions; then he fixed his gaze with a melancholy sigh upon the glowing coals.

His sister drew a tartan lap robe from the sopha and spread it across Mr. Garthwaite's knees. "If only, Richard, you have not taken a chill!"

"It matters little," he replied with indifference. "The storm that is coming shall make these bitter rains appear as the merest shower, and the cold *then* shall be the chill of the grave. Repentance is the sole remedy, and but a false warmth against the fires of Hell's imagining."

I lifted my brows. I had not expected a sermon on a Monday.

"The brutal winter—the stillborn spring; there shall be no summer, and the autumn shall fall in violence upon our heads. Flood, famine, the crops rotting in the fields, and lamentation rising a thousand-fold from gaping, wounded mouths! The child plucked from the mother's arid breast shall be thrown into the pit; and the serpent devour the godless."

"An Evangelical, I perceive." I had met a few such souls among the Devout in the course of my life—indeed, they were in some circles the high kick of Fashion—but I could not like their fervour. They took too grim a pleasure in detecting Sin, assuring others that they were themselves quite free of it, and assigning retribution to the rest of us.

"A man of Science, rather." Mr. Garthwaite's dark eyes, set

deep in sepulchral sockets, met mine—and I was startled at
the anguish I read there. "A Fellow of Learned Societies, tho'
I confess I am indeed a clergyman. Would that I had never
strayed from Holy Writ! I have tasted too deep of the Tree
of Knowledge, Miss Austen, and dread what I have learnt
there. I delved into arcane studies of Natural Philosophy,
when I ought better to have been upon my knees, praying
for salvation! Are you aware—or as yet ignorant of the intelligence—that the warmth of the sun has been wrapped in a
veil; that no man may say when it shall be torn asunder; and
that perpetual winter shall wither crops in the fields, bringing
desolation upon the multitude?"

My eyes strayed to the windowpanes, streaming still with
wet, and involuntarily I shuddered. The weather *had* been
uncompromisingly wretched for months; but surely . . . there
was nothing *apocalyptic* in it?

"Shall I fetch you a cup of tea, Richard?" Miss Garthwaite's accent was rallying, as tho' she cajoled an infant in the
nursery. "Or a pot of chocolate, perhaps, if Mrs. Potter may
be prevailed upon to boil it?"

But her brother paid no heed, his long fingers plucking
anxiously at his knees as he fixed his gaze upon mine. "You
must prepare, Miss Austen—indeed you must prepare! The
Devilry began months since, on the far side of the world.
The belly of the earth erupted with fire, and spewed the ash
of eons into the Heavens! The light of the sun was blotted
out; the seas heaved, and o'erwhelmed the land; countless
pitiful innocents were swept to their deaths, along with the
Damned—"

I frowned a little. "Do you refer to a *volcano*, sir? —And to a particular volcano that I collect erupted last year, somewhere in the Pacific?"

My brother Frank had exclaimed over the disaster, I vaguely recalled, when he learnt of it from a fellow officer: a horrific explosion and lava flow near Java, in the Dutch East Indies. He later read news of it aloud from Naval reports, during our evenings together at his home in Alton. The eruption utterly destroyed an island and killed the majority of its inhabitants.[2]

Coming as it did after the far more sinister intelligence of Buonaparte's escape from Elba, the Act of God on the far side of the world could not be accorded very much attention in England. Last June's three-day battle at Waterloo, devastating in its losses tho' a triumph for Buonaparte's enemies, had banished every rival thought of disaster for the remainder of that summer. Indeed, I had heard nothing of the distant volcano or its effects in over a twelvemonth.

"The eruption was but an instrument of Divine Ruin," Mr. Garthwaite assured me. "The filth of an hundred thousand years—gases, ash, molten stone, all spewed from the bowels of Hell—gushed forth such smoke into the air, as blotted out the sun! None of us may predict when warmth

---

2 The eruption Jane vaguely recalls was of Mount Tambora, on the Indonesian island of Sumbawa, which in 1815 was part of the Dutch East Indies. On April 10, 1815, it experienced one of the most powerful volcanic eruptions in human history, with a Volcanic Explosivity Index of seven. Mount Tambora continued to erupt in a minor fashion for the next three years. The cloud of ash that encircled the globe caused a brief period of worldwide climate change, crop failures, and famine, particularly in 1816, which was known as the Year Without a Summer.—*Editor's note.*

shall return. Useless to hope for crops or harvest, this year or the next. No blessed fruit or blushing flower—perhaps for the remainder of our days! But those shall be brief, and numbered in weeks. Repent, Miss Austen—*Prepare*. The end of all things is upon us."

The pug broke the silence that followed this outburst with a humid snort. Mr. Garthwaite started, and clutched at his tartan lap robe.

"Do you make a very long stay in Cheltenham, Miss Austen?" Miss Garthwaite enquired, as tho' her brother had never spoken.

"A fortnight or so," I stammered. "And you?"

"As long as may be required to effect improvement in Mr. Garthwaite's condition. It is serious in nature. *You* do not appear to suffer. *You* cannot claim ill-health," she said appraisingly.

I frowned at the impertinence. "There may be as many reasons to visit Cheltenham, surely, as there are persons to enjoy it?"

"Oh, *aye*—the frivolous will always seek dissipation in a watering-hole!" Miss Garthwaite retorted disparagingly. "I had not been here a half-hour before I recognised the sort. Men-of-the-Town, intent upon attaching an heiress; women of uncertain origin and morals, who live I dare not say how; *actresses*; card-sharps; and aging spinsters who fancy themselves ill, in a shameless bid for notice and indolence! But my brother's malady is otherwise."

Miss Garthwaite stepped close and lowered her voice. "His nerves are sadly disordered. You see how it is. The slightest anxiety may imperil his reason. You must respect the gravity of my situation, Miss Austen, when I ask you to leave us to the *solitary* enjoyment of this parlour."

I had no great desire for more of Mr. Garthwaite's interesting conversation, but his sister's presumption wearied me. "I beg your pardon," I said. "I had not understood the room was privately hired."

Miss Garthwaite reared back in disapproval. The intended effect—which was to put me in my place—was somewhat spoilt, by the difference in our comparative heights. She was forced to peer up at me like a schoolboy, and resembled nothing so much as her dog, begging on hind legs.

"You are aware, Miss Austen, that my brother is a man of God—a clergyman quite worn down by the cares and anxieties of a numerous parish. But can you comprehend that his life hangs by the veriest thread? —That there was a time not so long since when I despaired of gaining Cheltenham and its restorative waters, before he should have *expired*? I am sure you will apprehend the seriousness of my demand for peace and refreshment. It cannot be a sordid question of *expence* or *funds*. I am sure you could not be so determined in selfishness. You would not wish to harry him to his grave."

"Indeed not," I assured her, "if attention to *his* comfort did not deprive me of *mine*. But it is no great matter; I shall rely upon Mrs. Potter's judgement. It must be the landlady's concern to arrange indulgences among her lodgers, in a fashion that assures general peace. Shall I step downstairs and have a word with her? Pray enjoy the parlour's solitude while I do."

"Unfeeling woman," Miss Garthwaite muttered as I quitted

the room. "Upon my word, Brother, I have rarely met with so waspish a creature!"

"The fall is always the farthest for those who cling to the heights," I heard the gentleman reply. "Perhaps Thucydides will bite her."

6

OUR LITTLE FAMILY

Monday, 27th May, 1816
Cheltenham, cont'd.

"I trust that not all our fellow-lodgers are so disagreeable, Jane." Cassandra selected an iced cake from the assortment on the table before us—we had paused in our promenade about town for a trifling refreshment at Gunton's confectionery—and closed her eyes in bliss as the morsel passed her lips. I preferred a simple apple puff to swirls of marzipan—but then, few things agree with me at present, other than plain black tea.

I was saved the trouble of carrying tales to Mrs. Potter by the appearance of my sister on the boardinghouse landing, clutching a letter that required posting. Observing the rain to have abated to a mizzle, I left the Garthwaites in sole possession of the sitting-room and joined her in a trice. The post office is mere steps from Mrs. Potter's door, and a trifling bout of wet should not deter us from exercise. One cannot allow what is uncontrollable in Nature to dictate what must be well-regulated in the soul. Particularly when there are shopwindows to study.

Having deposited Cass's missive in the bag, and retrieved

a brief note from Martha Lloyd, we determined to view the Royal Crescent, as lovely a modern range of dwellings as its namesake in Bath. The golden stone and elegant proportions duly admired, we strolled past silk-mercers and goldsmiths, perfumers and the Cheltenham Library—whose reading room is eighty feet long, and much patronized by visitors to the town. It is but one of many on offer, but easily the largest; and from the appearance of its racks, nearly every newspaper or journal published in the Kingdom might be perused there. I promised myself an early return for a quiet hour in a comfortable chair; it is not often I am afforded the luxury of so much print, and now that Henry has fled London, I must seize the opportunity for steady and indulgent reading.

Cassandra purchased a card of lace, and wasted at least a quarter-hour fingering Irish linen, for which she has a decided weakness; then, when my patience was nearly at an end, had us overlook the builders' site of the new Assembly Rooms. They promise to be commodious, in the current modern stile, and fitted along every side with a considerable number of tall windows, which should make the Summer Balls blessedly airy.

"If one could but observe the Duke to open the dancing!" Cassandra mourned.

Having met with Wellington on a previous occasion, I could not repine; and so carried my sister to Gunton's Confectioner and Ice Shop, not far from Bedford Buildings, to rest our aching feet. The hour being somewhat advanced, we were so happy as to secure seats in the window, where we might observe all of Cheltenham hurrying about their business.

"I could be happy with no additional lodgers," I mused. "The Garthwaites shall provide vexation and amusement enough."

"Mrs. Potter assures me that all her rooms are to let, however." Cassandra assessed a chocolate biscuit on the dwindling confectioner's platter. "And there are *seven bed-chambers*, Jane."

Taking into account the two allotted to the clergyman and his sister, as well as the one accorded to ourselves, we must assume an additional four lodgers *at least* vying for position near the sitting-room hearth. It was a lowering thought. And if one or more were married . . .

"I daresay the rest are somewhat more amiable," I asserted. "That is why we have not yet met them. They have been avoiding the Garthwaites' conversation."

"Jane!" Cassandra suddenly grasped my arm. But her gaze was fixed on a figure beyond the window. "Is that not the lady from the Royal Well? —The companion to the Tragic Figure in the basket-chair?"

I peered past the edge of Cassandra's bonnet. Despite the intervening scrim of rain, I judged she was correct. It was indeed the sober young woman we had glimpsed in the Long Room, progressing down St. George's Place without a cloak or an umbrella. Miss Williams—or perhaps Miss Fox. The shoulders of her grey spencer and the brim of her hat were dark with damp. "She is intent upon the Quaker Meeting House."

"But she cannot be a *Friend*," Cassandra said blankly. "I have not met with one before."

"You have not met with one now," I pointed out.

"But where is her interesting charge? And the dashing Captain?"

"Returned to his ship? Or perhaps they have eloped together." I tucked Martha's letter into my reticule. "If you have quite finished, Cass—"

"I do not think the Royal Navy would allow such a thing as a clandestine union. Although Frank assures me that he is permitted to perform marriages at sea," my sister replied doubtfully. "I cannot regard such a bond as entirely legitimate when performed upon *oneself*."

But the answer to these mysteries was partly secured once we regained Mrs. Potter's, three-quarters of an hour later. Drawn up to the hearth was the lovely young invalid from the Royal Well, fresh as a new-opened daisy in white muslin and lace; and tending the fire, all solicitude, was Captain Pellew. He had traded his ebony walking stick for an iron poker with no diminution of looks or honour.

"I begin to like these lodgers very well, Jane," Cassandra whispered, as we passed on to our bedchamber to remove our wet things. "Only see how they have routed the Garthwaites!"

WE WERE NOT SO fortunate as to take our dinner with the interesting pair, however. It soon became evident that the sole private parlour in Mrs. Potter's establishment had been claimed by the Misses Fox and Williams—and that Captain Pellew was a favoured intimate of their charmed circle.

Their dishes were borne to their table under separate covers, and tho' we caught the murmur of voices from behind the closed door, not another glimpse of the party did we earn. Upon sitting down to table, Cassandra and I were treated to the clergyman and his sister presiding at head and foot, for all the world as tho' they had welcomed us into their parsonage. We must be content with the Garthwaites' wearying conversation; but in the event, the lady's intelligence proved more apt and interesting than we had any reason to hope. On the subject of the invalid and her friends, Miss Garthwaite was replete with information. I suspected her of having interrogated the sober companion in an unguarded moment, to the gratification of her enforced acquaintance.

"Miss Rose Williams is from Cornwall," Miss Garthwaite declared as she partook of a dish of fresh peas. Thucydides waited at her chair leg, hopeful for a slip of the spoon. "An heiress, I believe—tho' sadly unlucky in health, however blessed by fortune. Brother, will you not sample the mutton? It is not nearly so tough as yesterday."

"Tin," Mr. Garthwaite murmured reflectively. His gaze was fixed mournfully on the middle distance, his plate untouched.

"I beg your pardon?" Cassandra's aspect was all sympathy. "I did not perfectly hear you, sir. Do you require something?"

"Tin," he repeated. "A vulgar term for *coin* among the lower orders—but in Miss Williams's case, decidedly apt. Her father's fortune was gained from tin mining. Copper also, I believe. Mr. Aloysius Williams was a despoiler of Cornwall, Miss Austen. Which is to say: an intimate of rogues and thieves, and now that he is dead—of Beelzebub. No doubt the daughter's ill-health is a judgement of Divine Providence.

Do you have any notion of the present conditions among the Cornish people?"

My sister glanced helplessly at me. I concentrated on the serving-girl and the dish of stew she offered.

"I have not had the pleasure of visiting Cornwall—" Cass attempted.

"Dreadful," the clergyman pronounced. "In every particular, *dreadful*. My own parish, you will understand, is in neighbouring Devon. There is want, and misery, among those who go down into the mining-pits. The exposure to arsenic alone—you will know it is one of the chief metals unearthed in tin-mining—kills scores of men before their time. Pit bosses like Aloysius Williams are no better than executioners. His daughter's frail prettiness cannot disguise her fortune's poisonous taint."

"But is not tin a valuable commodity in Britain?" Cassandra attempted. "And a miner's wage necessary to the miner?"

"Pish! There is more honour and safety in sweeping a street! But there will come a time when all the mineral wealth of the Kingdom will be as ashes. Now that crop-failure and famine are unleashed upon the land—"

Fearing a reversion to Mr. Garthwaite's zeal for prophecy, I broke in, "And the lady who travels with Miss Williams? She is also from that part of the country?"

"Indeed." Miss Garthwaite savored a bite of Mrs. Potter's potatoes. Thucydides, his nose lifted to the scent of braised mutton, edged from her chair leg to mine and gargled hopefully. I lowered a stealthy bit of bread to the black muzzle. "The Williamses and the Foxes have long been intimate, I believe—the men of the family (I cannot call them gentlemen) being partners in the mining trades and banking."

"Heretic," observed Mr. Garthwaite serenely.

"Richard." His sister set down her fork. "You know that I *deplore* that term. It is *popish*, and thus has no place in respectable English conversation. Miss Fox is *Nonconformist*. She *dissents*. That is how we must regard her tendencies, and speak of them. The young woman is a Quakeress, Miss Austen," she added for my benefit, "and I believe serves as a *paid companion* to the unfortunate Miss Williams."

"Have you an idea of the nature of that lady's indisposition?" Cassandra enquired.

"A wasting disease of some sort."

"She is decidedly slender," Cassandra agreed. "Her beauty appears undiminished, however. Some might deem her countenance pallid. She is otherwise all that is charming. But for the basket-chair, I should not have known her for an invalid."

"An indiscriminate indulgence in finery may disguise all manner of ills," Miss Garthwaite replied, "and where dress is concerned, Miss Williams spares no expence. Indeed, did I not observe her to drink the waters each day, I should suspect she is come to Cheltenham merely to promenade at her ease, with Miss Fox to propel her, and Captain Pellew to pay pretty compliments!"

The note of acid in this speech was not lost on my sister, who drew back a trifle. However engrossed by gossip, she recoils from appearing so. But our party was disrupted at that moment by the opening of the parlour door, and the quiet entrance of a young woman neatly and unobjectionably dressed in a high-necked, dark blue gown of twill. With a strangled bark, Thucydides trotted to greet her.

The lady bent and patted the pug's chest, while his tongue lolled in ecstasy. Although still in her middle-twenties, I suspected, she wore a plain muslin cap over her hair. The dowdiness of this touch suggested a desire to discourage notice, or heighten respectability.

Both, perhaps.

The possessor of Mrs. Potter's last bedchamber, I surmised; and by all appearances, a lady of quality, although from her modest raiment, not of means. Was she an instructress at an academy for young ladies? —A confirmed spinster? —Or possibly, even, a *war widow*?

"Thucydides!" Miss Garthwaite's tone was quelling. The pug's corkscrew tail faltered perceptibly; his head dropped; he slunk back to fling himself beneath his mistress's chair.

The stranger merely inclined her head to the Garthwaites. Her gaze hesitated wordlessly over ourselves. Then she drew out a chair from the far end of the dining table and seated herself.

"Mrs. Smith," Miss Garthwaite said abruptly, as though the lady had been another incorrigible dog. "You are late for dinner. Your work detains you, apparently. I wonder Mrs. Potter does not have you take your meals in your room! Here we are, on the point of adjourning for coffee, and you will be expecting mutton!"

"My habits cannot be your concern, Miss Garthwaite," the lady replied composedly, without lifting her gaze. I noticed then the compression of her lips and the lines of weariness about her mouth. "No tardiness of mine is allowed to delay your dinner; therefore it cannot be allowed to be your business."

"But your incivility must," the older woman returned, "particularly before new acquaintance! Miss Austen, and Miss Jane Austen, have joined our little family, Mrs. Smith."

At that, the lady raised her head with an expression of defiance. Had we offended her unwittingly? "I am happy to make your acquaintance," she said, "but contrary to Miss Garthwaite's claims, I belong to no family. And I long since outran the censures of a parent! Now, if you will excuse me—I believe I *will* take my dinner in my room."

Mrs. Smith rose and left us as quietly as she had appeared—tho' with the forcible impression of leaving storms in her wake.

Cassandra glanced at me with lifted brows.

"An actress," Miss Garthwaite proclaimed with distaste.

"Fallen," her brother added succinctly.

In unadorned dark blue, and a plain muslin cap! *Mrs. Smith* to tread the boards in a Cheltenham tragedy? I revolved the image of Sarah Siddons in my mind. Impossible!

"What Mrs. Potter can be thinking of, to foist such a creature on us all—" Miss Garthwaite spluttered.

"The lady appears the soul of respectability," I observed.

Miss Garthwaite smiled, but there was no kindness in it. "I *have heard* she has not the slightest claim to reputation. We may be certain her name is not *Smith*, at any rate. Nor that she is married. Wanton, benighted creature! I have considered a change of lodgings, rather than expose my dear brother to scandal."

"Is Mr. Garthwaite susceptible, then, to fallen women?"

Cassandra enquired, with a dangerous appearance of concern. "I have heard there are any number of clergyman with a similar tendency. It is borne of a desire, I believe, to rescue such women from Sin. Although demanding the *indulgence* of it, of course—"

I rose somewhat hastily from the table. "I do not think coffee will answer my indifferent constitution this evening, alas! We will defer the pleasure for another occasion, Miss Garthwaite. Until tomorrow! *Adieu!*"

7

LEARNED OPINION

Tuesday, 28th May, 1816
Cheltenham

"Your case is a not unusual one," Dr. Hargate assured me. "Pains in the back, disordered bowels, and an indifference to nourishment . . . you are a spinster, of course."

Our Alton apothecary, Mr. Curtis, had recommended Hargate as a distinguished man of physick, trained up in Edinburgh, that seat of medical learning. Immediately after breakfast this morning I sent round my card to the fellow's consulting room, along with Curtis's note of introduction— and received the reply that I might call upon the doctor at midday.

At his pronouncement, my chin rose and my brows drew together in a frown. "I am *unmarried*, sir, but how that condition should bear upon my health—"

"An excess of uterine influence," the doctor said comfortably. "The unencumbered, untried womb releases all manner of poisonous humours into the blood, weakening the female brain and body. Denying the organ its proper function of childbearing precipitates a fouling of the internal matter, and eventual decline. The uterus is to blame for every kind of affliction common to your sex, Miss Austen—nervous complaints, lassitude, strong hysterics, a dangerous desire for excessive learning . . ."

"Witchcraft?" I suggested.

The doctor smiled thinly. "Come, come, Miss Austen. I trust you are a member of the Established Church?"

"Our father was a clergyman, sir," Cassandra said crisply. She had accompanied me into the consulting room, as protection against scandal when Dr. Hargate peered at me closely through his spectacles, and listened gravely to my list of indispositions.

"Do your monthly courses persist?" He scrutinised my countenance. "You are barely above forty, and I have known women to suffer from the expulsion of blood well into their fifth decade."

I felt myself flush. "I have not had my courses in over a year."

"Then your imbalance of humours is acute. An obvious solution is available to you—a swift course of bloodletting or the application of leeches might restore you to perfect health. I also advise cupping. There is an excellent cupper, Nancy Lewis, at the Freemen's Bath and Cupping. You will find the establishment between the High and Back Road, not far from the Mill."

I have a profound distaste for bloodletting, which leaves me tired and listless. I have never been cupped, but it was one of the last remedies my father was afforded, in his final illness: glass vessels, heated at the rim, and placed burning on the naked flesh of his back. Despite them, he passed from this life in an apoplectic fit.

"And the waters?" I asked the physician, in hope of an easier solution. "Do you recommend *them*?"

"Among the wells, your choice should be the Montpellier," he said decisively. "There are five pumps, but I must insist that you draw from Number Three, as it offers the most chalybeate draught. The metallic nature of the waters will fortify your blood. I advise three glasses each morning, taken before breakfast, between the hours of seven and nine. Your sister should follow your example, Miss Austen, as her womb must be similarly afflicted."

"Three glasses?" Cassandra faltered.

Hargate peered at us, his lips pursed. "The waters have a decided loosening effect on the bowels. You will wish to remain close to your chamber pot for the better part of the morning. And I must advise you to partake heartily of breakfast each day, once the bowels are purged. You are both far too thin about your persons."

"Such arrogance!" I seethed as we quitted Dr. Hargate's rooms in St. George's Place and made our way towards Montpellier Grounds. These stretched southwest of the High, beyond a bridge over the bare trickle of the River Chelt, a pleasant enough walk when the weather is clement, but decidedly bone-chilling this morning. Graveled paths formed a genteel perimeter to a sodden rectangle of park, bordered by mud-churned rides; a solitary horseman trotted circumspectly in the distance. Otherwise, the spa grounds were nearly deserted. Our visit to the physician's chambers had delayed our sampling of the wells; we met a number of patrons returning towards their lodgings, and very few headed in our own direction.

"To suggest that my unmarried state is responsible for my ill-health! When you know, Cassandra, that excessive child-bearing is the ruin of so many women among our acquaintance!"

Unbidden, Lizzie's elegant dark head and generous mouth, curved in laughter, rose before my eyes. She had been but five-and-thirty when the birth of her eleventh child destroyed her. Tho' nearly eight years have passed, Edward has not ceased to mourn his late wife, and has yet to find comfort in another.

Charles's Fanny is recently dead at four-and-twenty, and her last babe with her.

James's first wife passed from this life after agonizing labour, giving birth to her only child, Anna . . .

. . . and that same niece Anna, married not yet two years, is in the family way *again*. Poor animal, she will be worn out by the time she is thirty.

"But Dr. Hargate must know a great deal more of such matters than we," Cassandra said reasonably. "He is a learned man, of deep study and considerable experience. Even the waspish Miss Garthwaite can find nothing ill to say of him— and assures me he has done much good among Cheltenham's poor, in company with James's friend, Dr. Jenner. You must know, Jane, that the two physicians are the chief patrons of St. Mary's dispensary, which is credited with returning many of Cheltenham's ill to useful life."

This should have silenced me—that no less a genius than Jenner esteemed Dr. Hargate's understanding—but one man's acclaim as a physician could not be taken as proof of his friend's.

"Cassandra," I sighed, "to be informed that I want for health because none of the male sex has desired to do more than *dance* with me, is to add injury to insult. I will not credit Dr. Hargate, however much he laments my untried womb. I may drink a few glasses of these waters—"

My sister halted suddenly on the paving, her gloved hand shading her eyes. I stopped short and glanced at Cass. A tear slid down her cheek, and her thin lips trembled.

"My dear. What is it?"

"The injustice," she said thickly. "I longed for nothing so much as to marry Mr. Fowle, and the pain of losing him was almost more than I could bear. I would gladly have exchanged my single estate for even a few days with Tom, and given all my family so much happiness—"

He had been a handsome enough fellow, Tom Fowle, when Cassandra lost her heart to him between the space of two Basingstoke balls. They formed an engagement when she was but nineteen, and he seven-and-twenty. Tom was once my father's pupil, a graduate of Oxford, the son of a close family friend, dedicated to a life in the Church; a kind-hearted and high-couraged fellow with all of life before him. He had sailed off as chaplain to his patron, Lord Craven, on that nobleman's harebrained expedition to the West Indies, certain that the woman he loved would await his return.

But he did not return; after two years, a letter arrived in

Tom Fowle's place—the blow falling with Lord Craven's first words: Tom was dead of yellow fever, along with any number of the soldiers he had intended to serve.

I remembered Cassandra's anguished cry and the sheet of crumpled paper I had pried from her clenched fingers; the persistent wretchedness that followed; the weeks and months of oppressed spirits.

Like Edward, she has never formed a second attachment.

"I am sure you should have been glad to do your duty also, Jane, as wife and mother, had any man appeared who was worthy of you," she said.

"Perhaps." My perception of a gentleman's worthiness, I found, had changed with the passage of time; those whose suit I might have accepted eagerly at nineteen, I should have spurned at nine-and-twenty.

We had been such giddy girls! Gossiping behind our hands with our friend Martha Lloyd at those same Basingstoke assemblies; arranging one another's hair; glorying in a length of ribbon to trim our bonnets afresh—the only impulsive finery our slim purses could afford. Now Cassandra's face was lined; Martha's hair had begun to grey. The weeks and years passed unvaryingly, yet every particle of our former selves was changed.

"Having consulted Dr. Hargate, however, you ought not to spurn his counsel," Cass persisted.

"Absurd!" I frowned at her. "How am I to act upon it?"

She drew forth a linen handkerchief and delicately patted her nose. "There is a recourse open to you, my dear. A gentleman who undoubtedly admires you. If only to improve your health, Jane, you ought to try the waters at Bath . . . and renew your acquaintance with Mr. Raphael West. I am ready to accompany you, should you desire it."

I nearly laughed. Cassandra, to throw her sister at a gentle-man's head, at Hargate's earnest orders! Here was selflessness, indeed! But I would not wound her with easy mockery; nor could I accept her sacrifice. She might be ready to give me up for my health's sake, but what kind of sister should I be, to abandon her to an elderly parent, uneasy financial circum-stances, and an abyss of loneliness—while I pursued a man who, had he truly loved me, should have presented himself in Chawton months ago?

There. The truth was seared in my thoughts; Mr. West had not come in search of me. Why should I risk my self-possession and my heart, in running headlong after a man of indifferent feeling?

I smiled and slid my arm through my sister's. "I have a better idea, Cass. Let us drink from the detestable Pump Number Three at Montpellier's Well, and then repair to the Cheltenham Library. There *must* be a novel tantalizing enough to banish the aftertaste of sulphur!"

IT APPEARED THAT CAPTAIN Pellew had been visited with a similar inspiration. He was seated on a brocade settee, the *Cheltenham Chronicle* spread open before him, a solitary figure amidst the desultory groupings that circulated among the reading tables. As I lifted a volume of *Guy Mannering*, by the author of *Waverley*—which, tho' published anonymously, is undoubtedly from the poet Mr. Walter Scott's pen—the

Captain's eyes passed over me without recognition, only to fall on a figure behind me. His expression lightened, and he rose from his seat, obviously intent upon paying a courtesy. I half-turned, suspecting to see Miss Williams in her chair— and found Mrs. Smith, instead.

She was dressed as simply today as she had been the previous evening, in unadorned dove-grey wool. The edge of her muslin cap peeked from beneath her bonnet; on its plain straw she had permitted a length of green ribbon. Neither cap nor bonnet could quite disguise her beautiful hair, however; a length of it, mahogany in shade, curled near her left ear. In one hand she clutched the strings of a reticule; in the other, a copy of Mr. Sheridan's *The School for Scandal*. Was the actress contemplating a turn as Lady Sneerwell?

"Mrs. Smith." Pellew had removed his tricorn and now bowed to his fellow-lodger. "I hope I see you in good health, ma'am?"

"Captain," she replied, "I am very well, I thank you." At that instant, she perceived me standing at a little remove from them both, and stepped impulsively in my direction. "Miss Austen. I must beg your pardon, I was very rude to you last night! Only think, Captain, this lady is our fellow-lodger—may I introduce Captain Pellew to your notice, ma'am?—and I had barely made her acquaintance before I ran away in a fretful temper!"

"You had barely eaten dinner, too, I warrant," Captain Pellew replied shrewdly. "Miss Austen, your servant."

I dropped the gentleman a curtsey. "I detected no rudeness, Mrs. Smith, I assure you. Only perhaps a certain disinclination for company, which any of us might feel at the close of a long day."

"You are very good," the young woman told me. Her eyes, which were moss-green flecked with amber, studied me gravely for an instant, then warmed. "You will have detected Miss Garthwaite's disapproval, I am sure. I shall forestall that excellent lady's gossip, and warn you myself that I am a scandalous creature, an intimate of Mr. John Bowles Watson's Cheltenham Theatre, undeserving of genteel notice. I give you leave to cut me direct, and shall never reproach your taste."

"Nonsense," Captain Pellew said roughly. "I have known Mrs. Smith nearly all my life, Miss Austen, and I may assure you there is no one more respectable. Her humour, perhaps, is capricious." He gestured at her volume. "Do you undertake to master comedy, ma'am? I had thought Shakespeare more your suit. *Caesar*, wasn't it, last week?"

"Indeed. And my work was rewarded—the play is to be mounted in two days' time, and Jasper bids fair to be a charming Brutus. But this," she explained with a wave of the Sheridan, "is next week's bill—and Tess is to play Lady Teazle."

"Good Lord!" A smile suffused Pellew's countenance, transforming it instantly. "Watson doesn't ask much. Lady Teazle! He might as well demand you turn loaves into fish."

"She'll look like an angel."

"Tess always does," he agreed. "That isn't the trouble. She'll also open her mouth."

I must have knit my brows in confusion, for the Captain explained, "Mrs. Smith is charged with a heavy duty, ma'am.

She is required to instruct the members of Mr. Watson's company to speak the King's English."

"Are they . . . French?" I suggested.

"No, no," Mrs. Smith replied on a laugh. "Merely unschooled."

"Mrs. Smith turns any number of sows' ears into silk purses before the curtain rises." Captain Pellew's lips pursed. "She makes the worst Back Alley Tom sound like a lord, and every barmaid a duchess. Gives them proper airs, too, and notes on how to raise a quizzing glass."

"You instruct the travelling company," I said wonderingly, "in . . . elocution? And genteel behaviour?"

"Someone must." The young lady's features were alight with mischief. "And I will own that, save for those lacking all talent, actors are in general quick studies. Most are ambitious—and to acquire refinement, in voice and air, is to gain a distinct professional advantage. The theatre is unforgiving. Pretty faces age, but graces do not."

"Tess has not the slightest scrap of talent," Captain Pellew said. "I wish you joy of her."

"You're sadly correct." Mrs. Smith's mouth curved. "And as I am already a quarter-hour behind in my duty, I have not another second to waste. *Adieu!*"

She parted from us with a friendly nod.

Pellew's eyes followed her through the throng of library patrons, as tho' he had forgot my presence. But in this I was mistaken.

"There goes one of the most admirable women of my acquaintance," he said. "I do not know what Miss Garthwaite may have said of her—all manner of nonsense, no doubt!—but I would urge you to form your own opinion."

"I make a habit of doing so," I replied. "Have you come to Cheltenham for your health, Captain? A brief respite between commands?"

He returned his gaze to my countenance. "Worse than that. I have been paid off, ma'am, and must look forward to a life ashore." He gestured ruefully with his ebony stick. "This game leg gives no end of trouble. I should have allowed the ship's surgeon to relieve me of it when he had the chance, and replaced it with good English oak."

"You sustained an injury while in service, I collect?"

He inclined his head. "On the North Atlantic Station, during the recent hostilities."

"Indeed! One of my brothers served on that station more than six years. Perhaps you are acquainted with him? — Captain Charles Austen? He commanded the *Indian*, the *Swiftsure*, and at the last, the *Cleopatra*, which he then brought home."

Pellew's grey eyes widened in surprize. "Charles Austen, begad! I know him very well! How is Charles? We have not met this age."

"He was so unfortunate as to lose his wife," I told Pellew, "a year since. And most lately he lost his ship, which foundered in a hurricane."

Dismay and surprize overspread his features. "I remember the year he was married, in Bermuda. But that is dreadful news! Mrs. Austen was a lovely creature—and so young . . . It is beyond belief, however, that Austen should have lost the

Phoenix! He meant to earn such prizes in her, I recollect, when named to her command. How came it about?"

"The error of his pilots. They drove Charles's frigate onto the rocks, it seems—off Smyrna."

"The Mediterranean? —He was chasing pirates?"

"I see you know something of that Station."

"I am in some wise related to the admiral who commands it. Sir Edward Pellew is a distant cousin of mine."

As I had hoped. "My brother is even now embarked for London, to answer to an Admiralty Board."

"Then I must write a letter immediately," Pellew said, "as testament to his character and skill. Pray send your brother my compliments when next you communicate with him, Miss Austen—and be assured of my sympathy at the loss of his wife. His little girls must be sadly bereft."

"They are. I thank you, Captain."

"It is only what Austen should do for me, in his turn, if our situations were exchanged."

He raised his chapeau-bras, and I moved on—giving quiet thanks that opportunity had thrown him in my way. I do believe there is no better set of men in England, than those of the Royal Navy.

8

AN UNEXPECTED CALLER

Wednesday, 29th May, 1816
Cheltenham

Whether it was from the noxious effect of the Montpellier Well's waters, which had proved no less awful than Hannah Forty's, or whether Mrs. Potter's mutton stew failed to agree with me, I was indisposed with a bilious attack and aching head for the remainder of yesterday. The weather continuing in wretchedness, Cassandra found no temptation to set foot out-of-doors, and remained in our bedchamber to attend me—setting a hot water bottle at my back, which flared in pain; and soothing my head with a handkerchief dipped in lavender-water. She also read aloud from *Guy Mannering,* which we had taken from the Cheltenham Library, and despite being unwell I found the story engrossing and diverting. A Scottish heir kidnapped at birth, raised in Holland, and left for dead after a duel in India—only to follow his lady love back to the Highlands, and be revealed as said heir by his gypsy nurse . . . ! That a poet and critic as renowned as Mr. Scott should turn his hand so readily to novel-writing is an injustice to the rest of the writers set with pretensions to the art, as I told my sister in some heat.

"Mr. Scott ought to confine himself to verses, rather than take the bread from other people's mouths," I said indignantly. "How is a lady to compete with his forthright, bracing stile? And have we time for another chapter, Cass, before you must sit down to dinner?"

"I shall beg Mrs. Potter to furnish me with a tray here in our room," she told me, "so that we may not miss a word."

THIS MORNING FOUND ME much quieter, and amenable to taking some tea and toast, although disinclined to attempt the waters of *any* of Cheltenham's wells.

The simple breakfast being allowed to settle, I went so far as to *dress*—although an eye to the dripping eaves and a sharp sense of my own weakness dissuaded me from any greater activity in the rain.

"I will recruit my health on the sitting-room sopha," I informed my sister, "and turn the pages of Ackermann's *Repository*. Mrs. Potter's latest volume is not above two years old, and I might regale myself with the study of fashions already generally acknowledged as hideous, this twelvemonth at least."

"I shall hasten to the theatre," Cassandra supplied, "and secure our seats for tomorrow evening's performance of *Julius Caesar*. Provided, of course, that you believe you will be well enough—"

"I have it on excellent authority that the part of Brutus is to be played by a lord," I told her, "by the name of Jasper.

Or at least, by a fellow who apes the lord to perfection—and that is all you or I may require for the length of an evening's entertainment. I should not miss it for the world."

Mrs. Potter, at my appearance in the sitting-room at the early hour of ten o'clock, exclaimed her sympathy for my dubious condition, and urged me most sincerely to avoid imbibing *any* water drawn from the ground in Cheltenham for the remainder of my visit, unless it had been strongly boiled and used to steep tea.

"And the best Bohea—it shall always be in my house, make no exception," she declared. "Tho' you ought to consider ale with your toast each morning, ma'am. Mr. Potter insists it is more fortifying than milk to those who are poorly."

I had not entirely believed Mrs. Potter possessed a husband, but forbore to comment, choosing instead to hasten her on her way with a request for more tea. In her absence, I settled myself among the sopha cushions and commandeered the tartan lap robe previously tucked about Mr. Garthwaite's bony knees. I had barely opened the covers of Ackermann's *Reposi tory of the Arts*, solely with an interest in its fashion-plates, when the sound of heavy footsteps on the stairs heralded a fellow-lodger. Too heavy to be my sister; Captain Pellew, perhaps?

But it was quite a different tableau that met my eyes as the figure achieved the last step—Miss Fox, the Quakeress, in her usual dark grey gown, presenting her narrow back to my gaze. She was stooped over her charge's chair, which was being borne upwards by the combined efforts of herself and Mrs. Potter's housemaid, Lucy—both women straining with exertion. As Miss Fox pulled upwards, Lucy heaved from below, and in this fashion, by slow inches, the invalid achieved the lodging-house's first floor.

"Good Lord, Sarah!" Miss Williams, the chair's pitiful occupant, cried aloud as Miss Fox stepped backwards at last onto the safety of the sitting-room carpet. "Will you never have done shaking me?"

"There, there, my lamb," Miss Fox crooned, her hand releasing the chair to rest an instant on Miss Williams's right shoulder. "We shan't go out again today, as your pains are so great. Do you wish to lie down for an interval, while I read to you?"

"I wish you at Jericho," Miss Williams retorted, and plucked at the fingers of her kid gloves, drawing them off in a near-frenzy. "Had I known how miserable I should be, confined in endless boredom with such a poor creature, I should have elected to stay at home."

"You are tired, and perhaps hungry. Let me ring for Mrs. Potter—"

"I have not the *least* inclination to hear that woman lecture me, on the qualities of her own sordid kitchen, or the best things to *eat,* or *drink*!" Miss Williams's rapid fingers now tore at her bonnet strings. "Carry me to my bed, the pair of you, and then leave me blessedly to myself for a while!"

Miss Fox looked speakingly at the housemaid, Lucy, who grimly said, "You take her under the arms, miss, and I'll shift her ankles."

Without another word, the two attendants grasped each end of Miss Williams. The lady went rigid as a board in their clasp, and commenced a shrill screeching that put me in mind of nothing so much as a boiling teakettle. Disregarding, or perhaps indifferent to, her audience, the lady was borne through the private parlour door to her inner apartments, the sound of her anguish diminishing with the abrupt closure of an oak door.

"Lord love us!" muttered Mrs. Potter, appearing in this natural phenomenon's wake with a tray bearing my tea. "How we are so fortunate as to win that lady's custom, I'm sure I *don't* know. Do you take sugar, ma'am?"

"I do." I thrust aside the tartan lap robe as the landlady settled the tray on a side table. "Miss Williams seems decidedly ill. It must be dreadful for those who care for her welfare."

"Sick in the head, if you ask me," Mrs. Potter retorted. "There's nothing much ails her, other than willfulness."

"How can you say so?" I glanced up. "She suffers a good deal. Her limbs appear insensible—a paralysis of some sort—"

Mrs. Potter shrugged. "She summons the energy to do as she likes. But the doctor promised to call today, and Miss Williams cannot abide him—he's told her the truth once too often, I daresay."

"Then why does she consult him?"

"It's Miss Fox as called in Dr. Hargate. 'I am determined to make her well, Mrs. Potter,' so she told me, 'even if she hates the very sight of me when I am done.' She's a quiet one, Miss Fox, but they're generally the most pig-headed."

"It is unusual for a paid companion to direct whom her employer may chuse to see," I said thoughtfully.

"Paid! Miss Fox is never *paid*," the landlady objected.

"Devoted friend, is what she calls herself; and a deal of devotion is necessary, I vow, to put up with Miss Williams's megrims and carryings-on."

I must confess to surprize at the intelligence. I had assumed that the soberly-dressed young woman who propelled the basket-chair was subservient to the invalid, but indeed, why had I judged it to be so? Miss Garthwaite's gossip, possibly; or the lack of desire for notice Miss Fox exhibited whenever I chanced to observe her. Yet, at first glance I had thought the two ladies might share a family connexion. I had detected an intimacy that was now readily explained.

Was it possible, I wondered as I sipped Mrs. Potter's cooling Bohea, for a physical ailment to exist solely in the mind? I knew full well that spiritual ones often did—witness James's Mary, and her constant phantasy of deteriorating health. But such pantomimes of decline and *nerves* were everywhere among the ladies of my acquaintance; these imagined disorders conveyed a certain distinction, an interesting complication, to an otherwise mundane life. I could detect such childish bids for notice at a hundred paces.

Miss Williams's condition was otherwise, however—her figure gaunt from want of appetite; her countenance, however perfect the features, notable for its pallor; her strength apparently reduced to immobility. Yet Mrs. Potter, who must have known a parade of invalids in her years in Cheltenham, described the lady's indisposition as *willful*.

"Does Miss Fox share your view of her friend's condition?" I asked.

Mrs. Potter paused in building up the fire. "In a manner of

speaking. She says that Miss Williams's illness arises chiefly from the fact that she refuses even the smallest morsel of food, and retches into the chamber-pot what she does take; and if that ain't mulishness itself, I don't know what is."

I frowned over this; for after all, I was driven to Cheltenham myself for relief from an uneasy stomach and want of appetite. Most of those making a trial of the waters should say the same. But I did not debate Mrs. Potter; the condition of my fellow-lodgers ought not to be my close concern, any more than *my* indisposition should be theirs. To probe further was to risk indelicacy.

"Jane!" Cassandra mounted the last of the stairs and paused in the sitting-room doorway, her nose reddened from the chill and damp of this insipid May. "You have procured a tea tray! Excellent creature!"

I rose a little against my sopha cushions. "And have you procured the theatre tickets?"

"I have done better. I have secured seats in a private box—and an escort to attend us tomorrow evening." She stepped further into the room, revealing a figure in the passage behind her. "Only think—Mr. Raphael West is come to Cheltenham, Jane, and was so good as to recollect our acquaintance!"

If I could have commanded the floor to collapse immediately and swallow me in its dust, I should have been tempted. As it was, I suppressed the impulse to wail at Cassandra, draw the tartan lap robe completely over my face, or dash peremptorily into an adjacent room, preferably one with a looking-glass, where I might rearrange my cap.

Instead, I stiffened in helpless mortification, felt myself flush, and attempted to smile. "Mr. West! What an unexpected pleasure!"

"I must hope it is not an unwelcome one," he returned, drawing his hat from his unruly dark head and bowing. He was as heart-stoppingly handsome as ever in an iron-grey driving cloak of considerable dash. "Forgive me, Miss Austen, for calling without first sending up my card. Your sister encouraged me to be selfish—so great was my pleasure at learning of your presence in Cheltenham."

Selfish. He could use that word to describe his desire to see me—when I had been charging him in my mind, in my bleakest moments, with selfishness in staying away.

"Pray sit down, sir." Cassandra was beaming as she loosed her bonnet strings, as tho' congratulating herself on having conjured the very person to physick my diagnosis of female neglect. "Mrs. Potter, would you be so good as to bring a fresh pot? I shall just hasten upstairs, and discard these wet things. I shall not be a moment!"

Cass, of course, could not know how much I had dreaded meeting Mr. West again. She had not been present in London during our last protracted period of acquaintance—and no one but ourselves knew of the gentleman's charged words at parting from me last November. I would not think of them now, I silently vowed; one look at my altered person must be enough to send every thought of past intimacy from Mr. West's mind.

He was unchanged. His dark hair was a trifle shorter than I remembered, his face perhaps slightly more lined—but no degree of difference in the penetration of his gaze, or the supple grace of his mouth. A straight blade of a nose, brown eyes deeply socketed beneath a high forehead, lips full and bowed above a strong chin—tho' in his late forties, he retained every personal charm capable of bewitching a woman. He looked what he was: a gentleman of ease and accomplishment, his intelligence and decision writ upon his countenance.

He did not immediately dispose himself in a chair, but came instead to stand over me, gazing down into my face. "You have been unwell, my dear. It was a cruel winter, was it not?"

"And no less challenging spring."

He extended his hand, and I placed mine into it. He raised my fingers to his lips. The grazing touch sent a surge of warmth through my breast.

"What brings you to Cheltenham, sir?"

"The urging of a friend. You will not have heard of Mr. George Dinsdale, perhaps, but I shall make him known to you—a painter who studied with me long since. He has newly hung an exhibition of his works in his home here on North Street, and opens it to the publick free of charge for a few hours each day. I shall escort you to see them, by and by, when you are strong enough."[3]

---

3 George Dinsdale (lithographer and painter, active 1809–1829) offered the exhibition of his works free of admission to the Cheltenham public between 2 and 4 P.M. each day during the 1816 season at his home in North Street, according to Carolyn S. Greet in her article "Jane and Cassandra in Cheltenham" (Jane Austen Society Collected Reports, 2001–2005, p. 237). The *Cheltenham Chronicle* of May 30, 1816 lists Dinsdale's address as No. 5 North Street.—*Editor's note.*

"I am very well, I assure you. A trifling indisposition—a meal that did not agree with me."

"Your sister informs me you have not been yourself some months. I blame myself—I ought to have come into Hampshire and called upon you, on my return to London, at Easter—but for the claims of one dear to me."

"Indeed?"

Had he given his heart to another lady, then, and meant to break the news to me while I lay swaddled in a tartan blanket?

"My daughter Charlotte was delivered of a son at about that time—stillborn, sadly." He turned his head, and chose one of the armchairs near at hand, settling into it. "She felt the blow deeply. Her spirits were so oppressed, in fact, that her husband and I feared for her reason—and then, over a period of some weeks, for her life. There was her elder child to consider as well, a girl of nearly three years, who badly wanted her mother's notice and interest. I was detained in Bath some two months past Easter—longer than I intended or hoped."

"It sounds a sad and difficult time," I ventured. "Your daughter has improved?"

"Enough that I felt it safe to part from her for a time, but not enough that I am entirely free of anxiety."

"What parent may ever be that?"

He dipped his exquisitely-molded head, a feathering of silver at the temples, to concede the point. "I hope your family is well? Your lovely niece, and your excellent brother?"

"If you would enquire after Henry," I said lightly, "not even bankruptcy and the utter ruin of his career may long keep him bowed. As for Fanny, she goes along much as ever—increasing in wisdom and accomplishment, without one whit of vanity."

"She has learnt much from her time with her aunt, I perceive."

Mrs. Potter then appearing with the tea tray refreshed and amplified, by the addition of two cups and a plate of cakes, further exchange of an intimate nature must be at an end. Cassandra stepping into the sitting-room with her hair redressed beneath a fresh cap, and launching instantly into a discussion of the Cheltenham Theatre, which she had not known before was a favourite of the late Mrs. Jordan's—a comic actress Cassandra preferred above all others—we three spoke on general matters; and not long thereafter Mr. West took his leave. But in parting he contrived to say, in a lowered tone for my ears alone, "I am putting up at the York Hotel adjacent, and am to be in Cheltenham at least a week. Will you and your sister dine with me there, tomorrow, before the theatre? I shall bespeak a private parlour, so you may be comfortable."

Mrs. Potter's mutton stew is very well in its way, but not worth the risk of constant repetition. The York Hotel is Cheltenham's finest, and must employ a French cook. I accepted on behalf of both Austen ladies with relief; and at Mr. West's departure, turned my thoughts to choosing which of my gowns I should wear for the adventure.

If there was a shade more colour in my cheeks when next I glanced in the mirror, I am sure the local waters were not responsible.

9

THROWN FROM HEAVEN'S GATE

Thursday, 30th May, 1816
Cheltenham

To our surprize, the storm clouds over Gloucestershire broke long enough today for a brisk jaunt along the Elm Walk. Tho' we did not leave off our woolen spencers and stout boots, the stroll was so pleasantly airy that it might *almost* have been spring! Cassandra was daring enough to open her sunshade, while I drew off my gloves, and caressed the petals of a late-blooming tulip.

The warmth and sun had drawn most of the intimates of Mrs. Potter's house to the pleasure grounds of the Royal Well. Miss Garthwaite and her brother marched purposefully up the steps to the Long Room, Thucydides trotting beside them, his tongue lolling from his droll black muzzle. Unbidden, Cassandra slowed her gait a little to afford the pair a few moments' grace; we had encountered the shadowed clergyman and his forthright sister over the breakfast table, and could not be blamed for avoiding a second meeting within as many hours.

Providentially, a voice called out a greeting—I turned, and saw Captain Pellew not three paces distant.

"Good morning, sir!"

"Your servant, Miss Austen." Leaning on his stick with one hand, he raised his chapeau-bras with the other.

Beside him was Miss Fox, her hands on the basket-chair; and arranged quite prettily within it was Miss Williams. She wore a celestial blue gown embroidered with daisies, so fresh that it might have come direct from her modiste. A charming bonnet of chip straw, fastened under her left ear with a silk bow of primrose, framed her blond curls. Despite her apparent thinness and languor, her eyes were alight as they glanced up at Pellew; they were the same shade of blue as her gown, and rimmed with dark lashes.

"May I present my sister Cassandra?" I enquired. "This is Captain Pellew, who is acquainted with our brother Charles."

"How delightful." Cassandra curtseyed. "We are disposed to regard every officer of the Royal Navy as an immediate friend."

"The Misses Austen lodge with us at Potter's," Pellew offered in turn to his party. "Miss Fox, Miss Williams—"

We inclined our heads all around.

"Are you come to Cheltenham for your health?" Miss Fox asked as we turned back together to make a circuit of the grounds.

"I must suppose that is the general purpose among visitors to the town, although I confess for my own part an equal desire for a change of scenery," I replied. "The miserable winter, too long endured, was a powerful inducement for quitting Hampshire."

"I was similarly inspired in my desire to leave Cornwall. Do you make a long stay in Cheltenham?"

"A fortnight only. And yourselves?"

"Our plans are not definite."

"But Sarah," Miss Williams interjected, "now that the weather has turned, we shall certainly remain another month at least. Having made a trial of Cheltenham at its worst, I do not wish to leave when all the delights of the Season are promised."

"Then you must endeavour to recruit your strength," her friend replied. "A little gruel, perhaps, with your tea—"

"I may decide to remain here for the summer entire," Miss Williams persisted, as tho' Miss Fox had not spoken. "It would be something, would it not, Captain—to witness the Duke of Wellington open the new Assembly Rooms?"

"A pleasure, indeed!" cried Captain Pellew. "But I had heard the Duke was not to waltz in Cheltenham until the end of July. I shall have returned to Plymouth by that date, I daresay."

"Such paltry courage!" Miss Williams observed, gazing up at him from under her lashes. "You might have induced me to dance."

"But with this leg," Pellew returned, "I should have done you no credit."

The remark, in referencing an instance of *undoubted* courage in the gentleman's life, must be felt as a rebuke; it silenced the invalid. If she intended her raillery as flirtation, Miss Williams judged sadly; the Captain's looks were grave.

Into the little awkwardness, I said: "Plymouth—Are you a Devon man, sir?"

"As are most of the Pellews, ma'am." He took up my words eagerly. "Tho' so many of us have spent our lives at sea, Devon will always be home. Do you know that part of the country?"

"I have been so happy as to visit it some once or twice. Now, Cornwall, on the other hand, I have never seen."

"Then you are fortunate," Miss Williams tossed over her shoulder. "It is a miserable place, filled with wretched people. I could not hasten from it too quickly, and hope I may never return."

Her accent had gone from playful to petulant, and Miss Fox swiftly intervened. "I fear you are tired, my dear. Do you wish to return to our lodgings, or visit Gunton's for a strawberry ice?"

"You know I abhor strawberries, Sarah."

"Will you not take at least one glass from the Royal Well, now we have walked all this way?" Miss Fox urged coaxingly. "You know Dr. Hargate advises it."

"The Royal Well was favoured by the King, was it not?" Miss Williams mused. "And he has since run mad, I believe— these five years at least. No, Sarah, I do *not* wish to sample the waters. But by all means fetch me a cup of tea from the Long Room, and I shall do my best to swallow it. No milk or sugar, mind! I cannot abide them!"

"Allow me to go," Captain Pellew said. "It would be an honour."

"As if you could carry a tea tray, walking as you do with that stick!" Miss Williams retorted. "Sarah may do it; she is the stoutest of us all, and cannot mind the exercise."

Miss Fox's eyes met the Captain's over the top of the basket-chair, and I thought I perceived the lady to give an almost imperceptible shake of the head. She turned towards the spa's open French windows; the strains of a Bach concerto drifted to our ears.

Pellew managed, despite his game leg, to propel the chair from the gravel path to rest in the shade of an elm. Miss Williams lifted her face to the light that shifted among the leaves. Her long-lashed eyelids closed. "How delightful is the sun," she murmured, "after so many months of grey! Delicate as the brush of an angel's wing, when one from Heaven strays."

"Miss Williams is a poetess," Captain Pellew offered in a lowered tone. "Of some ambition, I believe."

"Nonsense." The lady retorted firmly. "Women are constitutionally incapable of ambition. I have been informed so, by no less an authority than my physician, Dr. Hargate. Our poor frames are unequal to the ravages of an excited mind. We may safely listen to *some* verses, when read aloud by a gentleman— tho' never Lord Byron's, which dangerously overset the nerves. Any attempt at private composition is strictly forbidden, and all pens and paper confiscated until such time as one consents to drink iron and sulphur, or choke down a hearty breakfast."

"You are joking, of course," Pellew smiled.

"Not for a moment." Miss Williams's accent was sweetness itself. "I never jest about those forces that would attempt to stifle or control me. Which poets are *your* favourites, Miss Austen? I do not know your Christian names, and therefore cannot distinguish between the two of you; but either sister may answer, as you chuse."

Cassandra looked dismayed at this careless speech; it was at once too playful and too caustic; she did not know whether to be amused or offended. But I took up the challenge.

"My Christian name is Jane—and I do not hesitate to read Lord Byron, no matter how unsafe the practise may prove. If there is a mortal danger in words, I have yet to discover it."

"You admire *The Corsair*, I imagine, or even *Childe Harold*. Do you read *female* poets, Miss Jane?"

I hesitated. The mocking challenge in her voice was disconcerting.

"Catherine Maria Fanshawe, perhaps?—for she is much praised by Mr. Walter Scott. Or do you know Charlotte Lennox—an intimate of Samuel Richardson and Samuel Johnson?"

"I have, of course, read her *Female Quixote*."

"That is a novel, however, and therefore cannot signify."

"I have been a dedicated reader of Charlotte Smith," I attempted.

"Another novelist, at heart. Have you looked into Mary Robinson, who excelled so much in the dramatick arts, or Anna Seward, the Swan of Lichfield?" Miss Williams pursed her lips and shook her head disapprovingly. "If not even a professed admirer of poetry condescends to read her fellow women, how are we ever to find our just audience?"

"That is unfair!" Cassandra cried. "There is no one more likely than Jane to understand the scorn that is heaped on female writers—"

"Cass," I muttered warningly. I had no desire to expose my work to a virtual stranger.

"The person, be it gentleman or lady, who has not pleasure in a novel, must be intolerably stupid," my sister persisted. "Indeed, you do novels an injustice, Miss Williams, if you regard them as so much inferior to verse."

The Beauty in the Basket Chair turned her contemptuous gaze upon Cassandra. "Do I, indeed? I merely voice a criticism I hear unceasingly on the lips of every reader, women chief among them. Poetry is declared the most sublime, the most exalted, and the most uplifting of all the literary arts, because it is fortified with male vigour; whereas novels are fit only for such dull minds as require sensation and outrage to transport them. It can be no accident that *women*, who both produce and consume such frivolous fictions, are chiefly dismissed by the critical journals."

To my mortification, I felt colour rise in my cheeks.

"Come, now," Miss Williams rallied, "how many times have you heard a lady of your acquaintance turn her book face-down among the sopha cushions, and declare in an accent of boredom that it is *only a novel*, not very worth reading?"

"Far too often," Cassandra replied quietly, "to do justice to the pleasure such works provide."

Miss Williams laughed harshly. "You are unrepentant, I see, in your literary tastes! Far be it from me to suggest they may not merit such regard. I should not wish to insult your experience or understanding, Miss Austen."

"I should certainly never condemn *yours*. We must agree, Miss Williams, to disagree."

Cass slipped her arm through mine. "Now, Jane, is it not long past time we bid our friends *adieu*, and took a draught from the King's Pump?"

"And if we are *very* fortunate," I murmured as we moved on in the direction of the Long Room and its orchestral crowd, "it may even drive us mad."

10

DRAMA AT THE THEATRE

Thursday, 30th May, 1816
Cheltenham, cont'd.

The York Hotel, Mrs. Potter informs me, is owned by one Mr. Sheldon, the son of a local publican who aspired to something more. Perceiving in his youth that the notice of the Royal Family might do much to change the fortunes of his village, he added two storeys to what had been a simple coaching inn, called it after the Regent's brother, and stiled it an hotel—by which Mr. Sheldon gave notice to Cheltenham's growing crowd of visitors, that they might be honoured to pay him handsomely for the sort of accommodation they had come to expect in such fashionable watering-holes as Brighton and Bath.

"And then Sheldon acquired Mr. John Bowles Watson's old theatre," Mr. West informed me as he drew out my chair at table in the private parlour, "and expanded his building to incorporate it. We are even now sitting down to dine in what was once the pit, I believe."

"Do you dare suggest, sir, that Mrs. Jordan once tread the boards in this very room?" Cassandra demanded.

"She is known to have played in *The Merry Wives of Windsor*, before His Royal Highness, when King George stayed in Cheltenham to take the waters," Mr. West replied, "so I must believe it to be so, ma'am. You are an admirer of Dora Jordan?"

"Emphatically." Cassandra permitted West's friend, George Dinsdale, to seat her. "Without question, she is the greatest comic actress of our age. I was so happy as to see her once in Drury Lane. A breeches part, of course—she excelled in them."

"I am relieved that we are to view a tragedy this evening," Mr. Dinsdale observed, "as there can then be no possibility of an unfavourable comparison."

Mr. West's friend is very gentleman-like, though rather short in stature and thick in girth. As if in compensation, his tailoring is exquisite. Nothing could be snowier than his cravat, and his collar is calculated to a nicety—neither rakishly high nor priggishly low. If I suspected the creaking that emanated from his person, as he settled my sister in her chair, was due to a whalebone corset, I would keep such amusing thoughts to myself.

Mr. West had called at two o'clock, in a barouche hired from the York's hostelry, and invited Cassandra and me to drive out to Mr. Dinsdale's house, the ground-floor rooms of which he threw open for two hours each day, in a publick exhibition of his art. The fair weather had held, and we were privileged to sit opposite one another, enjoying the open carriage and all the interest of the passing scenery, as a hired coachman conveyed us to our treat. I had not felt so well in months.

Alighted at Mr. Dinsdale's home—a modern villa in the Palladian stile, on North Street—I was interested to discover that engraved prints vied for place with watercolours on his walls. Knowing him to have studied with Raphael West, whose family tradition is in the grand historical mode, I had expected oils to be chiefly on view. But I had forgot; all true painters must acquire a mastery of the charcoal sketch from life, and learn to control the subtle wash of pigments clouded and diffused with water. Works in oil are the final height only achievable from such skills; and it should not be wonderful that many artists are satisfied with lithographs, or swift colour sketches that capture a passing moment or scene. Certainly the modest prices of these, relative to a study in oils, must find eager buyers and their purses.

Mr. Dinsdale's subject is chiefly Cheltenham itself. I find one engraving of a city, viewed from its surrounding hills, to be very like another; and Mr. Dinsdale's habit of framing his view with a single tree, invariably at the left foreground of the composition for perspective, seemed studiously contrived. It succeeded, however, in lending a raw town a falsely Classical air, which must have greatly increased the prints' value among his admirers. I found the gentleman's watercolours more natural, and was able to be warm in my praise—a subject I took up again now, as the York Hotel's serving-man shook out our napkins, and draped them over our laps.

"Natural!" Mr. Dinsdale replied. "You must know, Miss Austen, that there is no one to equal our friend West, here, for sketches in the natural line; the freshness he captured, during his youthful journeys through the primitive American landscape, is a constant inspiration for my work. He was so good as to present several drawings to me, and I keep them displayed in my workroom."

"Pennsylvania is hardly primitive, George," Mr. West observed with amusement. "It is my father's birthplace, recollect."

"He did not chuse to remain there overlong, however."

"True; tho' I have known a time when he regretted his defection to the courts of kings and autocrats."

"Great paintings demand greater patrons," Mr. Dinsdale declared, throwing up his hands, "but if you are going to discuss *politics* before the ladies, I despair of your manners."

"On a night when we are to see *Julius Caesar*, sir, can anything *but* politics be the subject?" I countered. "I am perfectly ready to debate you on the subtleties of power, faction, conspiracy, and murder, having been an English subject all my life; our history, you know, is rife with such examples."

Raphael West laughed, but his friend looked grave. "I would never try your patience with matters so involved, ma'am, and so beyond your accustomed sphere. Let us discuss instead the late nuptials of Princess Charlotte and Prince Leopold of Saxe-Coburg! I am sure you must have read of them, and seen the colour plates of both ceremony and dress. A lady must always love a wedding."

"Ten—*thousand*—pounds!" Cassandra uttered in stringent accents. "That is the reported cost of the Princess's wedding gown—silver lamé on net, over a silver tissue slip, embroidered with shells and flowers. How a single dress may demand so vast a sum is inconceivable; for myself, I think it positively wicked, when so many in the nation suffer from want."

There was a political statement, if Mr. Dinsdale liked; for however "involved" the Kingdom's matters might be, as he chose to put it, women will always understand the cost of finery.

"I could have wished the ceremony were in an actual church," I added, "rather than the Red Drawing Room at Carlton House—but perhaps the Regent was afraid he might be struck dead by lightning bolts, if he attempted to enter the Chapel Royal at St. James. I daresay he has not found occasion to do so since his own wedding."

Mr. West's eyes glinted with laughter. "Ladies! You will shock poor Dinsdale! Do you not know the subject of the Royal Wedding is dear to his heart? I wonder you did not exhibit your transparencies to our friends, George, when opportunity offered."

"They are not yet completed to my satisfaction," Mr. Dinsdale replied with discomfiture, "and moreover, ought not to be glimpsed until the night in question."

"Dinsdale is preparing a remarkable series of illumina tions," West explained, at my look of enquiry, "from prints of his own design, on a magnificent scale, to be displayed at Monday's Assembly. The ball is to be a celebration, you know, of the Princess Charlotte's recent nuptials."

"—And of course, of her grandfather His Majesty's Natal Day, which falls on the Tuesday," Dinsdale added.

"And your prints commemorate both?" Cassandra asked.

"They do. Eight scenes to be exact, including His Majesty's

cherished pursuits: Statecraft (in his Royal Robes, holding a Globe), Agriculture (holding a scythe), Astronomy (with a telescope), and Family Life (surrounded by Her Majesty and Their Fifteen Dear Children). Of Princess Charlotte, we will have: Her Royal Highness as a Child; the Meeting with Prince Leopold at Carlton House; First Interview at the Pulteney Hotel; and of course, The Royal Nuptials."

"Did you actually witness the *ceremony*, sir?" Cassandra cried. "And what is your opinion, then, of this outrageous dress?"

I cast her a quelling look. "You have undertaken a prodigious amount of work, Mr. Dinsdale."

"I count the labour as nothing, dear ma'am. It is a privilege to honour the Royal Family, while bringing delight to all Cheltenham!"

"I could wish, now, that we had stolen a glimpse of the prints—but I respect your desire to display them to superior advantage."

Dinsdale nodded gravely. "One cannot be too careful, if one desires the greatest effect. At exactly midnight Monday, by the clock, the transparencies shall be illuminated for the Assembly-goers' delight, in a special interior pavilion erected in the ballroom for the purpose. An octagonal structure, with the images affixed to screens at intervals, and illuminated from behind."

"And what an excellent spur to your engraving sales that shall be, if the spectacle comes off as planned," I murmured.

Dinsdale beamed around the table. "It should be most edifying! It cannot help, I think, but be well-received!"

He was so obviously proud of his scheme, and the occasion

on which it was to be unveiled, that I could no longer sport with his good humour.

"Well! I wish you every success, Mr. Dinsdale, as I wish Princess Charlotte every happiness. We may all agree, I think, in pitying a lady reared by such ramshackle parents, whose only common ground was scandal."

"Here, here," West said.

The serving-man having filled my glass with good French wine, I raised it in a salute to the table; and any hint of discord was at an end. But I vowed to seat myself by Mr. West during *Julius Caesar*—there was no gentleman less likely to instruct me in the vein of conversation most proper to ladies, or the enjoyment of a play.

JULIUS CAESAR, IN THE event, proved all that we could desire.

"Mrs. Smith has performed her duties to perfection," my sister observed, as the curtain fell on Act III. "This Brutus speaks so nobly, he might be mistaken for a duke. I almost prefer him in the part to Kemble himself—so laboured are that celebrated man's speeches, I have sometimes lost myself in attempting to follow them."

"I wonder if Mrs. Smith's enjoyment of the play is diminished by familiarity," I mused.

"—Or from viewing it always from the wings, as I suppose she must. It is a pity she is not able to join the rest of this evening's party from Mrs. Potter's."

Cassandra was referring to the occupants of the box almost directly opposite our own. When the lights came up during the interval, we had observed Miss Williams, looking frail but lovely in a robe of white satin with a silver-net overskirt. Her shoulders were too prominent, a testament to the wasting of her condition, but her golden curls—unadorned this evening except for a spray of hothouse flowers—shone in the reflected light of the candle-lustres. Beside her was Miss Fox, arrayed unusually for her in dark green. They made an interesting pair—one so fair, the other so dark. Beside them, Captain Pellew was all that was distinguished in his dress uniform. He certainly spent a good deal of his time in the pair's company.

I amused myself with conjectures on the gentleman's motives. Was he a friend of long standing, who escorted the two ladies into Gloucestershire? Or had he scraped an acquaintance with the heiress and her companion in Mrs. Potter's establishment? Was his intimacy evidence of a native gallantry, or was his heart actually engaged? And if the latter, which lady had won his affection—Miss Williams, or Miss Fox?

I happened to catch the Captain's eye, blushed with a consciousness of my own wayward thoughts, and was rewarded by the sight of him rising from his seat with a word to Miss Fox, and exiting the box. A moment later the door to our own loge opened, and there was Pellew, offering his compliments and begging to be introduced to our friends.

I presented him to Mr. West and Mr. Dinsdale; he had seen the latter's exhibition so recently as last week, and was able to offer some praise, although he admitted he preferred a fine sketch of a Naval engagement to any landscape.

Then, in drawing me a little aside, he said in a lowered tone, "I wished to inform you, Miss Austen, that I have written both to your brother Charles and to my distant cousin, Admiral Sir Edward Pellew, in testament to Captain Austen's character. When I have the Admiral's reply—whatever the news, of good or ill—I shall hasten to relate the whole to you."

"You are very good, sir," I replied, in heartfelt accents. "I have not yet had word of my brother's arrival in London, but as he is unaware that I am presently staying in Cheltenham, that cannot be surprising. I must hope to be greeted with the best possible intelligence of his panel's result, when I am returned to Hampshire. I shall always be grateful for your energy on Charles's behalf."

Whatever he might have said in answer was forestalled by a little flurry of activity in the box nearest at hand. It had sat empty throughout the first three acts of the play, as tho' in expectation of those who had reserved it; but now a couple had entered the loge, the gentleman drawing out the lady's chair. He was perhaps near thirty, the lady of indeterminate but no very advanced age; his appearance neat and unremarkable, hers distinguished by the number of fine jewels she wore at her neck, ears, and wrist. Her hair was fiery, and her ruby-coloured gown hardly less so; in such a town as Cheltenham, her appearance must draw every eye.

Except, it seemed, Captain Pellew's. His gaze was fixed instead upon the box opposite, and the reaction of its occupants to the interesting couple's arrival.

Miss Fox's countenance, normally unruffled and under the strictest self-command, bore an expression I may only describe as *alarm*, from her widened eyes to her parted lips. But it was Miss Williams whose appearance shocked me most. The invalid's pallid face had flushed to the roots of her hair, and in defiance of her usual immobility, she had half-started from her chair. For an instant she clung with both hands to the box's gilt railing, and then with a pitiful little cry she collapsed to the floor, her golden head disappearing from view, in a dead faint.

11

REVELATIONS OF A VISCOUNT

Friday, 31st May, 1816
Cheltenham

The theatre was one of the newer buildings in Cheltenham, having been constructed for the purpose by Mr. Bowles Watson on a plot of land south of the High. It was mere steps from Mrs. Potter's door, but Mr. West and Mr. Dinsdale insisted upon escorting us to our lodgings once the play was done, and parted from us on the threshold.

"I hope your young acquaintance has recovered from her fit of illness," Mr. Dinsdale said, "and that a cheerful report greets your return."

"I am sure that if there is any intelligence to be conveyed, Captain Pellew will offer it," I replied.

That gentleman had hastened immediately from our box at Miss Williams's sudden swoon. As the curtain rose on the play's fourth act, I observed Miss Fox on her knees, a vinaigrette in her hand; but her efforts to revive her friend seemed unavailing. Within seconds the lady's insensible form had been carried from the box by two footmen, and her party followed her.

I saw as well that the gentleman in the box beside us had risen from his chair and quietly slipped through the loge door. His lady remained, however, her eyes fixed tranquilly upon the stage, and before long the gentleman returned and resumed his seat without comment.

"Poor Miss Williams," Cassandra whispered. "It is as I thought; Mrs. Potter is entirely wrong. Her illness is not a figment of an overindulgent mind, but of a failing constitution."

I thought it rather the result of a shock. But as I spied Mrs. Smith hurrying across the street at that moment to join us at the boardinghouse door, I did not dispute with my sister further.

"I must congratulate you," I said to Mrs. Smith. "Brutus was everything one could desire in the role, the very image of Roman gentility, and makes me long to hear the charming vowels of your Lady Teazle."

"I fear Tess is not so apt a pupil as Jasper," Mrs. Smith replied, "but perhaps I shall work a miracle. Mrs. Potter's door is always locked at this hour, but she has pressed upon me a latchkey. Pray, allow me to gain our admittance."

Eager at this advanced hour to find our own beds, we parted gratefully for her trim figure and mounted the steps behind our new friend. But in gaining the sitting-room, we discovered the whole house in upheaval.

Miss Garthwaite was sitting by the fire, arrayed in a dressing-gown, nightcap, and slippers, with Thucydides held firmly on her lap. Her expression was one of outrage, as yet unvoiced; I judged her to be listening too avidly to the conversation of others.

Captain Pellew leant heavily on his stick in the middle of the room, in apparent support of Miss Fox, who was engaged in vociferous debate with Dr. Hargate. Of Miss Williams or her basket-chair there was no sign, but the door to the ladies' private parlour was thrown open, and the spill of candlelight revealed a room in disarray: trunks flung wide, gowns piled willy-nilly on chairs, a quantity of silver papers strewn about the floor, and a travelling desk overburdened with books. Mrs. Potter's serving-maid, Lucy, was endeavouring to pack the ladies' things, but it was clear she had been summoned from bed for the task, and was nearly stumbling with fatigue.

"Under no condition should I allow her to be moved," Dr. Hargate said. "Indeed, Miss Fox, I regard you as foolish beyond permission to suggest it."

"But move she must," the lady retorted crisply. "It is impossible for us to remain safely in Cheltenham another moment, sir."

"Captain Pellew will support me." Hargate turned in exasperation to the only other male present. "You will represent to this headstrong girl the idiocy, sir, of travel by night, when the moon is barely at its quarter, in the company of a lady whose pulse is so tumultuous she might expire within a mile of this house!"

"Oh, dear," Cassandra uttered in failing accents.

"I do not know, Miss Fox, if you will find any coachman for hire who will submit to such conditions," Pellew said. "No man of sense will trust his horses to an ill-lit road. I cannot believe, moreover, that you would wish Miss Williams's health to suffer from this precipitous flight."

"I tell you, her very life is at risk if she remains." Miss Fox turned her back on Dr. Hargate and appealed solely to the Naval officer. "Have you ever had cause to regard me as unsettled in my reason? Or susceptible to strong hysterics? Before God, Captain, I speak only with such urgency as Miss Williams should herself, if she were not laid down upon her bed in a swoon."

"And yet you do not explain that urgency," he said. "You offer no reason why your departure cannot wait until morning."

"Exactly!" Miss Garthwaite cried, to general surprize. From her expression I concluded she was wholly engrossed in our domestic drama; her hand furiously smoothed her pug's sleek coat, tho' I judged her unaware of the repeated action. For his part, Thucydides seemed lost in an ecstasy of contentment.

"To say more would be to betray a confidence." Miss Fox's countenance was strained and white; she seemed barely to contain her temper. "I may only beg you, sir, to hasten to the nearest livery stable—one that is *not* attached to the York Hotel, mind—and hire whatever closed carriage you may discover, along with a man to drive it. You should be doing your friends the very greatest possible service—"

"May I be of assistance, Captain?" Mrs. Smith stepped forward. "I am acquainted with all the best stables in town"—at this, Miss Garthwaite emitted a contemptuous snort—"and may direct you, or preferably one of Mrs. Potter's servants, to the nearest."

"Hannah," Captain Pellew said gently. "Do not be abetting this mad flight, I beg of you."

"I will never fail a desperate woman, Harry," she said fiercely, "as you very well know."

From the ground floor, came a sudden loud knocking at Mrs. Potter's door. With an imprecation barely suppressed, Miss Fox threw up her hands and hurried into the private parlour, where Lucy was carefully tucking silver paper among the gowns in the trunk.

"Never mind that!" Miss Fox cried. "It does not matter if they are creased—only that we get away!"

She disappeared into Miss Williams's bedchamber, drawing closed the door.

"Such carryings-on!" Miss Garthwaite declared. She glared at Mrs. Smith, but her pronouncement was for me. "You are fortunate to be only now returning from your evening's entertainment, Miss Austen—for had you attempted to sleep, I assure you it must have been impossible! I myself was awakened by the most atrocious noise not an hour ago, and as all possibility of peace was clearly at an end, I ordered tea for myself and Thucydides here by the fire—which order has *not* been attended to!"

Below me, in the hall, the door bolts were drawn back, and there was a murmur of male voices. Then all the bustle of an entry, and footsteps mounting the stairs.

"It's a respectable house," one of the men said, "and Mrs. Potter insists on no callers after ten o'clock. But if it's as you say, my lord, I don't see as how I can do anything but rouse the ladies. Unless it be the case they have not yet retired."

A frowsy, silver head and a formidable set of whiskers appeared in the doorway; this must be the rumoured Mr.

Potter, whom Cassandra and I had not yet glimpsed. He was bare-legged beneath a nightdress, and held a tallow candle from the kitchens.

Behind him, not much greater in height, was the gentleman of modest appearance who had taken the box beside our own, at the theatre that evening.

I glanced at Captain Pellew and saw that he, too, had recognised the patron of the neighbouring box. "Good evening, Potter," he said. "What brings you out of bed at this hour?"

The landlord gestured with his light. "Viscount Portreath, sir."

The gentleman stepped into the sitting-room and drew off his tall black beaver in a gesture of civility to all of us. "Pray forgive my intrusion. I should not have disturbed you, were it not a matter of grave importance."

Pellew moved forward, as tho' to place himself between the visitor and the closed door of the private parlour. "My name is Pellew, my lord. I believe you have been the cause of considerable distress this evening, for two ladies of my acquaintance."

"Distress?" The Viscount's mild gaze swept over the Naval officer. "How can that be, Captain, when one of the ladies is my wife?"

1 2

THE NIGHT-WALKER

Friday, 31st May, 1816
Cheltenham, cont'd.

I think I may speak for every intimate of Mrs. Potter's boardinghouse when I say that his lordship's words stunned us to silence, and indeed, impeded almost every thought except astonishment. But the paralysis was brief; and two of our number recovered at almost the same instant.

"Your *wife?*" Captain Pellew cried. From his expression of shocked bewilderment, I concluded that he had known nothing of any marriage. Pellew was *not*, then, an old friend of either lady—he must have become acquainted with both so recently as Cheltenham.

"But which of the ladies is it?" Miss Garthwaite demanded.

The Viscount moved further into the room, suddenly in command of all our attention. His compact frame and mild features belied a depth of authority—the habit of birth and rank. But as his countenance came fully into the lamplight, I felt rather than heard Mrs. Smith gasp. She retreated a step behind me, as tho' to keep her distance from the gentleman.

I glanced at her face; it was as closed and shuttered now as it had been under the influence of Miss Garthwaite's conversation at dinner Monday evening.

"I gather, then, that she is not presently using her title in Cheltenham," Lord Portreath said. "When I married her, Miss Rose Williams was less inclined to shrink from the world's notice. Where is she?"

"Miss Fox and Miss Williams occupy the set of rooms beyond that door," Captain Pellew replied with a brief nod towards the private parlour. "Miss Williams is indisposed, and Miss Fox is attending her."

"Yes, I saw her swoon at the theatre. It is her preferred answer to an undesired meeting." He drew a case deliberately from his coat and offered a card to the landlord. "Potter, you will inform Miss Fox of my arrival, if you please, and add that I wish to speak with her immediately."

"Yes, my lord. Very good, my lord." Potter turned hastily to rap upon the door, spilling tallow on the floorboards at his feet.

"I am relieved you are come, sir," Dr. Hargate said impulsively. "I am no longer required to countenance a foolishness that must place your wife's very life in danger. Miss Fox is determined to remove her ladyship from this house, against every word of advice I may offer—and some in our presence would have encouraged it!"

Lord Portreath's gaze drifted over him. "And *you* are?"

"Lionel Hargate. A physician in this city, whose honour it is to have her ladyship under my care."

"She still refuses all sustenance, then?" the Viscount

enquired. "No wonder she swoons. Rest easy, Hargate—there is nothing truly wrong with her."

The parlour door was pulled slightly ajar, and the house-maid's thin face thrust through the gap. "Fetch Miss Fox, Lucy," Potter instructed, "and present this card."

The maid snatched the token and vanished.

"Jane," my sister whispered in my ear, "ought not we to retire?"

But at that moment Miss Fox strode forthrightly through the parlour door, her eyes overbright and her cheeks aflame with indignation. "My lord," she said abruptly, and closed the door behind her.

He inclined his head. "Miss Fox. It has been some weeks since we met."

"Three weeks and five days precisely," she returned. "We have not met since Sunday the fifth of May, when Rose and I quit the manor forever."

"I believe you are correct."

"Sunday travel!" Miss Garthwaite hissed from her place by the fire.

The sound of her voice drew the Viscount's eye; he said to Miss Fox, "We had much better speak in private."

The lady's gaze did not waver. "You can have nothing to say to me that all may not hear. Indeed, I require Captain Pellew's support, as guard against violence."

Portreath's eyebrows rose fractionally. "Are you intending, then, to strike me, madam?"

"If I were, it should be no more than you deserved." Miss Fox's hands were clenched at her sides, and her generous lips twisted with anger. "If my dear friend were not laid down upon her bed this moment she must agree. The mere sight of you has deprived her of sense. If she passes from this life this evening, my lord, her death may be laid at your door."

"Such wild imaginings!" Dr. Hargate broke in. "Lord Portreath, pay no mind to this woman's ravings. I assure you, she has parted from her reason; that can be the only explanation for wishing to fly from this house, and for so abusing a nobleman to his face."

"Is it true, Miss Fox?" Captain Pellew demanded. "Is Miss Williams indeed the Viscountess Portreath?"

Miss Fox hesitated an instant, then said with apparent unwillingness. "She is. But—"

"Enough." Viscount Portreath strode towards Miss Fox, who placed her back resolutely against the door. "I demand to see *my wife*, madam. You will take me to her at once."

Miss Fox sought Pellew's eyes over the Viscount's shoulder, her expression one of supplication. The Captain made no move.

"Harry," Mrs. Smith murmured softly.

I saw him almost imperceptibly shake his head.

"If I must have you hauled before the Assizes on a charge of kidnapping, Sarah, I will do it," Viscount Portreath said.

For a moment, no one moved.

"I am her nurse," Miss Fox attempted. "I must remain in the room while you speak with her."

His lordship shrugged indifferently. "As you wish."

Again, Miss Fox looked imploringly at Captain Pellew, but the gentleman remained impassive. From the rigid aspect of his entire form, however, I guessed at what this cost him. His knuckles, where his fist grasped the head of his ebony stick, were white.

With a sag of her shoulders, Miss Fox reached for the latch and stepped back to permit the Viscount's passage. Then she followed him into the room, and softly closed the parlour door.

"I should never have credited it, not for an hundred years, had I not heard the truth with my own ears," Miss Garthwaite uttered with an expression bordering on triumph. She rose from her chair, depositing Thucydides on the carpet in an outraged heap. The little dog emitted a nasal bark of protest. "I must inform my brother of this intelligence immediately. I bid you goodnight."

My sister and I inclined our heads without a word, and moved towards the stairs to seek our bedchamber above.

"What does it all mean, Harry?" Mrs. Smith said softly.

"I do not know," he replied, "but I mean to find out. Now, try to get some rest—it is exceedingly late."

Mrs. Smith dipped her head and gained the staircase; but she paused with her hand on the newel post. "You shall not desert her?"

"I shall not," he replied briefly, "until the door is bolted behind that fellow. You may be easy, Hannah."

I HAD REASON TO consider of bolted doors some three hours later, when I awoke with a start to the sound of stealthy foot-steps in the passage outside my door.

I glanced over at the other bed in my shared room:

Cassandra's. The humped shape of her body beneath the bedclothes reassured me. She was lying with her back to me and was breathing in the deep, insensible fashion of those who dream.

Why, then, had I awakened?

There was nothing extraordinary in such a disturbance—the sound of another person pacing a passage at night—when one lodged in a boardinghouse. One of the guests might seek the privy, although we had chamber pots against that necessity. Someone might be restless in the night, and wander downstairs to the sitting-room and the comfort of a book—although it was more natural to simply light the candle by one's bedside, and read while warm beneath the bedclothes. It was possible that a fellow-lodger had been abroad in Cheltenham and returned to rouse the household well after midnight; but which lodger might that be? We had all of us been within-doors when I myself retired for the night.

The footsteps, still tentative and stealthy, were diminishing down the hallway. At its end, the passage turned sharply right, and gave onto the gentlemen's bedchambers. Mr. Garthwaite and Captain Pellew were lodged there, but the footsteps were too light for either one. Garthwaite's tread was shambling and heavy; Pellew's marked by his limp. It was possible that Miss Garthwaite, whose room was opposite ours, had determined to visit her brother in the middle of the night; but in that case, I should also have heard Thucydides's paws, for Miss Garthwaite never stirred without her pug.

Mrs. Smith, whose room was next to ours, paying a clandestine call upon the Captain?

Startling thought—was it possible that the two were lovers?

He had called her *Hannah* in my hearing, and the freedom of a lady's Christian name must always be an intimate privilege; but then, the Captain had as much as told me that he had known Mrs. Smith from youth. I had certainly thought Pellew's attentions entirely Miss Williams's . . . but she was suddenly revealed as another man's wife . . . Was *this* why Miss Garthwaite spoke contemptuously of Mrs. Smith, as a *fallen woman*?

I gave way to consuming curiosity and crept out of bed. I tiptoed to the door and unlatched it quietly, then peered out, towards the far end of the passage.

A lady, indeed, was moving towards the turn in the hall that led to the gentlemen's rooms. Mrs. Potter kept an oil lamp burning low in the passage all night, as a consideration to her guests. As the figure passed under it, I glimpsed her hair, loose down her back. Not Mrs. Smith's deep chestnut; but molten gold.

I felt myself go rigid, breath suspended.

The crippled Miss Williams—or rather, Lady Portreath— was *walking under her own power* towards Captain Pellew's bedchamber in the middle of the night.

What could it mean?

That the lady was stronger than she looked, certainly—and healthier than she pretended.

Soundlessly, I eased the door closed and gentled the bar into its latch. I reclaimed my bed and pulled the blankets over me, my entire frame taut for a sound.

Within a few moments, scarcely longer than the interval

of a few breaths, the light footsteps returned past my door. Nothing of great moment had possibly occurred, then—a sentence exchanged, a note slipped across a threshold.

I listened as the careful steps diminished down the stairs. But it was long before I fell asleep.

1 3

ENTRANCE OF THE OTHER WOMAN

Saturday, 1st June, 1816
Cheltenham

Morning brought a swift and early reengagement of arms between the noble combatants; the token of a peace offering in the form of fruit; and the appearance of new figures on the field of battle, in the form of Miss Williams and the unknown lady observed under Viscount Portreath's escort at the theatre last evening.

As daylight also brought a renewal of rain, gushing from the heavens with a fury that bid fair to confirm Mr. Garthwaite's worst predictions, Cassandra and I elected to remain within-doors much of the morning, along with the rest of Mrs. Potter's lodgers—thus providing the requisite audience for our own particular domestic farce.

It was Lucy the housemaid, peering at us from under her cap as she made up the fire in our bedchamber grate, who offered the first intelligence. "He's come back," she pronounced without preamble, "and this time he has the Missus to deal with."

"You mean—Mrs. Potter?"

"Aye. Right canny the Missus is." The poor girl is not above eighteen and suffered a broken night, yet there she was on her knees in an earnest effort to banish the damp chill riffling along the floorboards. "She won't have him invading the ladies' private parlour, but says as how he can meet with them decent-like in the sitting-room, and she'll undertake to keep it free. I only tells you, miss, so as you'll know the sitting-room is spoken for."

"That is wretchedly inconvenient," Cassandra sighed from her bed, "when one has determined to remain at home against inclement weather."

"I daresay as his lordship won't require the room *all day*," Lucy said doubtfully, "and the rain may end, in any event. You might have the treat of walking to the wells, and taking a draught of water! I'll fetch your tea, shall I?"

I WAS BEFOREHAND IN my dress, and thus arrived at the breakfast table in advance of my sister—but was so unfortunate as to encounter Mr. Garthwaite in solitary enjoyment of the repast. He nodded at me distractedly and returned to his mournful pursuit: the crumbling of a piece of toast with his left hand, while his right moved in a desultory fashion in midair, as though he conducted an orchestra inaudible to all but himself. I contented myself, therefore, with buttering a piece of toast.

"Ashes," Mr. Garthwaite muttered thoughtfully.

After a moment, I added: "To ashes?"

"Dust," he said, with a penetrating look.

"To dust," I offered.

"World without end—"

"Amen. But I thought that was exactly what you anticipated with some enthusiasm, sir? —The end of the world?"

Mr. Garthwaite's right hand drooped disconsolately to his lap. He clutched fretfully at his napkin. Chastened, I took a sip of scalding coffee, and Cassandra joining me in another moment, I was less exposed to the clergyman's hollow stare.

Mrs. Potter's kitchen is neither elegant nor varied, but it offers a comforting supply of honest, wholesome English fare. Set out on the sideboard were eggs and sausage, bread and butter and jam, porter and tea, with the addition of a fine Gloucester cheese under a glass dome and some of last year's pippin apples, stewed. Cassandra is an enthusiast of breakfast, and partook heartily; I poured a second cup of coffee and toyed with my toast.

"Has Miss Fox been seen this morning?" Miss Garthwaite asked as she entered the room. "I do not enquire of Miss Williams—I should say *her ladyship*; I am sure she is still prostrate, the better to avoid a meeting with her husband!"

"Sit you down, Miss Garthwaite," Mrs. Potter said as she advanced rapidly into the room bearing a blue Staffordshire bowl filled to the brim with—extraordinary sight! Strawberries! This she set reverently on the sideboard beside the stewed pippins. "Sent up for Miss Williams—her la'ship, I *should* say—from his lordship this morning. Brought especially to tempt her appetite from the Viscount's own hothouses. But she's sent them back; wouldn't sample even a one, and says as we're welcome to them, with her compliments. There's macaroons, too, baked by the York Hotel's chef—I'll set those out directly."

"No champagne?" murmured Mrs. Smith, who had followed hard on Miss Garthwaite's heels. Her countenance, so usually brilliant, was pale this morning, and her eyes shadowed. "No chocolates brought, at breathless expence, direct from Paris? *Pooh*."

"That unfortunate man!" Miss Garthwaite lamented as Mrs. Potter placed a tray of macaroons on the sideboard. "Every consideration shown, every comfort thought of! And still she rejects him!"

"Has she, though?" Mrs. Smith drifted towards the proffered dishes, surveying them. "I certainly thought I glimpsed her just now, drawn up in her basket-chair by the fire, awaiting his lordship's appearance, with Miss Fox and poor Captain Pellew dragooned to support her."

"When I was a girl we *knew* what respect was." Miss Garthwaite affected not to have heard Mrs. Smith. "We were reared to deference. We should not dream of flouting authority, or the natural order ordained by God."

"Is that what Miss Williams has done?" Mrs. Smith enquired, with a satiric look. "Good lord! My opinion of her increases."

"I do not expect *you* to recognise the behaviour becoming to a gentlewoman." Miss Garthwaite rose from her place and stalked to the sideboard. She filled a bowl with strawberries, doused liberally with cream. "Such examples cannot have come within your sphere. But Miss Williams has been an intimate of *Godrevy Manor*!"

She uttered this with the sort of ecstasy usually reserved for the veneration of saints.

"Is it a handsome estate?" I enquired politely.

"The grounds are only moderately extensive, in running a good deal along the sea-coast; the home park is thus bereft of woodland," Miss Garthwaite said almost hurriedly, as tho' I might regard a windswept cliff as contemptible. "But the manor itself—portions of which date to the twelfth century—is all that is admirable in its progression of architectural stiles, representing the greatest advances of beauty in the building arts, and yet encompassing a something *more*, that cannot be expressed in mere beam and stone—in having been the seat of so illustrious and ancient a family as the Viscounts Portreath. There have been Bassets at Godrevy in unbroken line since the Restoration; and they are allied with some of the first families in the Kingdom."

Miss Garthwaite, I understood from this ecstatic account, prized rank and birth above all else. It no longer mattered that the fathers of Miss Williams and Miss Fox had been in trade—and that trade, having to do with tin works, copper pits, and as Mr. Garthwaite had noted accusingly, an unfortunate exposure to arsenic. Miss Williams's blood was washed clean, her virtue spotless, by her possession of a title.

"Godrevy Manor cannot have been all that worthy of admiration, ma'am, if its Viscountess chose to flee." Mrs. Smith plucked a few macaroons from the tray and carried them to an empty place at the table. Thucydides, scenting a treat, stood on his hindlegs, and pawed at her knees. She drew out her chair and paused to pat the little fellow's head. "And Miss Fox describes the Viscount as a death-sentence."

"Foolish woman! I will not listen to words uttered in all ignorance! The exertions of Miss Williams's friends should be entirely in support of restoring her to her proper sphere, her domestic circle, the security and comfort of her husband's governance. You express opinions, Mrs. Smith, on what you cannot possibly understand."

"Do I, indeed?" The young woman turned to face her. "And what possible claim may *you*, madam, have to—"

Whatever she might have said was forestalled by the sudden appearance of Captain Pellew at the dining parlour door. "Where is Mrs. Potter? We must summon Hargate at once. Miss Williams has fainted again."

IT WAS MRS. SMITH who moved instantly to the boardinghouse's back staircase and hastened to the kitchens below, already calling out for the landlady. Her celerity in aiding a relative stranger must be commendable, although I surmised she should not have been so swift if Miss Garthwaite or her brother had spoken, rather than Captain Pellew.

I must confess to a curiosity regarding their acquaintance, which in unguarded moments appears intimate. The use of each other's Christian names, for example, when neither is attending overmuch to their surroundings; the easy raillery that derives from a knowledge of character that is years in the making. I had not forgot the Captain's eager testimonial of Mrs. Smith's worth, delivered at the Cheltenham Library, and should have suspected a *tendre* on one or both sides, had Viscountess Portreath not been in the case.

But either from compassion for her frailty, or admiration for her virtues, Captain Pellew has danced attendance on that lady from the first. He has lost no opportunity to dine with Miss Williams and Miss Fox, to stroll with them in the Long Room or Montpellier Grounds, to escort them to the theatre, or to defend them against disturbance; indeed, his behaviour has been all that is required of a gallant suitor.

I paused an instant to wonder how Mrs. Smith regarded the Captain's widely-bestowed affections—and how the existence of Viscount Portreath, and the truths he had disclosed last night, had affected Pellew's dearest wishes. His countenance should never betray his feeling. He remained, to my eyes at least, bluff, confident, and determined—his only anxiety for others, never for himself.

Miss Garthwaite hurried from the room in the Captain's wake, without regard for the frankness of her curiosity. Mr. Garthwaite, after a moment's vague hesitation, rose from the table and donned his cloak—determined, it appeared, to venture out of doors in the streaming rain. Thucydides ignored them both, and collected himself at the foot of my chair, in obvious hope that I might feed him a crust of bread. I gave him a slice of toast entire, in fact, so that Cassandra might not notice how little I had felt able to stomach; either the York Hotel's rich dinner, *Julius Caesar*, or the continual swoonings and dramaticks of my fellow-lodgers had utterly banished my appetite. Tidying my fingers with a napkin, I rose from the table. Cassandra joined me.

"What now?" she demanded. "Another chapter of *Guy Mannering?*"

I shook my head. "Stout boots and umbrellas, rather. I am desperate for some air."

WE HAD, PERFORCE, TO pass through the common sitting-room on our way to collect our cloaks from the bedchamber above. As we crossed the threshold, we attempted to appear insensible of the party collected near the fire, but total ignorance of the tableau was impossible. Miss Garthwaite loitered at the foot of the stairs, as tho' undecided whether to remain or go. Captain Pellew leant on his stick, his free hand gripping the mantel and his gaze bent upon a little grouping of women—Miss Fox, waving burnt feathers beneath the nose of an unresponsive Miss Williams in her chair. Her ladyship's pallor was dreadful, her golden locks undone and tumbled about her shoulders, her eyes determinedly closed.

On her knees beside that chair, both hands chafing Miss Williams's pulse, was the lady who had attended the theatre with the Viscount the previous evening. Her eyes were trained on Miss Williams with a beseeching earnestness; her whole heart appeared engaged in her activity. The Viscount stood before the sitting-room window, his indifferent back turned to the room and his interest fixed on the torrents of rain wetting the street below.

Ahead of me, Cassandra hastened her steps and achieved the staircase, but when I would have followed her, a slight disturbance caused me to glance instead over my shoulder. It was Lucy, the housemaid, with Dr. Hargate on her heels.

"Stand aside, Miss Fox, if you please," he said without a word of greeting, "and you, there, ma'am—cease to chafe her ladyship's hands. I wish to take her pulse."

With one accord, every person in the room, including Cassandra and me, stood stock-still and fixed our eyes on the medical authority. He stood gravely over Miss Williams's form, his fingertips pressed against the slender white wrist. After a few seconds, without word or glance, he reached into the leather saddlebag he had set on the floor beside him and withdrew a glass bottle.

"Miss Fox," Hargate commanded, "place your hand beneath her neck to support her head. I shall now administer a paregoric draught."

Setting the flask to Miss Williams's lips, he tipped a little dark amber liquid into her mouth. She remained inert an instant, then swallowed, coughing slightly, and her eyes fluttered open.

"Dearest," murmured the unknown lady kneeling at her side.

Miss Williams turned her head and studied the lady's face in apparent confusion. Then without warning, she began to scream.

14

DUBIOUS MACAROONS

Saturday, 1st June, 1816
Cheltenham, cont'd.

The unknown lady reared back from the hysterical invalid's chair and scrambled to her feet, aghast. The Viscount turned from the window and was at her side in an instant, one arm raised protectively to the lady's back.

Miss Fox grasped her friend's shoulders and said firmly, "Rose. It is all right! *Rose.* I shall not let them hurt you—"

But Miss Williams paused only to draw breath, and then screamed shrilly again. Captain Pellew said tensely, "Hargate! Cannot you do something?"

Without hesitation, the doctor slapped Miss Williams across first one cheek, and then the other. Abruptly, her shrieks dissolved into heartrending sobs.

"Wheel her into her bedchamber," Hargate ordered Miss Fox. "I shall examine her there."

With an expression of relief, Miss Fox hastened to comply, but Viscount Portreath set himself between the chair and the private parlour's door.

"Unnecessary," he said in a colourless accent quite at

variance with his wife's scene. "If she disappears again into that room, we shall never pry her out; and I intend to leave for Cornwall in an hour's time."

"I cannot permit her to be moved," Hargate returned. "A journey of any kind should be the end of her, as I informed you, my lord, last night."

"I do not believe the Viscountess to be so poor a creature, as must be mortally deranged by two hundred miles of good road," Portreath said. "She has fled from me once, and I will not permit a second such outrage. Examine her here, doctor, or send me your bill for the paregoric draught—and leave us."

"My lord—"

The shocked utterance was Captain Pellew's.

The Viscount's bored gaze drifted over his countenance. "Remind me, sir, by what right you interfere in my wife's affairs?"

"He does so at my insistence," Miss Fox burst out, "and because you are a monster."

"—Says the lady who is guilty of no less a crime than abduction," Portreath returned coolly. "Pray, Miss Fox, how should you defend your actions in a court of law?"

"No court would condemn me," she spat. "I came to the aid of a defenceless woman, a prisoner in her home and in fear for her life, as any feeling person must do."

"A *prisoner* in her home," Portreath repeated softly. "With her family, I take it, in the guise of gaolers? Fine words, Sarah, but unpersuasive. By absconding with my wife, you have deprived me of the use and enjoyment of my property; and under English law, that is a capital offence."

"Your *property!*" Miss Fox breathed, incensed. "Aye, you have always regarded her as nothing more than a convenient source of funds."

"Which means that you have necessarily added the crime of *theft* to your other sins. You may take it as evidence of my good will that I do not chuse to prosecute. Now stand aside from her chair."

Rose Williams feebly clutched at Miss Fox's skirts. "Do not desert me."

"You have no cause for fear while the Captain and I am here," Miss Fox soothed.

"I must insist, my lord, on examining my patient in private," Hargate interjected. The deference to rank he had displayed last evening was absent now in the presence of a failing young creature; the physician's frowning visage was replete with indignation. "This prolonged discord is dangerous to her ladyship's heart and her nerves. I will undertake to leave the parlour door open, and shall ensure that it remains unlocked against you."

There was an instant's fraught silence, and then the Viscount bowed his head. "Very well. You may have a quarter-hour."

With an expression of contempt, Miss Fox wheeled the basket-chair into the adjoining room, the doctor at her heels.

Viscount Portreath drew an enameled box from his coat and refreshed himself with a pinch of snuff to each nostril. He offered the box to Captain Pellew, who declined it.

"I have no notion of whom the rest of you may be," the

Viscount observed, to the room in general, "but I must beg you all to depart at once."

Cassandra instantly turned to mount the stairs, but Captain Pellew, his face flushing, retorted, "Allow me to introduce these ladies to your acquaintance, sir, as they are certainly known to your viscountess. Miss Garthwaite, Miss Austen, and Miss Jane Austen—Viscount Portreath."

Pellew indicated each of us with a sweep of his broad arm. Although I was inclined to detest Lord Portreath for his brusque manners and indifference to his lady's feelings, I offered a grudging curtsey in acknowledgement. Captain Pellew bowed to the unknown lady and said: "Ma'am?"

She appeared as one still dazed by the ringing of Miss Williams's screams, her aspect troubled and her eyes overbright with tears. A finely-dressed woman in a day gown of bottle-green silk, with a matching spencer and a bonnet ornamented with pheasant quills—but a few years older than Miss Fox, I now perceived.

"I am Mrs. Williams," she said quietly. "Stepmother to the Viscountess, and her father's widow."

Miss Garthwaite drew an audible breath. Pellew darted a glance at the Viscount, whose countenance remained untroubled.

I had suspected the lady must be a near relation—of the Viscount, perhaps; a ward, a cousin, a sister. My surmises at the theatre last night—that she was the gentleman's wife—had been revealed as impossible. I had briefly revolved the idea of a mistress, but the lady's appearance in our midst, chafing Miss Williams's hands, banished the thought. Now, however, I was bewildered. The wife of Miss Williams's late father—inducing shrieks of terror in her prostrate stepchild?

"Extraordinary," Cassandra said under her breath.

At that moment, Mrs. Potter appeared in the doorway, her aspect all agitation. "Miss Garthwaite! The little dog is in a fit, and I can do nothing to soothe him!"

"A fit?" Miss Garthwaite hastened towards her. "I am sure it is merely one of his tricks. He is cunning, Thucydides—and will think to coax a lamb-bone out of you."

Mrs. Potter set her fists on her ample hips. "If retching up the macaroons he had off Mrs. Smith's plate, which she left behind when the Captain disturbed her, is a dog's way of raiding the pantry, then I'm a duchess. See for yourself, ma'am."

With a grimace, Miss Garthwaite followed her from the room.

"Jane," Cassandra said softly.

No other word was necessary; it was time and more since we should be quitting the present company, and scenes never intended for our ears or eyes.

"You will excuse us." I offered the phrase to Captain Pellew; he inclined his head distractedly.

The Viscount, however, surprised me by giving voice. "Stay," he commanded. "I would beg a favour of you, ma'am. Mrs. Williams is sadly overset by the behaviour of her step-daughter, and I am sure would benefit from an interval of quiet in her own rooms. I cannot spare a moment to escort her back to the York Hotel, my attention being demanded here; and we left her maid to packing our trunks, being determined to quit Cheltenham now the Viscountess has been found. I wonder if you ladies would be so good as to walk with Mrs. Williams to the York?"

I lifted my brows in wonder, and stared from the Viscount to the lady. The hotel was directly adjacent, the distance but a few steps. Was Mrs. Williams so fearful of unfamiliar streets, that she dared not set foot in one alone? Or was her distress in the moment so profound, as to weaken her sensibilities?

"Oh, yes," the lady murmured eagerly. "I should like it above all things. You are not otherwise engaged?"

"Not at all," I replied. "Allow us merely to fetch our spencers and bonnets."

Cassandra and I hurried above, my sister frowning a little. "What can it mean, Jane? Does that—that *monster*, as Miss Fox chuses to call him—hold all the women of his acquaintance in thrall? —And are we now to be added to the number?"

Her words were interrupted by a sharp cry of misery emanating from below. I stared at my sister, transfixed.

"The Viscountess?" Cassandra whispered, her hand gripping her bonnet strings.

I shook my head. "If I do not mistake—Miss Garthwaite."

WE DISCOVERED OUR FELLOW-LODGER kneeling on the dining parlour floor over the lifeless body of her pug. Thucydides lay on his side, his four limbs splayed and his black muzzle flecked with red-tinged foam. He had been foully ill on the carpet, and had voided his bowels. The stench rose to our nostrils so violently that Cassandra retched, and stepped backwards.

"Impossible!" Miss Garthwaite cried, her palms lifted to Heaven. "He cannot be gone. He will awake in an instant. It is one of his tricks!"

"Miss Garthwaite—" I touched her back consolingly.

"Fetch the doctor!" she ordered.

"But—" I stared at Thucydides. His prominent eyes were fixed and without spark. I could detect no sign of breathing.

"At once!"

Cassandra fled in the direction of the private parlour.

"Now, give over, miss, do," said Mrs. Potter. She had retrieved a flour sack from the kitchens and bent down to cover the little dog with it. "I'll shift him to the scullery, and we'll bury him in the back garden once I've got the potatoes set to boil."

"We shall do no such thing!" Miss Garthwaite cried. She began to strike poor Mrs. Potter about the arms and shoulders, driving her away.

"What is all this?" Dr. Hargate, whom Cassandra had succeeded in summoning from her ladyship's private parlour, hastened into the room, my sister at his heels. "Miss Garthwaite! Endeavour to control yourself, ma'am!"

"But, Thucydides!" she cried, in stricken accents.

Hargate's ragged grey brows furrowed irritably. "Has the dog eaten one too many sweetmeats?" He lowered heavily to his knees on the carpet, seemingly impervious to the stench, and placed his fingers on the inert creature's neck. "Poor fellow. I'm afraid he has left us, Miss Garthwaite."

"But *why*?" she cried. "*How*? He was quite a young dog. Not above three years. Perfectly stout in every way."

Dr. Hargate frowned, and examined Thucydides's mouth. The tongue and gums were livid and pale. "He appears to have vomited a deal of blood. What have you fed him, ma'am?"

"Nothing as yet this morning. There has been so much to distract one!"

Mrs. Potter interjected. "He's had a few of those macaroons, I warrant. I found him standing on Mrs. Smith's chair when I came to remove the breakfast dishes. He'd nipped up canny as anything to steal from her plate. Never had a chance to touch it, Mrs. Smith didn't, on account of her la'ship's fainting-fit."

Dr. Hargate rose from his knees. "Unlikely."

"But I saw him with my own eyes," Mrs. Potter protested.

"You misunderstand me, my good woman. I am perfectly willing to believe that the pug stole food; I am simply unwilling to credit the idea of poisoned macaroons."

"Poisoned?" I repeated.

"Yes." He glanced around the room, his gaze lighting on the platter of remaining biscuits that still rested on the sideboard. "Has anyone else partaken of these?"

Mrs. Potter shrugged.

"I have not." I turned to Cassandra.

"Nor I," she said. "I do not recollect Mr. Garthwaite sampling them. Miss Garthwaite?"

"I ate some strawberries," she whispered. "But I cannot abide macaroons. Oh, Thucydides!"

I offered her a handkerchief from my reticule. She buried her face in it.

"Did you bake these, Mrs. Potter?" Dr. Hargate enquired.

"No, sir. Brought over from the York, they were, for Miss—for her la'ship."

"By her visitors?"

The landlady nodded. "Her la'ship wouldn't have nothing to do with them. She can't abide victuals, Miss—her la'ship. Eats nothing, most days, and I reckon she meant to teach his lordship a lesson, by turning up her nose at his gift. Told me to carry the whole platter away to the dining parlour for the rest of the guests, and so I did."

Poison. It was a term from a Gothick novel, too absurd to entertain when surrounded by the drab walls of a perfectly ordinary boardinghouse.

"Do you mean to suggest that the hotel's kitchen is somehow unwholesome?" Mrs. Williams faltered. "Pray accept my apologies! I should not have had the little doggy hurt for worlds!"

I gazed into the lady's earnest visage. There was a faint pucker between her brows, and her lip trembled slightly from sympathy or confusion. Was her mind so innocent, as to conjure nothing more dangerous than a tainted pantry or a spoiled confection? The macaroons had been brought especially for her stepdaughter. At the express wish of that lady's husband.

I tell you, her very life is at risk if she remains. So much had Miss Fox declared, only last night, as she implored Captain Pellew to secure a chaise. But the intelligence that her friend was in fact a viscountess, in flight from her lawful husband, had banished the warning from our minds.

Did Lord Portreath intend to be rid of his wife? Why, then, had he come in pursuit of her?

"A napkin, Mrs. Potter, if you please." Dr. Hargate held out his hand. The landlady pressed a square of linen into it.

Hargate carefully covered the macaroon dish and turned with it towards the door. "Under no circumstances should the Viscountess be moved today, Mrs. Williams. I have informed his lordship of my opinion. And now—an interval of natural philosophy is in order. If you require me—I may be found examining these dubious cakes in the stillroom of my friend, Dr. Edward Jenner."

1 5

CONFIDENCES TOO
FREELY IMPARTED

Saturday, 1st June, 1816
Cheltenham, cont'd.

The York Hotel has, in addition to its private dining parlours, a publick tap room, a coffee room, and a writing room furnished with tables and ink for the correspondence of its guests. It was to this latter room that Mrs. Williams, after the slightest of hesitations, drew Cassandra and me; she had glanced through the entryway and ascertained that at this hour of the morning—it was now nearly noon—the place was deserted.

I had expected her to bid us *adieu* in the lobby, and ascend the stairs immediately in search of her maid. She extended her gloved hand impulsively, however, and said, "I am grateful for your escort. I hope I do not impose—but you have such *kindly* faces. Would you care to recruit your strength before going back out into the rain?"

We had braved the downpour for barely five paces, between the boardinghouse and the hotel, but I perceived a desire to converse on the part of our new acquaintance, and I was curious to hear whatever she wished to tell me. I looked to Cassandra, whose aspect was all interest.

"Are you indeed at leisure?" I asked. "I had thought you preparing to return into Cornwall."

"Indeed, and I hope not, as we only just arrived. I am *not* the best traveller—I am always plagued with the head-ache; and I am sure the Viscountess will require a deal of care on the journey home." She smiled and gestured towards a divan done up in deep blue velvet, ranged before the fire. "Will you not sit down?"

We submitted with alacrity.

"I shall ring for tea," Mrs. Williams said, reaching for a heavy bell-pull near the writing room door. "There is a decided chill, tho' it *is* the first of June."

For my part, I had drunk enough tea to float myself to China; but the fussing over cups and pots and waste-bowls should provide a foil for any awkwardness. Mrs. Williams was not so much of an innocent as I had thought; her countenance might be fresh with youth, but her knowledge of Society was not.

"Viscount Portreath appears determined to quit Cheltenham, however," I observed.

"I shall do my best to persuade Granville to remain here a few days." The lady drew off her bonnet and set to work on her gloves. "He is not nearly so tiresome as he likes to appear when arguing with Miss Fox, you know—I find he usually accedes to my wishes."

But not his wife's, I thought with a sharpening of interest. "Granville?"

She met my gaze directly, her own guileless. "Viscount Portreath. It is a family name; there have always been Granvilles among the Bassets."

"I see. And are you also a native of Cornwall, Mrs. Williams?"

She shook her head. "I was reared in Plymouth. That is where I met my husband, in fact—Mr. Williams was often in Devon for the conduct of his business."

"And do you reside there now?"

"Oh, no," she replied, frowning a little. "I have not lived in Plymouth for some years. When I was married, Mr. Williams and I lived in Penwith—but I make my home at the manor, now."

"Godrevy Manor?" Cassandra enquired, all politeness "Its beauties are much talked of."

As she had never heard of the Basset family's ancestral seat before Miss Garthwaite's fulsome ecstasies, I found this amusing. "And have you been resident there for long?"

"Some three years." Mrs. Williams's face lighted as a servant appeared. "Ah, how timely. Might we have some tea?"

The man bowed and withdrew.

"You accompanied Miss Williams there after her marriage?" I persisted.

Mrs. Williams inclined her head. "And was only too thankful to do so, I may assure you. Mr. Williams died two years after his daughter's marriage. I should have been in a sad way, had Rose not desired me to join her—shifting for lodgings among the other widows in Bath or Brighton, I daresay!"

This was decidedly odd; I had understood Miss Williams's

father to have been a warm man, and she a notable heiress. Surely this lady had not been cast out of her home at her husband's death?

And if Miss Williams had begged her stepmother for companionship, why had she shrieked upon first seeing her this morning?

"But what of you ladies?" Mrs. Williams enquired. "What part of the country do you claim?"

"Hampshire," Cassandra said quickly. "Our home is not far from Alton."

"I know only Basingstoke, in that county; and that, viewed only from a coach window," she returned, with a merry laugh. "Ah! Here is our tea!"

The servant poured out; and having thanked him and seen him set the tray on a side table conveniently to hand, Mrs. Williams abandoned all pretence of being interested in ourselves. She had a purpose in drawing us aside, as I had suspected; and it was to learn whatever we might be willing to tell.

"I do not need to inform you that this breach with Rose has been excessively distressing." She set down her cup and leant earnestly towards me. "You have overlistened her scenes. You have witnessed her swoon. She is not to be reasoned with; her unsoundness of body and mind have progressed beyond what is tolerable. We are told that to remove her must be perilous; but to encourage such reckless folly, and the malicious interests of her companion, is madness!"

"By companion, you would refer to Miss Fox?" I asked. "She appears all devotion to the Viscountess."

"I cannot say what her feelings or motives *may be*," Mrs.

Williams replied. "I know only what she is—an admirer of the late Mary Wollstonecraft and her radical ideas. Miss Fox abhors the male sex, and believes her duty in life is to thwart all men."

"Indeed? How singular! And does your stepdaughter share her friend's dislike?"

"As her ladyship's distaste for Lord Portreath has only increased as her friendship for Miss Fox has grown, I must assume so," Mrs. Williams informed me. "The ladies' acquaintance predates the marriage. The two girls were at school together. Miss Fox is a member of the Society of Friends, as you will know, and the women of that sect are dangerously devoted to learning; they are mad for independence of thought. My stepdaughter fancies herself a poetess, and as a result of Miss Fox's encouragement and meddling, she is now determined to renounce her marriage and devote her life to composition. The Viscount has not had one moment's peace since his wedding-day. Miss Fox has schemed to endear herself to the Viscountess; has poisoned her ears against her husband; has divided my stepdaughter from my affections; and contrived, in the end, to persuade her to desert her home in a senseless flight to Cheltenham, of all places, when she might better have been supported and cared for at Godrevy Manor!"

"You sanctioned Miss Williams's—Lady Portreath's—visit to this neighbourhood, however?" I asked.

"Not at all. Miss Fox spirited her out of Cornwall while the Viscount and I were on a visit to London; we discovered his wife's defection upon our return home, and were at our wits' end to know where she was gone. Had we not learnt from our banker—who is also Miss Fox's family man of business—that the abductress had drawn funds from his Cheltenham branch, we should not have had a notion of their direction."

This was imparting a careless deal of information, indeed; but I suspected Mrs. Williams hoped to stoke our horror and interest, and thereby win our sympathies to her own ends. "The alienation of affection must be a heavy charge," I observed, "but when poor health and decline are added to the sum of injury, appears almost criminal. What can be Miss Fox's motive?"

"Revenge against the most illustrious male of her acquaintance." Mrs. Williams looked candidly from my sister to me. "She will drive the Viscountess to her grave, thereby depriving Lord Portreath of every happiness, and so be satisfied."

I found this pronouncement, tho' rendered in the calmest accent, to be wildly improbable. Miss Fox was unceasing in her promotion of Rose Williams's health. It was Cassandra, however, who interjected: "What exactly is the nature of her ladyship's illness?"

Mrs. Williams hesitated an instant. Then she placed her hand over my sister's and pressed it gently. "You both will respect this confidence, I am sure. The creature is not of sound mind. She has taken the greatest dislike to her husband; sets him at a distance; and when forced to answer the expectations of her position in Society or marriage, enacts the most violent protests. Since the beginning of this year, she has refused all sustenance. For a time, nothing more than bread and water passed her lips, and that only at infrequent

intervals. She refused to sit at table with her friends or relations; confined herself to her rooms; locked her door against
the Viscount; and permitted only Miss Fox to see her. In
short, she means to starve herself if Lord Portreath does not
submit to her whims."

"And what are those, pray?" Cassandra asked in a lowered
tone.

There are times when having an ardent gossip for a sister
is uncommonly useful; it saves one a deal of trouble. With an
expression of absorbed interest, I sipped my tea.

"She demands freedom," Mrs. Williams said. "—A large
allowance—an independent establishment in Town—an
end to the marriage bond. In short, anything and everything
designed to rob a gentleman of his patience. Having failed
to win the Viscount's consent with tantrums, her ladyship
has attempted desertion! I suspect the plan was to recruit her
strength for an interval in Cheltenham, before moving on to
London and setting up her household, in flagrant disregard
of his lordship's pride and reputation. But the Viscount is not
to be so humiliated. He is not to be trifled with."

"I am sure he is not," I murmured under my breath.
However humdrum the gentleman's looks, his air of abrupt
command revealed a spine of steel. He was accustomed to
ordering his world without regard for the feelings of others;
I should never wish such a man to have the ordering of
mine. His wife's desertion—and Miss Fox's defence of it—
might be a desperate bid for self-preservation. Certainly
Miss Fox had spoken solely in terms of life and death. But
Mrs. Williams's candour—her tone of indignation and

chagrin—urged us to view her stepdaughter as a spoilt child, wayward and misguided by false friends. Was the woman insensible of the Viscount's capacity for cruelty? — Or had she *another motive* in securing her ladyship's return to Godrevy Manor?

"I must beg you, Miss Austen—*and* Miss Jane Austen . . ." The pressure of the lady's hand was now applied to mine. "You apprehend how we are circumstanced. You see the dangers of my stepdaughter's situation. She is on the verge of throwing herself away—without regard for position, security, or respectability. I do not speak of the havoc she has done to the reputation of a most estimable man, or the damage to his domestic felicity. But I believe I may appeal to you. I believe you are women of sense and probity. You are lodged in the same house—you observe her ladyship hourly. If my dearest is on the verge of some mad act—a sudden flight or self-harm—will you not send word to me immediately?"

I glanced at my sister, whose expression was wooden.

"I have only the Viscountess's interest at heart," Mrs. Williams concluded, pressing her hands to her breast with a pathetic air of entreaty.

I was not entirely persuaded of this, and remained dubious of the true circumstances. But I said merely, "We are honoured by your confidence. You may be assured of our discretion."

I rose and curtseyed; Cassandra did the same. Mrs. Williams smiled at us, and reached once more for the teapot. There was a plate of the York's macaroons on the tray beside it. If only an hour ago she had lamented over the hotel's unwholesome kitchen, I daresay she had forgot it, as well as Miss Garthwaite's poisoned dog.

Would she sample the confection, I wondered, once we were gone?

"Miss Austen!"

The tall, dark gentleman who nearly collided with us on the hotel threshold was instantly recognisable, elegantly clad and superbly self-contained, a soft-crowned beaver set rakishly over his left eye.

"Mr. West," I said. And felt a surge of warmth thrill through my body as he reached to steady me. His touch fired along my arm; I stepped back with a shaky breath.

"Did you stop here in search of me?" he asked, his gaze fixed on mine.

"We have more than one acquaintance lodging at the York, sir," I returned carefully.

"Do not dash *all* my hopes!" His smile glanced over my shoulder to rest on Cassandra. "Where are you ladies bound? May I cajole you to visit the Cheltenham Library? I mean to peruse the London papers; I have ruralised in ignorance long enough."

Cassandra declined, with a faint colour to her cheeks; she meant to leave me in sole enjoyment of Mr. West's attentions. For my part, I had breathed enough of stifling rooms, and wished for a turn in the damp air. I accepted his left arm with alacrity; with his right, he raised an umbrella.

"What have you been about this morning, Jane?" he demanded, as we set off.

I regaled him the length of our walk with my fellow-lodgers' histrionics, and the strange affair of Thucydides's poisoning.

"No one else fancied the macaroons?"

"Mrs. Smith—a fellow-lodger you have not yet met—perfectly intended to sample them, but was prevented from doing so by the appearance of Captain Pellew, and his urgent desire to summon the doctor. I believe she went in search of Hargate herself; she had not yet reappeared when I left the boardinghouse, so perhaps she went from Hargate's surgery to the theatre."

He looked puzzled. "Was there a performance this morning?"

"Not at all. Mrs. Smith exerts herself *behind* the curtain. She is a sort of instructress, of elocution and politesse. She teaches actors to appear as genteel as the characters they represent."

"Remarkable," West murmured. "But these biscuits, which the doctor appears to believe may be poisoned—they were not served directly to the lady?"

"Mrs. Smith was not the intended target of malice," I confirmed. "Her choice was as random as the result. Any one of us might be suffering Thucydides's fate, had breakfast not been interrupted." The conclusion was bleak but indisputable. I, who consumed little at that hour of the day, was happily preserved from the murderous threat; but my sister or Mrs. Smith, Mr. Garthwaite or Captain Pellew, even Mrs. Potter herself, might have fallen victim to the anonymous poisoner. Tho' I had not canvassed the hideous danger with my fellow-lodgers, I remained acutely sensible of it. The villain—Lord Portreath?—responsible for Thucydides's squalid death must be exposed, lest another life be taken.

"That seems a reckless action, even for one resolved to murder." My companion's tone was thoughtful. "If we entertain for a moment the idea that the Viscount meant to poison his wife, and came armed for the purpose, bestowing his strawberries and cakes on the general crowd should expose him in a most alarming manner. It is not a plot founded on sense."

"His wife is the one who sent the food into the dining parlour," I pointed out, "in Mrs. Potter's care. Perhaps his lordship could not protest, for fear of betraying a damning anxiety?"

"Do we know why he should wish to be rid of his lady?"

"Only that he *was* already safely rid of her, but nonetheless journeyed into Gloucestershire—a journey of some two hundred miles!—at the first word of her discovery. Is that the action of a murderer?"

Our progress slowed as we came up with the Assembly Rooms, where a knot of gentlemen had collected under the pedimented marble doorway to shelter from the rain—fashionable patrons intending to play at billiards, perhaps, in the building's upper rooms. West held back as I negotiated the crowded paving, then regained my side.

"The action of a *subtle* murderer, perhaps," he replied, "—one who intends to look the part of dutiful husband before the world, but schemes in private. Should you describe Portreath thus, Jane?"

I revolved what little I had observed of the gentleman. "His looks are deceptively mild and unprepossessing, which blinds one at first to his potent character. He is a cold man who places little value on amiability; to be *liked* appears his least object. His lordship is studiously calm, not unintelligent, and distressingly frank—as when he referred to her ladyship as his *property*. I should never describe him as wishing to win her affections, or attract her to return to him from the ardency of his feeling. He dealt with her desertion as one might a business matter. There was not an iota of passion in it."

A passing cart, heavily laden with barrels of ale, lurched drunkenly into a rut at the edge of the High. A welter of mud splashed upwards, and West's arm came reflexively around my waist, turning me from the dirt. "And is passion required for subtlety?" he breathed into my ear. "I should rather have said the reverse."

I came to a halt and stared into his eyes. "It ought to be required for murder—anything less is diabolic."

He was mere inches from me, studying my face; his eyes darkened an instant, and then with a sharp intake of breath he released me. "I shall have to endeavour to meet the fellow at the hotel, and observe him myself. Viscount Portreath has never come in my way before, nor has any of his family. They must not keep a London house."

I resumed my unobjectionable walk to the library with the man who, my entire body informed me, should have demonstrated the meaning of *passion* had we stood anywhere less publick than the High. I tried to stifle my disappointment. "I cannot say; Mrs. Williams referred only to Godrevy Manor."

"That is another unusual circumstance—that a young and handsome widow, however nominally related, lives with the couple."

"She intimated that she did so at the Viscountess's request, as tho' they were intimate friends more than relations, quite dear to one another. Yet the lady screamed at first sight of Mrs. Williams this morning."

"A reaction that remains unacknowledged and unexplained. You know nothing of the widow's circumstances?"

"Her fortune, you mean? She was not so eager to share *those* particulars. She *did say*, however, that she was obliged to give up her home at Mr. Williams's death."

"—Which would suggest the leasehold was not part of her jointure," West concluded. "I wonder if the greater part of Williams's fortune went to his daughter? If that fact were publicized, well before the father's death, it explains the marriage, at least."

"—The trading of a title for a fortune, you mean?"

"Such unions are known."

"His lordship is a fairly young man, and I would guess has only lately come into his majority and his title," I said. "It is unusual for a viscount to bestow his hand on a tin miner's daughter; pride should forbid it. But if he were in need of funds—"

"—The demands of his estate might argue the pursuit of an heiress," West concluded. "So much for the dearth of passion, Jane, and the emphasis upon *property*."

There it was, again—a deliberate reversion to the dangerous waters of *feeling*; impossible to discuss the affairs of others without straying into our own. But we were nearly to the library, we were entirely exposed to Cheltenham's eye, and I must hold firmly to the arid and the analytic. There was a murderer to be dealt with.

"If his wife is once laid in her grave," I observed, "should not his lordship be free to enjoy title, money, and passion all at once?"

"In the company of the ravishing Mrs. Williams, perhaps?"

Is she indeed ravishing? West must admire redheads. A lowering thought. "They are on terms of remarkable intimacy. She told me without the slightest consciousness that they had visited London together—*without* the Viscountess—a month since, during which absence her ladyship fled the manor."

"Careless," West murmured. "But perhaps they preserve the fiction of separate bedchambers."

We had achieved the circulating library; I preceded him through the doorway, and perceived immediately that a crush of patrons had sought out the lengthy reading room on this wet morning, from a desire for diversion or shelter or both. As West shook out his umbrella in the vestibule, my eyes travelled over the desultory crowd: gentlemen seated in chairs, with newspapers spread before them; ladies in fashionable attire drooping before the newest fashion-plates, spread out on broad tables; and a few earnest bluestockings in spectacles and plain bonnets, sorting through recent publications on the library's shelves, in hope of a beguiling novel. It occurred to me to wonder if the volumes of my own *Emma* were on offer—a thought that was abruptly interrupted by the utterance of a brisk, "Good morning, Miss Austen! Is Miss Williams recovered from her swoon?"

I turned to find Mrs. Smith approaching, her glorious chestnut hair disguised by yet another drab muslin cap, her trim figure hidden by a voluminous cape. There could be no mistaking those moss-green eyes, however, or their sparkle.

"The doctor has just left her," I replied. This was not the place to canvass poisoned macaroons, or the fate of Miss Garthwaite's dog. "Are you preparing another play for our enjoyment? I hope to see the Sheridan next week—"

But Mrs. Smith was no longer attending. Her eyes had widened and fixed on Raphael West, who had just moved to join me, and I observed the colour to drain from her face. I glanced at him in surprize.

"Good God," he exclaimed. "Miss Vyvyan! But what brings *you* to Cheltenham? I had thought you fixed in Derbyshire!"

"Mr. West," she managed. "What an—an unexpected—"

She drew a deep breath, looked imploringly at me, and ducked her head. "I am sorry. I may not stay. Do forgive me, Miss Austen—Mr. West—"

And with that, she swept around us, and was gone.

16

PROCLAMATION OF A POETESS

Saturday, 1st June, 1816
Cheltenham, cont'd.

"I did not know you were acquainted with Mrs. Smith," I said.

West was staring after the lady, who had disappeared through the library door, his brows drawn down. "I know nothing of Mrs. Smith," he countered, "but shall swear that is Miss Hannah Vyvyan, formerly of Plymouth, and the ward of Sir Charles Markham of Derbyshire. I had the pleasure of taking her portrait some years since, when she was resident at Sir Charles's Town house in Mount Street, on the occasion of her come-out. Hers is a countenance not readily forgotten."

"No," I agreed, with a twinge of envy. "But it is possible, is it not, that the lady has married since last you heard of her?"

"Possible, but improbable," he replied. "She was the dearest friend of my own Charlotte, when the two young ladies were at school in Bath; that is how I came to receive the commission for her portrait. That she should hurry away without a word of interest for my daughter, or a few pleasantries for me . . . there is some great mystery, here, Jane, that I am determined to find out."

"Perhaps she did not like to canvass her history in so exposed a place," I said. "You might find her all that is amiable, did you call upon her in private."

"I should like to be able to give Charlotte a report of her friend." West still stared at the door through which Mrs. Smith had exited. "It might lift her spirits, to recall less anxious times, when there was no grief in her hours."

"Why do you not go after the lady now?" I suggested. "She is sure to be returned to Mrs. Potter's, or if not there, then to the theatre."

"I do not mean to desert you. I am not so fickle an acquaintance. There will be time enough later to meet with Miss—*Mrs.* Smith."

I did not press him. Raphael West is generally in command of himself; he does not require others' urging. He would find the lady at his preferred hour and in the proper setting—and learn everything there was to know about the interesting fortunes of Hannah Vyvyan.

My sister Cassandra was lying down in our bedchamber when I at last regained Mrs. Potter's. She roused herself, however, to receive a letter from my hands—I had stopped at the post office in my way back along the High and found two missives awaiting us. Hers was from Martha Lloyd. Mine was from our niece Fanny.

"How vexatious!" my sister declared as she eyed the direction. "I have just filled and crossed an entire sheet to Martha, replete with the interesting nothings of our visit, and should have been on the point of sealing it—but now I must absorb her communication, and respond to each of her idle questions, before dropping it in the outgoing bag. Would that her letter had been delayed a day! I might have been happy this evening in the knowledge of virtue, instead of haunted by a task undone."

I left her to irritated enjoyment, and broke the wax on Fanny's letter. It was the briefest of notes, which must always inspire anxiety—such things are reserved for urgent tidings, that may not wait for the fulsome lines of an easy correspondence.

Thursday, 30th May
Godmersham Park
My dear Aunt Jane,
I write to inform you that my Father has had an Express from Town this morning, at Uncle Charles's direction. He is at Gravesend, and means to be in London so soon as tomorrow. His Admiralty Board is to convene on the Monday, and my Father intends to post up to Town in order to support Uncle Charles. Papa may not attend the Review itself, as only Naval officers may be present, but he hopes at least to stand Uncle Charles his dinner afterwards, and learn what he may of my uncle's Fate. Uncle Francis is to post to London, too, and try what he can to influence his friends at the Admiralty. My Father means to write to you as soon as the Board is done, so that you and my Aunt Cassandra will not be left long in suspense.

I remain,
Your devoted Niece,
Etc., etc.

Here was news!

I thrust the note at Cassandra and hurried immediately below in search of Captain Pellew. He is the first person to interrogate on the subject of my brother Charles, although I confess I have doubts about the Captain on other matters that remain unresolved. Despite his appearance of bluff candour, Pellew guards an admirable silence regarding Mrs. Smith's past, tho' he enjoys a degree of intimacy with her and must certainly be aware that she is *not* married. He employs her assumed name before Mrs. Potter's lodgers, and not the more honest Hannah Vyvyan. Moreover, I have not forgot that it was Captain Pellew who interrupted breakfast with an urgent summons for the doctor, before that very Mrs. Smith could consume a poisoned macaroon! Pellew effectively dispersed the entire breakfast-table in advance of general harm. Happy accident, or deliberate intent?

I am not so mired in suspicion of Lord Portreath as to set aside those who were in his company when the macaroons were first produced. Captain Pellew is perfectly capable of killing his fellows—indeed, as an officer of His Majesty's Navy, one might say he has been trained up in the practise! If he were so bewitched by Rose Williams (or her fortune) as to hold the marital bond cheap, he might well have seized the Viscount's morning visit as opportunity to strike. The Viscountess would be sure to disdain the cakes, as she did all sustenance; and a deft hand might dust them with poison unobserved and direct the platter first to his lord-ship—thereby eliminating a rival. In the event, however, Lady Portreath spoiled the plan by sending the macaroons immediately into the dining parlour—to the Captain's horror and dismay?

I could construct a plausible case for culpability against almost anyone, given half a moment. But my doubts regarding Pellew did not prevent me from consulting him on my brother's affairs—if anything, they urged me to further our acquaintance.

I discovered the Captain established before the sitting-room fire. The door to the ladies' private parlour adjacent was half-open, and I glimpsed the back of the basket-chair, and the skirts of Miss Fox. Pellew was mounting Watch, lest Lord Portreath attempt a domestic abduction.

"Miss Austen." He groped for his ebony stick as tho' to rise from his chair.

"Please." I extended my hand. "Do not be troubling yourself, sir. I came only to offer intelligence of my brother, as you were so obliging as to write to your relation on his behalf. Captain Austen was at Gravesend so recently as Thursday, and is summoned to his Admiralty Board in two days' time."

"Is he, indeed? I must write again to my cousin, the Admiral, and underline the merit of the man about to present himself." This time, the Captain succeeded in thrusting himself to his feet, and moved directly to the writing table at the far end of the sitting-room.

"That is excessively kind in you, sir."

"Not at all. It shall relieve my mind of an unhealthy preoccupation—" This, in a lowered tone, with a nod towards the half-open parlour door.

"You remain anxious for her life?" I enquired, in a voice

as subdued. "I know so little of what ails her, that I cannot form an opinion."

"As to that . . ." He drew out the desk chair and seated himself before it. "I am no doctor. From what Miss Fox has related, however, Miss Wil—*the Viscountess*—will never be well until she abandons this morbid desire to starve herself."

"You regard it then, as a *choice*, not the symptom of a deeper disease?"

"Say a compulsion, rather, that drives her to self-destruction. I do not profess to understand it." A shy smile, disarming in its rarity, suffused his countenance. "We men of the Navy, you will know, never refuse a good meal."

"If she wishes to die," I said in puzzlement, "why flee her home in Miss Fox's company? Such an action suggests a desire to live. A desire for freedom, and a future of her own imagining."

"Knowing little of either lady beyond the impressions of recent acquaintance, I cannot hope to explain it."

"Ah!" I smiled faintly at his look of enquiry. "From your considerable intimacy, sir, I had assumed you were a friend of some years' standing."

Quick colour suffused Pellew's countenance, but he kept his frank gaze trained on mine. "I have only known the ladies from Cornwall some ten days. Perhaps I have been over-particular in my attentions to them—but an invalid will always inspire pity and solicitude, I believe."

Especially when she is young, pretty, and by all appearances possessed of a comfortable income, I thought to myself. He was certainly not dangling after octogenarians in basket-chairs.

But I said only, "You are all gallantry, Captain. I imagine time hangs heavy on your hands in Cheltenham. You are a man of action, accustomed to a greater charge. The tiresome rituals of a watering-place must only add to the tedium of being turned on dry land. But you have certainly found a use for your energy, in championing her ladyship's cause."

If I hoped he might explain his motives, or even what had drawn him to this spa town in the first place, I was to be disappointed. Pellew did not chuse to share his business, and a lady may not probe too narrowly into questions of a gentleman's health or heart.

"As to that—" He shrugged in dismissal. "I am only fit to amuse the ladies, and support their interests on occasion; Miss Fox is the true warrior. Even now she is cajoling her ladyship to take a little thin gruel, so that she might meet the Viscount with greater strength."

"Do you know whether that gentleman still intends her removal to Cornwall?"

"I believe he has agreed to a little forbearance. Her ladyship is allowed to remain in Cheltenham another day, at Dr. Hargate's insistence. In this, I think we may all congratulate *ourselves*—the vociferous alarm of her fellow-lodgers has effected the Viscountess's safety. Too many disinterested strangers have heard the physician's warnings of danger, should she be forced to travel, for Lord Portreath to be blameless if his wife comes to harm."

Disinterested strangers. I had not thought Pellew such. Had the intelligence of her marriage been a painful blow? And had that disappointment been channeled, perhaps, into a vow to secure her freedom?

"So long as the gruel is not from the York kitchens, we may safely promote it," I said thoughtfully. "But perhaps her ladyship feels her cause is better served by an appearance of weakness. So long as she is unfit to travel, her husband may not move her. Recover a little of her strength, and his object is satisfied."

"He was so unwise as to inform her of his intended return at four o'clock," the Captain replied. "You may well be correct, that if Miss Williams consumes anything, it will be only after he is gone."

"Is Dr. Hargate to return as well, then?"

"I cannot say. I sent round a note to his lodgings, to advise him of the hour, but have received no reply."

"Did you not know that he was to be closeted with Dr. Jenner," I asked in surprize, "for the better part of the day? I know little of natural philosophy, but I believe the two intended some sort of analysis, of the macaroons consumed by poor Thucydides."

"Miss Garthwaite informed me of her dog's death. It is surpassing strange that a tea-cake should prove so unwholesome. I could wish Hargate would leave off such foolishness, and devote himself to the living. Surely we have greater need of his advice than Miss Garthwaite!"

Captain Pellew making no mention of *poison*, I avoided the word as well; better that Dr. Hargate convey his conclusions once they were formed. Was the Captain's appearance of ignorance genuine, or meant to allay such suspicions of his

motives and actions as I had recently entertained? Regardless, I must be circumspect. It would not do to be spreading
the idea of a murderous attack around the boardinghouse. I
should only alarm the lodgers and put the murderer on his or
her guard. Better to reserve my speculation for Raphael West;
he understood how to answer it.

There was a rustle at the parlour door, and the figure of
Miss Fox appeared. There was a line of worry between her
brows, and her expression was sombre. She held a tray in
her hands with a porcelain bowl and napkin, discarded.

"Would she take anything?" Pellew asked.

Miss Fox shook her head. "She preferred to compose some
lines of poetry, which I have set down at her insistence. About
the sea cliffs below Godrevy, and the birds that circle there.
She has fallen asleep in her chair."

"You will wear yourself out in her service," the Captain said
gruffly. "Indeed, I wonder if you have had any refreshment.
Did you even attempt breakfast? Shall I call for a tea tray, or
some soup?"

Miss Fox smiled wanly. "You are very good, sir, but Mrs.
Potter brought me a nuncheon an hour ago. There is nothing
I require. At least—that is . . ."

"How may I serve you?" Pellew blotted his letter and folded
it, then drew a wafer from the desk drawer. Reaching for the
writing table's candle, he held the flame over the wax, and
pressed the seal closed.

"I should like to take a turn in the air, regardless of the
rain," she said impulsively. "Would you be so good as to sit
with her, sir?"

He glanced at me, the letter in his hands. I suspected he had intended to post it immediately, the outgoing mail being set in its coach a quarter-hour after four o'clock, when Lord Portreath meant to return, and there being no mail service on Sundays.

"Captain, why do you not accompany Miss Fox, while I sit with her ladyship for an interval?" I suggested.

Miss Fox's wan looks brightened. Curious, that a woman described as antipathetic to men should so clearly value the society of *one* of their number.

"Have you any correspondence to post?" Pellew asked her. "We might begin by walking in that direction."

"I shall just fetch my cloak." She looked at me, her eyes glowing. "I am in your debt, Miss Austen. We shall not tarry too long, I assure you."

"Pay no mind to that." I retrieved Mrs. Potter's volume of *Belinda* from the table where I had left it. "I have taken my exercise already today, and should infinitely prefer a book."

THE BASKET-CHAIR FACED THE parlour's bow window, which gave out onto Mrs. Potter's rear garden (a vegetable plot, faring poorly in this wretched June) and beyond, Back Street with its scattering of small buildings. On a fine day, the southeast exposure should admit a wash of sunlight, picking out the glint in Rose Williams's hair; but at present the atmosphere was dim and grey. A fire in the hearth prevented the seeping chill from invading the room, but otherwise it was fairly cheerless. Miss Fox had set up a screen between her chair and the patient, to shield her friend's eyes from the light of an oil lamp, its wick turned low.

I deliberately set the screen to one side and turned up the lamp wick, brightening the chair's immediate vicinity. If Miss Williams slept, I yet required stronger light for the enjoyment of my book; and if the glare woke her, better still! My purpose should not be served by a sleeping viscountess. If I meant to learn anything from her that might prevent a violent loss of life, I must seize such chances as fell in my way.

For a few moments, her breast continued to rise and fall in a shallow, indiscriminate manner that did not augur well for either health or rest. Then, with a faint mew like a kitten, she opened her eyes. She raised one hand against the light and peered at me narrowly.

"Why are you come?" she asked in a failing accent.

I smiled and leant towards her with a gesture of reassurance. "I am sitting with you while you sleep. Pay no mind; I shall be as quiet as a mouse."

"Where is Sarah gone?"

"She has gone out for an airing, but will return directly. She did not like to leave you unattended. I am happy to be of service."

"I imagine you often are," her ladyship murmured. "It is the way with poor old ladies—"

"One must be eager to support such a creature, whose attention and care are given over entirely to her friend." I was determined to appear vague and artless, the better to disarm her ladyship and lull her to a false complaisance; she might then reveal more than she intended. "Miss Fox is quite *self-less*—an example to us all. That is what I told my sister, your ladyship. 'Only think, Cassandra,' I said to her last night as we prepared for bed. 'Miss Fox has given up her life entirely for the well-being of her friend, left home and family, and risked the ire of so great a nobleman as Viscount Portreath! That is *selfless*, is it not?' And Cassandra agreed. We are both all admiration of Miss Fox."

"That will win you no favours from Sarah. She is indifferent to admiration." A blue gaze moved idly over my countenance, which I schooled to a vacant benevolence. "She is not nearly so selfless as you think, either. To outwit his lordship is a pleasure to her. I merely provide the means."

"I am sure she finds pleasure in setting down these pretty verses!" I cried affably, as tho' I had detected no edge to the lady's words. I reached for a tablet of paper near the lamp. *A coruscation of stone/that rears its brittle head/against the light that shone/where bird-wing fancy led—*

"Give me that!"

Whatever her flagging strength, Miss Williams summoned enough to rear upright in her chair and fling out a peremptory hand. Two bright spots of colour burnt in her cheeks.

"I beg your pardon, I had thought verses were intended to be spoken aloud." I lifted the sheet of paper on which the lines were scrawled and glanced at the next leaf. "Miss Fox is equally accomplished, I see! Tho' her talents run more to charcoal and paintbox—"

"Sarah learnt to sketch at school. But my poetry is a gift, not an *accomplishment*," the Viscountess fumed. Her pretty mouth, which she was used to form into a beguiling bow when Captain Pellew was near, was pinched into a contemptuous knot. "My gift is not akin to embroidering a pair of slippers or netting a screen. It is the deepest expression of my soul, my *art*—one the man who claims to *own* me would deny, if he could! Men do not speak of Byron's *pretty verses*, or Cowper's *accomplishments*, Miss Austen, as tho' they were frivolities reserved for an idle hour! Why, then, must the writing of a woman be dismissed as the product of a lesser mind?"

"Because we are the *weaker* sex," I said fatuously. "Only look at yourself, my dear! At the condition your tantrums and hysteria have reduced you to, regardless of your degree of Art! You are wasted to nothing, confined to a chair, unable even to stand when menaced by that very *man* and his ownership!"

Miss Williams gasped, and her mouth fell open in outrage. I braced myself for a shriek of fury, but none came. She merely drew breath, and steadied herself. "What you say, Miss Austen, is only the paltry charge I have refuted my entire life. *Women* are weak. *Women* are powerless. That is solely because we allow men to rule our purses, our beds, and our minds. I will no longer be a party to such martyrdom; I refuse to submit. In my verses, I roam far beyond this chair. In my verses, I am free."

"Well and good," I agreed. "I have reason to agree with you, tho' you might not credit it. I feel compelled to interrogate your motive, however. With such animus towards the male sex and its power, why did you ever consent to marry? It seems a blind act of self-murder for one such as you."

She lifted her shoulders indolently. "I had no choice."

"I do not understand you. It is choice that separates us from mere beasts."

"Miss Austen," she said, "have you ever been intimately acquainted with a man?"

"I have known six brothers, one father, and a wearying number of nephews," I told her serenely.

She lifted up her eyes in contempt. "I refer to the marriage bed."

I felt myself colour. "I have experienced the tender emotions, tho' my experience has not been *that* large."

"And yet, you retain the single estate."

"I regard it as affording greater freedom . . . of *choice*. Why did you exchange it for a title, my lady?"

"Not, as you appear to assume, out of a desire for notice," she flashed. "I married to win a different kind of freedom. By the terms of my wretched father's will—you see, Miss Austen, they control us from birth—I could not touch my capital until I was wed. And then, once got with child, I should lose control of my fortune entirely! Only if I *died* should I be free of conditions; and so—between the cords my father chose to bind me, and those my husband could work, I determined to strangle myself. I stopped eating. It was the last power left to me."

"That, and running away," I observed

"I owe Sarah everything." Her ladyship's voice softened. "I abuse her terribly, of course—it is the privilege of intimacy never to appreciate those one values most—but without her, I should not be alive today. She has given me a vision of a future, unencumbered by *men*."

"—Happily secured and sustained by the retention of your wealth." It was not lost on me that Rose Williams's greed, as much as her dislike of the Viscount, had formulated her plans; Miss Fox's views were perhaps less interested. "Why, then, reduce your body *now* to a useless husk? Weakness cannot further your hopes!"

"Because I am not yet free of him," she replied, fierce and low. "Self-control is the only weapon I wield. I am the sole creature under my command, Miss Austen, and I am determined to be ruthless. Whether I die or live, I mean to be an example to all men, of a woman's strength of will. There is protest in denial. Sunk in this chair, I am nonetheless rebellious; and I mean to effect a revolution from it, one day."

I should have accepted such words from the sober Miss Fox; her gravity was suited to the spirit of a Queen of Scots; but emanating from the mouth of this fragile blue-and-gold creature, they verged on the absurd. I might have pitied her, but she should abhor such an emotion from me—and my common sense forbade it.

"Revolutions, like battles, rise or fall on the bellies of their fighters," I said briskly. "I have two brothers schooled in the recent wars, and may claim to be educated on the subject. There are many forms of martyrdom, and if you wish to avoid the most sickening, I would advise you to *eat*, Miss Williams. I will not call you Viscountess, as you *are* a rebel. Eat, and recruit your strength for another day. And now I believe I hear Miss Fox and Captain Pellew returning."

I rose and shook out my skirts.

"Captain Pellew? —Captain Pellew has escorted Miss Fox on her walk to the post?"

"He has."

Her ladyship's countenance flushed red, then drained white with a suppressed fury. "I had thought both of them devoted to their vigil here. I had thought them ranged in support of *me*—not intent upon selfish pleasures!"

"One cannot always be a martyr to another's cause. I imagine the walk and the conversation of a gallant gentleman, afforded Miss Fox much-needed comfort." I held out the tablet of paper, which I had left turned to the second page. "Look how your friend has captured the Captain's likeness! Such a speaking sketch! Only the hand of affection could move so surely."

It was indeed an admirable portrait of Harry Pellew, as he looked on occasion when deep in thought—captured in profile, with his gaze fixed on something unseen, a quirk of amusement to his narrow lips. The expression of the eyes was remarkable. It was this artist, I suspected, who truly possessed a *gift*. That her heart was engaged by the gentleman, more-over, I did not doubt. But what were *his* feelings?

A sharply indrawn breath from Miss Fox's jealous friend. "Give me back my writing tablet," she demanded—and without a word, I complied.

17

HISTORY OF A FALLEN WOMAN

Saturday, 1st June, 1816
Cheltenham, cont'd.

"Miss Austen!"
The housemaid, Lucy, accosted me as I quitted
her ladyship's room. With a hurried nod for Captain Pellew
and Miss Fox, who were removing their headgear by the fire
before attending the Viscountess, I took the visiting card the
maid offered.

"Gentleman to see you," she said. "He's waiting below."

Mr. Raphael West. On the back of the card, he had hurriedly
penned the words—*A few moments of your time.* I glanced at
the mantel-clock: It lacked barely a quarter before four, when
Portreath intended to remount his siege upon his errant wife.
Given that he might already have presented her with poisoned
macaroons, I did not like to be absent for the interview. Perhaps Mr. West would join me in the sitting-room?

I hastened to follow the maid downstairs, where West
stood in apparent contemplation of a hideous framed sketch
of the Elm Walk, his hat in his hands. "Miss Austen," he
said, turning to bow in greeting, "I wonder if you would care

to take a turn in my curricle? The rain is at an end, and there are still two hours before sunset and your dinner—"

At that moment, Captain Pellew lurched down the stairs, his stick ineffectually negotiating its steepness and his stiff leg. "Lucy," he called to the housemaid, "you must send for Dr. Hargate. At once! Her ladyship has suffered another fit. I must leave this note for Lord Portreath at the York," he added, exhibiting a slip of sealed paper, "setting back his visit by an hour." He nodded at West, and moved heavily past us to the door. So much activity, for a man who is lame! Again, doubt as to his motives stabbed at my mind. But West was waiting—

"I will fetch my pelisse," I told him; and this swift errand accomplished in a trice, I was handed up into the neat equipage he had hired from the York livery.

It was a sporting curricle, with a single job horse, and quite likely to bowl along if the animal was given its head. West threaded his way through the traffic along the High in the direction of the Gloucester Road, and once free of the town's traffic, settled into a steady, trotting pace.

"I am grateful to you, Jane, for submitting to this wish of mine for open air," he said, as we ambled along. The recent showers had made the roadbed soft, and there were ruts from the passage of other and heavier conveyances; it was not to be a smooth passage, but I did not care—such exhilaration as I felt in my breast at being free of the narrow confines of the spa town, and in the treasured company of this excellent man.

"Not at all," I returned serenely. "You seem troubled in

your mind, Mr. West, and exercise as well as conversation are certain remedies for the relief of anxiety."

"I have just concluded an interview that disturbs me greatly."

"Indeed?"

He kept his eyes trained, perforce, on the surging neck of the animal between the traces, and his hands firmly gripped on the reins; but I was free to study his profile, which remained as superb as the first day I glimpsed it, in a snow-storm in a lane in Hampshire.

"I found Hannah Vyvyan—your Mrs. Smith—in her offices at the Cheltenham Theatre," he said. "Do you know that she consorts with all kinds of riff-raff there? And she, the niece and ward of a baronet!"

"Is she indeed? I apprehend you renewed your acquaintance?"

"At my insistence—although Miss Vyvyan would have it that there was not time enough to sit down before this evening's performance. It is to be *The School for Scandal.*"

"I am aware of it. And Miss Vyvyan's protégée, a girl by the name of Tess, is to play Lady Teazle."

He glanced at me sidelong, his eyes narrow and dark. "You have met this darling of the stage?"

"Not at all. I know her solely by repute. A pretty thing, apparently, but unable to distinguish her vowels from her consonants."

"A saucy guttersnipe with a cunning usually reserved for pickpockets," West concluded succinctly. "I sent the child away from her lesson in search of a pot of tea, which Hannah obligingly poured out."

"Mrs. Smith recalled your connexion?"

"Naturally. One cannot be subjected to the acutest study of a man's gaze, for a fortnight together, and fail to remember it."

For an instant, the idea of West poised before an easel, brush in hand, his eyes roaming over my form as he secured every detail to his painter's mind, left me suffused with heat—and not a little terror at such exposure.

"She has been cast out," he declared.

I angled myself a little towards him, my left knee brushing his right. "From Derbyshire? And her exalted relations?"

"Completely cut off, from her family and her proper station in life." He spoke with suppressed rage, imagining his own daughter Charlotte, no doubt, in such a friendless condition. "Without a thruppence in her purse, Jane, or hope of return."

"And her sin?"

"The usual one. She loved too recklessly, and loved a scoundrel, who left her with child."

I sighed.

"I had thought better of Sir Charles."

"Her guardian?"

"If such a term is applicable for one who so violates a sacred trust," West returned bitterly. "Hannah is the daughter of the late Richard Vyvyan, a gentleman of considerable property in Devon—the family holdings are just outside Portsmouth—and Augusta Markham, Sir Charles Markham's late sister. Her parents were killed when their carriage overturned at the hands of a drunken coachman. Hannah was their only surviving child, and by dint of her father's estate, was placed in the care of her Derbyshire uncle. Sir Charles sent her to a reputable ladies' academy in Bath, where she became an intimate of my daughter Charlotte—the two girls were of an age, and similarly animated in temperament. Upon quitting that institution, Charlotte remained in Bath under the care of a chaperon and companion I hired for her. Some two years later, she married a respectable young man—a solicitor with an excellent practise."

I nodded my encouragement; it was the most West had ever told me about his beloved daughter.

"Sir Charles took Hannah into his household at the age of nineteen, and launched her the next spring with a Season in London. He has no daughter of his own, and such conduct must be considered the least that a guardian of a ward, who was received with considerable property, ought to be expected to exert on her behalf. It was then that I was hired to take her portrait, a brilliant match being in view for the lady."

"Miss Vyvyan is an heiress?" I confess I was surprized.

"Indeed. Her father was a man of property, and her mother bequeathed to her a considerable fortune, derived from banking. Her funds are in trust until her majority at the age of five-and-twenty. Sir Charles, naturally, is her trustee, along with her late father's attorney."

"And how old is she at present?"

"Four-and-twenty."

"And her indiscretion—her fall from Grace—"

"Occurred about the time of my daughter Charlotte's marriage. As you may imagine, the two young ladies no longer moved in the same circles, being divided by rank and fortune; but they maintained a steady correspondence and sympathy.

From time to time, my portrait completed, I heard a little of Miss Vyvyan's social success. That slow stream of friendly intelligence ended abruptly a few weeks after Charlotte became Mrs. Evingrode; and as my daughter's life was full, I assumed the friendship had been allowed to wane, and did not enquire as to the cause."

He paused, and eased the curricle through standing water that bisected the road, careful lest the muddy water should splash my skirts.

"I know, now, that in her disgrace and shame, Hannah refused to tarnish the reputation of her friends," he added, "—and severed all connexion with those who had once held her in affection and esteem."

"I know your goodness too well," I said impulsively, "to believe that *you* would have abandoned her."

"I would not," he agreed, "and should have consulted her late father's executors on her behalf, had Sir Charles proved immovable."

"How did she survive? Support herself?"

"Sir Charles sent her back to Plymouth," he said grimly, "in the care of her former nurse, an elderly woman who had cared for Hannah as a child. The two were set up in a cottage, with the intention that the infant, once born, should be turned upon the parish, and put up for adoption."

I shuddered. "Abandoned as a parish orphan, more like."

He nodded. "In the event, the babe miscarried within a few months, and Hannah—unwilling to deal further with her guardian—paid off her nurse and removed to Cheltenham, under the name of Mrs. Smith."

"And found work as a theatrical preceptress?"

West smiled with sudden amusement, impossible to contain. "She meant to try her talent upon the boards, having always enjoyed the amateur dramaticks of her schoolgirl days in Bath. She meant to be the next Mrs. Siddons, I believe, and take London by storm."

"—A fine revenge upon her odious uncle," I said admiringly. "Having been assured that she was a disgrace, no longer to be acknowledged by respectable Society, she had, after all, no reputation to lose by becoming an actress—and everything to gain by fulfilling the worst suspicions of her relations!"

"It is exactly like Hannah's spirit," West agreed. "But she did not calculate on one lamentable fact. She suffers severely from stage-fright, a condition brought on by foot-lights and the presence of jeering strangers in the pit—neither of which were present at school."

"But being as clever as she is engaging, Mrs. Smith divined a use for her talents," I concluded, "and has supported herself very well. I must congratulate her—or should do so, were she aware that I knew her history."

"I can say nothing on that head." West guided the horse into a side lane, turning us back in the direction of Cheltenham. "She was most distressed when I discovered her backstage, and no doubt would have preferred that I leave her in peace; but my sense of justice could not be satisfied, Jane."

"What do you intend to do?"

"She has given me the name of her late father's solicitor— a London man. I shall write to him tonight, and arrange to meet with him on her behalf as soon as I am returned to Town. Tho' the bulk of her fortune is tied up another two years, she ought to be due a quarterly allowance, regardless of her guardian's animosity. Indeed, I expect she is in expectation of several years' remittance!"

"I am sure you will prevail. And I am relieved on Mrs. Smith's account." But my tone—like my spirits—had suffered a sudden oppression. West's return to his home in London—the house where his elderly father, the renowned artist Benjamin West, still lived and opened his rooms to patrons—was inevitable, of course. The fact inspired some anguish. Being once more in West's company taught me how dearly I regarded him. He was animation and vigour, understanding and beauty; whole worlds contained within, that I might have shared, given time.

I could not express my emotion, naturally. A woman does not speak her heart without assurance of return.

"When do you quit Cheltenham, Jane?" he asked quietly.

"In a week's time," I returned, striving for complaisance. "Or rather—not being given to Sunday travel—we depart on Monday the tenth of June."

"Then I shall make for London that same day."

We had regained the High, and the carriage traffic was, if anything, greater than when we set out. It was a slow progress to Mrs. Potter's, and I might have satisfied my love of observing humanity, the paving at either side being thronged with pleasure-seekers reveling in the cessation of the rain, had my heart been less full.

"Let us make the most of this week," he suggested. "There

is the Assembly Monday evening—will you dance with me, Jane?"

I drew in a deep breath. "I should be honoured, sir."

But would I have the energy? My heart quailed. Tho' I had enjoyed a week's rest in this spa town, and my appetite was a little restored, I yet experienced waves of weariness that came over me without warning, and would not be denied. The thought of the preparations necessary for a ball—I had brought no gown suitable for such an event—nearly overwhelmed me. But to dance . . . with *West* . . .

"It is to be a masquerade," he reminded me, as he pulled up before the boardinghouse. "In honour of the King's birthday, and the nuptials of Princess Charlotte."

"So it is," I said faintly. "We must go in *character*, then."

"Make this your reason for consulting with Hannah Vyvyan." He jumped from the curricle and handed the reins to a boy lurking in the doorway, along with a shilling. "Her theatre owner, Bowles Watson, has brought in a number of costumes against the event."

I grasped West's hand in my own and stepped down to the paving. He bowed low, brushing his lips over the back of my glove. "We should drive out more often, Jane," he said. "The wind has whipped colour into your cheeks. Indeed—I should like to paint them."

18

RAT THE FIRST

Saturday, 1st June, 1816
Cheltenham, cont'd.

Lord Portreath's visit to his recalcitrant wife had been
set back from four to five o'clock, at Captain Pellew's
insistence. Upon my return from my drive with Mr. West,
I enquired as to her ladyship's health, and sudden indisposition—and was answered by no less an authority than Miss
Fox, who had witnessed it.

"She did not swoon," the lady told me as she emerged from
the private parlour with a tea tray in her hands, "but appeared
rather to suffer a fit of temper. I cannot account for it. When
the Captain and I left her for the post, she was asleep; but at
our return, she was awake and in a rage! You were sitting with
her, Miss Austen—do you know what *can* have riled her so?"

Poor Miss Fox looked fatigued from her nursing. The skin
around her eyes was almost translucent with exhaustion, and
her lips were drained of colour. I reflected that it had probably
been my conversation that had upset the invalid's nerves; but
then I recalled the expression on her ladyship's countenance
when I displayed the sketch of Captain Pellew in Miss Fox's

notebook. Was it possible that *jealousy* had violently animated her temper?

"We spoke of her determination to starve herself," I attempted. "I urged her to recruit her strength, the better to advance her cause. Perhaps the subject was ill-advised."

"Dr. Hargate is with her now." Miss Fox sighed, and rubbed fretfully at the bridge of her nose. "I am glad of it; I hope he will remain while that monster conducts his interview, the better to safeguard Miss Williams."

"You do not employ her title, I observe."

Miss Fox's chin rose. "I do not regard her as that man's slave. Tho' he may have married her before God, she owes him no more duty or affection than he merits; and by his actions, he deserves neither."

"That is a heavy judgement." I seated myself at the writing desk and took up a pen. "You have known her ladyship long?"

"Nearly all my life," Miss Fox replied. "We were at school together, and continued our mutual devotion after her marriage."

"Indeed?" I selected a sheet of cheap writing paper from a pigeon-hole in the desk and set down the date. The less interested I appeared in Miss Fox's conversation, I suspected, the more freely she was likely to talk, as tho' conversing only with herself. She moved in a weary daze to a chair by the fire, and extended her hands to the warmth. She meant to rest a little before the next summons from her imperious charge; there should be no better moment for learning what I could of the two ladies' history. I held my breath that no one should disturb us.

"Did Miss Williams's marriage to the Viscount alter your degree of intimacy, once your school-days were done?" I asked.

"She did not, in fact, marry a viscount," Miss Fox returned, glancing over her shoulder at me. "She married Granville Basset, second son to Viscount Portreath—a cavalry officer in His Majesty's Seventh Light Dragoons, as he then was—and *not* the heir to the title."

"You astonish me!" I laid down my pen and sank back in my chair, gazing at Miss Fox. "There was another heir?"

"Granville's elder brother, Piers. I never met him; he died before Rose had been married a year."

"She had not expected, then, to live at Godrevy Manor as its mistress?"

Miss Fox shook her head. "It was an honour she never looked for, or indeed, desired. Her talents are not inclined to the management of a great house. She was not reared for it, nor suited to the shoring up of a noble line."

"I begin to understand Miss Williams's unhappiness."

"That is only the hundredth part! You must have seen there is no love between them; it was a marriage of convenience only, on both sides. Rose was determined to wed in her first Season—it being a stipulation of her father's that she should gain access to her fortune only upon her marriage. Granville Basset seemed the ideal husband, in being absent the better part of the year in the Peninsula, fighting for King and Country."

—*And likely to be killed as a result*, I thought, *leaving his bride in solitary enjoyment of her riches.* Rose Williams was revealed as a ruthless mercenary, indeed!

"For his part, Granville was only too eager to attach a wealthy wife," Miss Fox persisted. She rose from the heat of the hearth and took a desultory turn about the room, her eyes trained upon the floor. She had travelled far in memory, it seemed to me. "It was a condition of the marriage that Rose settle his gambling debts before his return to the field. That done, Granville embarked for Oporto the day after the wedding, and Rose on an interval of peace and enjoyment! How happy we were, then! She took lodgings in Bath, and invited me for several months' visit—until the sudden hour of the Portreath heir's death, and Granville's immediate return."

"A rude shock, indeed," I murmured.

"Her husband has done nothing since acceding to the title but spend his income in the pursuit of pleasure; and when it is all gone, he means to waste Rose's inheritance equally swiftly." Miss Fox came to a halt by my writing desk, her large dark eyes fixed miserably upon my own.

"You think to thwart that object, by helping her to escape?"

"Flight was necessary for more than one reason, I assure you. If it were merely a matter of Rose's fortune, we might have consulted lawyers at our leisure."

"But with limited result, I imagine? —A lady's wealth becomes her husband's as soon as she is married."

"That is true—but Rose's inheritance was left in trust." Miss Fox rested her palms upon the table-edge and leant over me. "Granville enjoys the income only *at present*. If she were to have a child, *or to die*, the terms of the Trust should alter, and Granville must benefit; but if she were to divorce . . ."

"Divorce!" I cried, shocked; for such an act is akin to death, for any lady. "Surely there can be no need for so drastic a measure? Tho' I admit, it does appear to be an unhappy union—"

"Unhappy? She has been made so wretched by his demands, as to starve herself in order to thwart them!"

"What sort of demands?"

Miss Fox shrugged. "The usual ones, where a nobleman is concerned. He requires a hostess to charm his political connexions, an ornament for Society, and a son to serve as heir. Rose has no interest in any of these. Her passion is for poetry alone, and composition."

I began to feel a trifling sympathy for Lord Portreath. Any man, upon his marriage, might be forgiven for expecting to have secured a wife.

"But it is not merely Rose's wealth that is at stake." Miss Fox sank into a chair near my table and put her face in her hands. "I have feared for her life, Miss Austen, this past year and more."

"Because of her determination to starve?"

"*That* is peculiar only to the past six months." Miss Fox smoothed her hands distractedly over her dark hair; it had come loose in places from its pins, and she was looking quite frowsy. Too much attention to the invalid, too little reserved for herself. "But for a period far longer, her ladyship has been dangerously prone to accident. There was an overturning of her carriage—a swing that broke as she sat upon it—a footbridge that gave out, and catapulted her into a stream . . . all survived seemingly by chance, or good fortune."

"Do you believe in either, Miss Fox?" I asked quietly.

"I do not believe that one may be so constantly in peril, absent a malicious design. That is why I carried her away from Godrevy, once Granville had quitted the place for London last month."

I made no pretense any longer of composing a letter. "Pray sit down," I told the young woman gently, "and speak plainly. You think the Viscount has repeatedly tried to kill his wife?"

Miss Fox drew forward a side chair. Her languor was gone; her whole attention was trained on her purpose. "No one else should benefit so clearly from Rose's death. For a man without scruple, what better answer than *murder* to a tedious problem? In one stroke, he should rid himself of a wife who refuses to answer his expectations—and free her fortune for his sole enjoyment!"

"What of Mrs. Williams? Rose's stepmother?"

Miss Fox snorted. "What of her?"

"Would she also benefit from your friend's death?"

"As his lordship might then be free to marry—can you doubt it?"

"There is an illicit attachment between them?"

"I am sure of it. His lordship insists on carrying Louisa Williams with him wherever he goes. And the creature offers not the slightest argument, or betrays the least sensibility. It is not for *her* to nurse her daughter when she is in decline; Mrs. Williams would rather secure the services of Rose's dearest friend, and journey to London in the stile of a viscountess!"

"As she did only a month since," I noted.

"Lord Portreath makes a habit of leasing a house in Town

for the Season. He sits in Lords, of course, but enjoys Society as much as policy. This spring he began to speak of looking about for a property to *purchase*, as tho' his funds ran to the maintenance of two separate households! But when he suggested Louisa Williams accompany him to consult with the house agents, and serve as hostess in his ailing wife's stead, I knew that he was intent upon replacing Rose. If Granville desired a London home, his wife's funds must be necessary to him—and what Granville desires, he secures. There should be further attempts on Rose's life once the Viscount and his mistress were returned to Godrevy."

"And thus, as her nurse, you determined upon a flight to Cheltenham while they were gone."

"This place was to be our first object only, on a longer journey that might well have ended on the Continent. But in the event, Rose proved too weak for protracted travel. While she drank the waters and consulted Hargate, we tarried here too long . . ."

And flirted with a handsome Naval officer, who had no reason to suspect Miss Williams was married, I thought. "Was she in better health when first you left Cornwall?"

"In truth, she was not—but I persuaded myself that travel and freedom might improve her. I dared not remain too long at Godrevy, and find her weaker still. His lordship's absence was a chance I could not let slip," Miss Fox admitted in a lowered tone. "I did not regard it as abduction. Rose was as wild to quit the scene of her misery as I was. I did not expect to see Lord Portreath returned to Godrevy until July, at least; and tho' I suspected word would reach him of our absence—the steward at least should inform him—I did not credit his lordship with excessive anxiety."

"I apprehend, now, your compulsion to fly from this boardinghouse the very night you glimpsed the Viscount in Cheltenham Theatre," I said. "But it will not do, you know, Miss Fox; you cannot run away forever."

She sighed in assent, and dropped her gaze to her clenched hands. "That is indisputable. We must face the evil as we find it. But what am I to do for her, Miss Austen? How am I to keep her safe?"

"Perhaps you will not need to," I suggested. "Perhaps Thucydides already has."

A bustle on the staircase precluded Miss Fox's reply. She moved forward in apprehension—and came face to face with Granville, Lord Portreath.

Behind him, still ascending the stairs, was Mrs. Williams.

"Miss Fox." His lordship drew a quizzing glass from his pocket and peered at us through it. "And, er—"

"Miss Austen," I supplied.

He inclined his head, and stepped aside to permit Mrs. Williams to gain the sitting-room.

Without betraying too frank an interest, I studied the pair with all the knowledge of Miss Fox's history. The Viscount was elegantly attired in evening dress—no doubt he intended to dine after this interview in Mrs. Williams's company—and his moderate looks were heightened to something more, by the snowiness of his cravat, and the excellence of his black coat of superfine. The lady in his escort wore a brilliant peacock blue this evening that set off her complexion to handsome effect;

on her head was an ornament with sapphires and feathers. They appeared all that was respectable and secure, steady and admirable; and the notion of murder at the hands of either seemed singularly ludicrous.

"I wish to see my wife," his lordship said, "and without further delay. We intend the theatre this evening."

Miss Fox did not honour her visitors with a curtsey. "Far be it from me to curtail any pleasure of yours. I shall convey you to her ladyship."

I MIGHT HAVE BEEN tempted to overlisten the interesting exchange of views that ensued in the private parlour, but its door is of oak, sufficiently stout; and I was aware, moreover, of a wind-blown condition to my hair and cheeks that demanded attention before I should appear at Mrs. Potter's dinner table. I hastened above stairs to my bedchamber. As I entered the passage leading to my room, a door at the far end was flung open, and Mr. Garthwaite's sepulchral form lurched forth.

His right arm was extended, and dangling from his thumb and forefinger—by its lengthy tail   was a rat.

I stopped short, unable to entirely credit my eyes. The clergyman continued his inexorable progress towards me.

"Good evening, sir."

"Dead," he said.

The rodent's teeth were bared in a grimace, and its forepaws drawn close to its chest.

"Forgive me—but you discovered *that* in your bedchamber?"

"In the passage just outside. Extinguished."

I pressed myself against the wall. Garthwaite marched deliberately past, without so much as a glance.

"A sign," he called, as he reached the head of the stairs, and turned to glare balefully in my direction. "We are but dust."

And to dust we shall—

"Pray, sir." I started forward impulsively, as my understanding kept pace with his runic words. "Dr. Hargate is below. I believe he would benefit from a view of your . . ."

"*Rattus norvegicus.*"

"Indeed?"

"Street rat, gutter rat, wharf rat, Hanover rat, Parisian rat . . . one of the largest of muroids." He blinked at me. "Its vomitus stains my drugget."

"Mrs. Potter shall be informed."

"We breathe poison." He groped for the stair-rail. "It is all about us. None of us shall escape."

I watched his grizzled head descend the stair, wavering from view.

"Repent!"

The single word trailed behind him.

"Dr. Hargate, sir!" I repeated, with some urgency—and then thankfully sought my room.

1 9

THE COSTUME-MISTRESS AND
HER TREASURE CHEST

Sunday, 2nd June, 1816
Cheltenham

For a wonder, dawn broke this morning without a curtain of rain, and tho' I should not characterise the day as brilliant, a fitful sunlight fought through the scrim of clouds from time to time, and made one giddy with the remembrance of what summers should be. Cassandra and I woke early, and did not break our fast, but walked to St. Mary's for morning service in quiet admiration of the colour to be found on every side, now that the dispiriting grey was banished. The peace of the ancient church—for it has been a home to worshipers full six hundred years—brought a welcome balm to my soul, and reminded me that I had come into Gloucestershire for rest and healing, not dramaticks and violent scenes.

As Raphael West said—Cassandra and I have one week remaining to us among the wells and walks of the various pump rooms; one week of concerts, art exhibitions, and circulating libraries—before we must return into Hampshire, collecting Cassie on our way and facing the result of Charles's Admiralty Board once we are returned to Chawton. As I sat in silent contemplation of the church's architraves, I vowed to turn my fascinated eye away from the tawdry spectacle of Lord and Lady Portreath, as well as their hangers-on, and enjoy Cheltenham while I am able.

"What would you say, Cassandra," I ventured as we curtseyed to the vicar, Mr. Jervis, and quitted St. Mary's for the warm, sun-splashed paving of the High Street, our prayer books in our gloved hands, "to attending the Assembly tomorrow? The ball is to be a masquerade; and Mrs. Smith is to bring some of her favourite gowns to the lodging-house for us to try."

"That is very kind in her," Cassandra said. "But do you not think, my dearest, that we are perhaps a little . . . past the age when such amusements must be agreeable?"

"We need not *dance*, Cassandra, and indeed I do not expect to," I said airily. "But we might enjoy the liveliness of the spectacle, if only for an hour, and have the satisfaction of telling all our acquaintance that we celebrated the King's birthday and the Royal Wedding in Cheltenham's Assembly Rooms."

"It will not tire you overmuch?"

I stopped short and stared at her. "When the alternative is to read aloud from *Guy Mannering* in Mrs. Potter's bedchamber, while the strains of violoncellos drift up to the window from the street—"

"Oh, very well, Jane." My sister threw up her hands. "When you put it so pathetically as that, I feel it is our duty as loyal subjects of His Majesty to attend."

"That is a relief, Cassandra—because Mr. West has already procured us tickets."

We had achieved the corner of the High Street and the Colonnade, which led the visitor past various merchants' vitrines to the Royal Well, and beyond it, to Montpellier. The shops were naturally closed on the Sabbath, but in glancing along the paving I noticed a grouping that surprized me: Miss Fox with the Viscountess in her basket-chair, Captain Pellew, and Mrs. Smith.

They were drawn up before a linen-draper's display, which cannot have interested the Captain overmuch, but on espying Cassandra and me at the corner, Pellew removed his chapeau-bras and bowed. At his notice, the ladies moved in slow progression to join us.

My brows drew down a little; I nearly trembled with the urge to speak; for I kept an idle secret from Cassandra, who sleeps soundest and farthest from our bedchamber door. I had awakened again in the middle of the night, to the sound of soft footsteps in the passage, and again had opened my door to find Lady Portreath gliding in the direction of Captain Pellew's room.

As before, she did not spend above a few moments in her nocturnal errand. Whether the Captain is even aware of the visitations, I cannot say. But some mystery surrounds the two, and I cannot cease to be puzzled by it.

"Is it not a capital day?" the Captain cried by way of greeting.

"Impossible to remain within-doors, as her ladyship informed me over breakfast."

The Viscountess affected far less languorous than she usually chuses, sitting upright in her chair, with her hair artfully arranged in clusters of side-curls at the temple, and her thin frame elegantly gowned in pale green and white. Perhaps she had benefited from her nocturnal exercise.

"I took your advice, Miss Jane," she sang out, "and drank some broth last evening, once Portreath was gone; and this morning I consented to a few mouthfuls of porridge, at the dear Captain's insistence, tho' it was nasty as dishwater."

She glanced sidelong under her lashes at Pellew, who smiled down at her.

"Mrs. Potter's porridge is unrivaled," he said. "If you knew what it was to consume hardtack and maggoty bread for a month together—"

"Dishwater," she repeated, and poked him playfully in the side with the tip of her parasol.

I glanced at Miss Fox as she observed this badinage, but her expression remained immovable.

"There is something in what you advise, I believe," her ladyship continued, with a look for me; "however much I may enjoy defying Portreath's attempt to regulate even my *diet*, a failing woman is a weak woman; and I mean to be strong."

"I congratulate you."

She beamed like a child who has confessed to naughtiness and been forgiven; then said crossly to Miss Fox, "Sarah! I am facing directly into the sun! Pray, turn my chair a little or I shall be brown as a heathen, before long."

The transformation in her ladyship from yesterday to this morning was remarkable. The patient had clearly derived benefit from being allowed to have her way, and for this I supposed we must thank Dr. Hargate.

Before quitting Mrs. Potter's yesterday evening, the physician had informed her ladyship's relations that if they were determined to move her, regardless of her precarious health and his sternest warnings, he should have the Law upon them. When Viscount Portreath asked him what crime could possibly be charged, in a gentleman's conveyance of his wife to her home, Hargate declared, "If she *dies*, my lord, I shall appear at an inquest to lay evidence against yourself of the grossest neglect! She is not to be moved before I adjudge her strong enough! —And I should *never* condone Sunday travel, in any case."

At that moment, Lucy the housemaid had appeared with a tray bearing her ladyship's dinner, which only Miss Fox would certainly sample; Lord Portreath consulted his handsome pocket watch, and informed Mrs. Williams that it was time they departed for the theatre; and the rest of the household, our spectacle at an end, adjourned to the common dining parlour.

We were treated to roast chicken, which thankfully bore no resemblance to *rattus norvegicus*, living or dead.

Impossible, of course, to enquire of Mr. Garthwaite if he had disposed of his prize, or consulted the doctor, as he morbidly contemplated his dinner. I was the sole person who appeared to know of his find. I confess the suspense was almost more than I could bear.

Now, Mrs. Smith, her serviceable gown improved by the sunshine, came up with me on the paving.

"Have you attended Divine Service?" she enquired. The discomfiture she had exhibited yesterday in the library was gone. Her interview with Mr. West must have cheered her.

"We have," I replied. "The church is a handsome one."

"And how did you find Mr. Jervis's sermon? He is known for an Evangelical."[4]

"Highly instructive." I glanced at Cassandra, who suppressed a smile. "He spoke on the wonders of natural philosophy, as the gift of a benevolent Providence for the improvement of mankind. I believe he intended merely to voice his approval—and the Lord's—of local physicians, who do so much good for St. Mary's poor; but it must be Mr. Jervis's misfortune that Mr. Garthwaite was among the congregants today, and took his fellow clergyman's words in bad light."

"Oh, dear!" Mrs. Smith's eyes widened. "Did Mr. Garthwaite disgrace himself?"

"He rose to his feet and cried aloud: 'I know your deeds; you have a reputation of being alive, but you are dead. Wake up! Strengthen what remains and is about to die!'"

"It is from the Book of Revelation," Cass supplied.

"I wonder poor Mr. Jervis did not expire on the spot." Mrs. Smith glanced at her companions. "Mr. Garthwaite

---

4 Charles Jervis, of Trinity College, Oxford, was the Perpetual Curate of St. Mary's from 1816–1826. He was an acknowledged member of the Evangelical movement, which sought to restore Protestant fervor to a lax Regency church.

ought rather to have come with us, to the Society of Friends' meeting; it is an interval for sacred contemplation, that might well have calmed his nerves."

"Are you also a Quaker?" I asked, surprized.

But she shook her head in the negative, her eyes sparkling. "I merely find Dissenters more welcoming to ladies of the theatre, than the Devout of the established faith. It is a relief, you know, not to be judged by my fellows one day at *least* among the seven!"

I could not help smiling at her, or admiring her spirit. "Not all the world is so harsh. In the present company alone, you appear to have any number of friends."

She laughed a little, and slipped her arm through mine as our conclave turned in the direction of Mrs. Potter's. "Ah, if you refer to Harry Pellew, you must know I have known him all my life, Miss Austen. If he cannot bear to hear me abused by others, it is because he reserves that privilege solely to himself!"

"It is not the Captain alone I would speak of. We have an acquaintance in common, I believe. Mr. Raphael West?"

A swift look from Mrs. Smith's candid green eyes. "So it was not mere happenstance that he entered the library immediately on your heels?"

"Rather, he escorted me there."

"Mr. West is my dearest schoolfriend's papa," she mused, "and an excellent man. It is astonishing, is it not, how very small the world may prove, Miss Austen? That we two, separated by every possible circumstance, should count the same gentleman among our intimates?"

I coloured a little. "I should not presume to call Mr. West *that*—"

"Ah! Then I conclude you have sat for a portrait?"

"No—" I paused in confusion. The gentleness of West's words as he studied the colour in my cheeks: *I should like to paint them.* Perhaps in his mind he already had; there are many ways to seize a likeness. "We met a few years since, at Christmastide, while both were guests at a country-house in Hampshire. The merest coincidence renewed our acquaintance here."

"I see. And do you know his charming daughter? Mrs. Evingrode?"

"I have not had that pleasure. Mr. West, I believe, has lately been visiting her in Bath."

"So he told me when we spoke yesterday—I do not think I mentioned that we met again, after I just glimpsed you in passing at the library." She spoke without the slightest consciousness of her awkward evasion in the Reading Room; her time as theatre apprentice had taught her a little of playacting, at least. "My poor Charlotte—Mrs. Evingrode—has had a sad spring."

"Perhaps you may go to her, and be of comfort."

"Perhaps." She flashed me her winsome smile. "But when I consider the scheme, I confess that I am assailed with doubt."

"Is it the distance that troubles you? Or the numerous demands upon your time?"

"Distance? What is fifty miles of good road? No, I call it a very easy distance. As for *demands*—I have answered enough of Mr. Bowles Watson's for a lifetime, I believe."

"Why, then, do you hesitate?" I asked.

She drew breath, her gaze fixed upon the paving at our feet. "Mr. West assures me that such a visit would not be at all unwelcome; yet I wonder whether *Mr. Evingrode* would agree. I am not acquainted with Charlotte's husband. My life, Miss Austen, has not always been perfectly regulated. I will say nothing of the past. I am aware that there are many— the world entire, perhaps!—who view my present choice of profession as scandalous, and the circles in which I habitually move as deplorable. I may be regarded as tainting an old acquaintance. I should not wish to add to Charlotte's troubles, or be a cause of division in her household."

"Mr. West may be much concerned for the state of his daughter's spirits, but he is not blind to everything else." I halted and placed my hand over Mrs. Smith's where it rested, still, on my arm. "I am sure he would never send you on an errand that might inspire humiliation. Think how sustaining it should be, to bring comfort to another, rather than attending too well to private anxieties! Mr. Evingrode, however little known his character or sentiments, should be a fool to shower you with anything but gratitude for your kindness."

"Very well," she said quietly, "I shall submit. I shall abandon my work, and revel for an interval in everything frivolous and restorative that Bath may offer. Do not be thinking me *too* much of a saint, Miss Austen, in my desire to serve others."

"I know enough of my own selfish motives to dismiss that idea," I returned with a smile.

"Now, tell me," she said as we resumed our walk, "—for I

detect unfathomed depths in your steady demeanour. —How do you and your dear sister mean to spend your remaining time in Cheltenham? We have not Bath's range of delights, but our entertainments, such as they are, are not entirely contemptible."

We were very nearly to Mrs. Potter's. The paving permitting only of the passage of two persons, Captain Pellew had fallen into place at the rear beside Cassandra, moving strongly despite his stick; Miss Fox lay between us, propelling her friend the Viscountess in her basket-chair. The suspension of general conversation must have incommoded her ladyship, for in the natural pauses of Mrs. Smith's conversation, I detected a peevish undertone, with rebukes and complaints of Miss Fox's exertions. Lady Portreath might appear all that was angelic and ethereal, but her nature was tumultuous. I should not like to be subject to her disfavour—and again, I felt a spurt of secret sympathy for her rejected spouse. Had he understood the creature he had chosen, at his marriage? Was this the natural result of a contract formed for convenience, rather than one predicated on love?

As for Rose herself—was the right to enjoy her inheritance reason enough to embrace a bond she must always have regarded with repugnance?

With such examples of marital discord all around us, it is a wonder any person of sensibility or understanding consents to matrimony.

"Miss Austen?" Mrs. Smith was scrutinizing my countenance. What had she asked? I attempted to unravel my thoughts.

"Our remaining week! I am tempted to commence it in the most outrageous manner possible, Mrs. Smith—by attending tomorrow night's Assembly. Do you recommend it?"

"I have never been," she said simply. "A woman with my occupation and negligible social standing should hardly be offered a ticket."

And *she* the ward of a baronet! It was unfortunate and almost incomprehensible.

We paused at Mrs. Potter's door, as the rest of our party came up with us. "Mr. West has procured my sister and me the necessary vouchers. I am sure he would be very willing to do the same on your behalf."

"Of what are you speaking?" the Viscountess demanded, as Miss Fox set her chair near the threshold. "What do you talk of? Is there to be a ball?"

"A masquerade, in fact," Mrs. Smith told her. "In honour of the King's birthday, and the late nuptials of Princess Charlotte."

"I *had heard* that you spirited a number of costuming out of the wings, Hannah." Captain Pellew looked at her with fond amusement. "Is there anything that might suit a Naval officer? Something in the rakish line, and thoroughly against type?"

"A highwayman," she retorted, "or perhaps a Bond Street Beau. I must look to my stores. I *think* I have taken your measure these twenty years and more."

"Do you mean to say that you have costumes *here*, at Mrs. Potter's?" her ladyship cried. "And that you mean to exhibit them to us all?"

"Rose," Miss Fox interjected, "this can be nothing to you.

There can be no question of your dancing. Captain Pellew, if you would be so good as to open the door, and call for Lucy, that we may lift her chair up the stairs—"

"What?" The Viscountess braced her hands on the arms of her basket-chair and raised herself up a trifle. "Are you determined to thwart my every pleasure, Sarah? Is this what you intended by urging my *escape*? —That I should be trapped and thrown back solely on *your* society? It is not to be borne! I shall be stifled with moping and despair!"

"The exertion required for such an undertaking as a publick ball should prostrate you." Miss Fox eased the chair over the threshold as Pellew held open the boardinghouse door. "I do not speak merely of your inability to dance. The heat of the rooms—the press of revelers—and the risk to your heart and nerves of so much dangerous excitement—"

"If it were left to you, I should be mouldering in my grave," her ladyship said resentfully.

"Rose! That is unjust!"

Mrs. Smith moved forward and lifted the front wheels of the basket-chair into Mrs. Potter's foyer. "Surely, Miss Fox, there can be no harm in rummaging through my false finery! There are paste gems and tawdry silks enough for the lot of us. Your ladyship may bedeck yourself with borrowed theatre feathers to your heart's content—play at Titania or Queen Mab if you will."

"That is very good of you, Hannah," Captain Pellew told her in a lowered tone.

"Not at all," she said with a smile for him. "Miss Austen instructs that there is happiness in serving others, and I mean to try her example."

"Do *you* mean to dance at the Assembly tomorrow?" he asked her. "For if so—"

"Captain!"

He glanced down at Lady Portreath, whose wide blue eyes were fixed beseechingly on him.

"I hope you will stand by me," she said, "for I mean to attend this masquerade ball, and enjoy the spectacle and the masquing, whether I dance or not. Say that *you* at least will not desert me!"

He hesitated, and I was aware for the first time of a frustration in his looks. "None of us is capable of that, my lady."

2 0

RAT THE SECOND

Sunday, 2nd June, 1816
Cheltenham, cont'd.

Miss Garthwaite was established in her brother's favou-rite armchair by the fire when we gained the sitting-room, a number of knitting spread over her lap. I observed that she was dressed entirely in black—a testament to her grief for Thucydides, no doubt. The unfortunate pug had been interred in the back garden yesterday by Mr. Potter. Miss Garthwaite was more composed than I had last seen her, but was unsmiling and pallid in her appearance. Her fingers stilled on her needles as the Bath chair cradling her ladyship was set down a little distance from the hearth.

"This is noise unsuited to the Sabbath, indeed!" she declared as her gaze roamed over our party. "Mrs. Smith is capable of anything; but I had thought better of you, Captain, and most certainly of the Austens. You are a clergyman's daughters, are you not?"

"We have that honour," Cassandra agreed, "and having borne it all our lives, may best judge for ourselves what is owed to the Lord's Day. I hope I find you well, Miss Garthwaite?"

"Not at all," she returned. "In truth, I am in expectation of Dr. Hargate. He brings a paregoric draught. The loss of my dear little dog has entirely overset me."

"That should not be surprising," I said gently. However absurd Miss Garthwaite's views, I could not ridicule her suffering, which I judged sincere. We must all love *something*, and her choices in life were few. "Is Mr. Garthwaite recovered from Divine Service?"

"He means to join us presently. He has found another rat, and wishes to offer it to Hargate."

This statement was intelligible only to myself. I observed my companions' looks of puzzlement. "Where did he discover the poor animal?"

"In the passage outside his bedchamber." Miss Garthwaite's expression darkened. "When I may summon energy enough, I mean to find other lodgings. It is an outrage that we should be plagued with vermin on the upper floors. They must run wild within the walls."

"Jane . . . ?" Cassandra's brows rose. She has a horror of rats.

"As soon as we have broken our fast, Mrs. Smith," I said hurriedly, "I hope that you will be of a mind to open your costuming trunk. I should dearly love to see what you have in store, tho' it *is* the Sabbath!"

"Why not bring the finery into the ladies' private parlour?" Captain Pellew suggested. "We might sort through the whole in private, and leave Miss Garthwaite free to consult the doctor here."

"If it will not incommode Miss Williams—" Mrs. Smith looked towards the basket-chair.

"I should love it above all things!" her ladyship cried.

Miss Fox bit her lip, and glanced at Captain Pellew. "You mean to encourage this foolhardiness, sir? Tho' she is not well enough to stand?"

"Nonsense, Sarah!" The Viscountess batted playfully at Miss Fox's arm with her glove. "You are jealous, that is all, for you know I shall outshine you in my costume dress, and draw away all your beaux. Is not that true, Captain?"

"You shall appear captivating, I am sure," he returned gallantly.

We parted in our separate ways towards breakfast. For my part, I intended to consume only black tea and dry toast, as a preservation against Thucydides's fate, and urge Cassandra to do the same.

WE RECONVENED A HALF-HOUR later in the private parlour, where Captain Pellew had helped to set out the theatre bandboxes—three in all—where the costumes were stored. When the lids were removed, I experienced a sensation absent since childhood, of being permitted to rummage to my heart's content through the remnants of my mother's girlhood, stored in her trunks in Steventon Rectory's atticks. She had been a beauty in youth, my mother—but the stiles of that period were so foreign to our own, involving powdered wigs, panniers, and chalk-white faces marked with black patches, that it was as good as a play to don her cast-offs. Surrounded as we were by a tribe of schoolboys, my father's pupils and my errant brothers, Cass and I repaired to the atticks during weeks of persistent rain or the frigid days of winter, and staged theatricals with the aid of a green baize curtain and a row of candles for footlights. I had written a few dramas, indeed, for our enjoyment, involving fainting-couches, abductions, and villainous suitors. My brother Henry and even sober James—being less of a stick before his marriage to Mary—had taken star turns on our makeshift boards. Scenes from decades past flooded my mind with a peculiar poignancy. We were grown so old, Cassandra and I—

"Here is a popish priest's gown and mitre that one of the ladies might attempt," Mrs. Smith suggested, laying out a robe of fine black silk with a brilliant pink sash, such as a Roman cardinal might own. "I do not think the colouring suited to you, Harry, but you should figure excellently as an Evil Conjurer, in this stuff of royal purple and a false beard."

"I mean to go as a Sylph," he countered, drawing forward a coat with silver panels, "and sport these wings of painted gauze. There is nothing else so entirely out of character with my usual display as a Spirit of the Air. My own mother should not know me."

"I wish to be similarly transformed!" cried the Viscountess, leaning eagerly towards the spill of fabrics from her perch in her chair. "Nothing less will do for me than the guise of a Roman Empress, or perhaps a Circassian slave!"

Smiling broadly at her, Mrs. Smith shook her head. "I have something altogether wonderful for you, your ladyship—you shall go as Cleopatra, borne upon her litter, kohl about your eyes and the blackest of wigs upon your hair. No one shall know you for Miss Williams, much less Lady Portreath!"

She drew out a shimmering length of gold tissue,

embroidered about the hem and bodice with a number of paste stones: emerald, sapphire, and ruby. "Look, there are gold bangles for your ankles, gold sandals for your feet, and a diadem to wear low across your brow. —Even the circlet of an asp to clasp about your arm."

"Enchanting!" her ladyship declared, fingering the stuff of the robe, which was light as a cobweb. "And Sarah shall go dressed as my page, in Turkish trousers and a scarlet vest, her hair bound up in a turban."

"But—" attempted Miss Fox.

I saw Captain Pellew shake his head warningly, his eyes on the Viscountess's face.

She was alarmingly flushed, her eyes glittering; she was dangerously excited, and might swoon with little provocation.

"What say you, Sarah? Shall you submit to acting as my slave?"

"When have I been anything more?"

Miss Fox offered the words in jest, but her countenance lacked all animation.

"Here is something you should enjoy, Miss Austen," said Mrs. Smith, in handing me a voluminous gown. "The raiment of a Spanish princess, complete with a black lace mantilla. I shall show you the trick of dressing your hair with these ebony combs, to display the veil to best effect."

The silk was the colour of fine French claret, with a square-necked bodice, and it was embroidered with flowers, birds, and scrolls for a full ten inches above the hem! The skirt draped like a bell over a light hoop, and fell just above the ankles. It should sway charmingly while I danced.

I held it against me and studied my reflection in the mirror as Mrs. Smith draped the mantilla over my head.

"Ravishing," she said.

I confess I coloured a little. It had been many months since I had merited such praise. I wondered what character Raphael West might chuse, and how he should regard my transformation—

"And for you, Miss Cassandra," Mrs. Smith concluded, "the ceremonial dress of Queen Elizabeth." She unfurled a stiff gown of copper-hued brocade, quilted with paste topazes. "The white ruff shall set off your remarkable cheekbones to wonderful effect. And these slashed full sleeves with saffron lining—"

"Are glorious," Cassandra whispered. "But do you not think that *you*, Mrs. Smith, should do such a gown greater justice?"

"I lack the necessary gravity," she returned, her eyes dancing. "I shall go as an Harlequin, with a French bodice of black and gold diamonds."

"Capital!" Harry Pellew cried, his countenance all animation.

"This is very well," Miss Fox interjected, "but for my part, I can form no plan for tomorrow until Dr. Hargate has seen his patient. It is for him, I believe, to say yea or nay to this ambitious scheme."

"Pish!" Lady Portreath said dismissively. "Hargate is an old woman."

"You did not think so, Rose, when he prevented your husband from returning you to Cornwall."

"Travel across two hundred miles is of a very different order than sitting quietly in my chair on the edge of a ballroom and observing the couples," her ladyship retorted. "Do not be so tiresome, Sarah! I cannot be immured forever in a single room with only *you* for company. I shall go mad of ennui before another week is out."

Miss Fox's visage paled, and she compressed her lips. Such careless ingratitude must be a constant trial to her temper. But before she could speak, I gathered up my Spanish gown and the breathtaking mantilla.

"A thousand thanks, Mrs. Smith," I said. "I count on you for the proper stiling of my headdress."

I pulled open the parlour door, Cassandra at my heels, only to stop short.

Mr. Garthwaite stood with his back to the sitting room fire, his right arm extended. Depending from his thumb and forefinger was his latest rat; and Dr. Hargate, spectacles fixed on his nose, was examining it.

"Where is Mrs. Potter?" the physician demanded.

"Attending the Chapel, no doubt," Miss Garthwaite sniffed. "She is decidedly non-conformist."

The Cheltenham Chapel, tho' occasionally appropriated for Church of England use, was claimed by the Baptists.

"Fetch the housemaid."

As neither of the Garthwaites sprang to action, I went to the head of the stairs and called out, "Lucy!"

"You may set the rodent on this newspaper," Hargate said, extending a folded edition of the day's *Cheltenham Chronicle* towards the clergyman. Mr. Garthwaite obliged. "I shall remove it to Mr. Jenner's stillroom for analysis, but I believe I understand the cause, now, of the pug's death."

Hurried footsteps on the stairs announced the maidservant's arrival.

"Well, girl, and has your mistress been poisoning rats?" Hargate demanded.

Bewildered, Lucy looked from one gentleman's face to the other's, avoiding Miss Garthwaite's outraged visage. "No, sir. Keeps a proper house and clean, Mrs. Potter does."

"How do you explain this?" the physician demanded, with a gesture towards the extinct rodent.

Lucy shrieked, and put a hand over her mouth. "Lord love us—you never found *that* in here?"

"Near one of the upper bedchambers. There must be a colony running through the joists."

I almost observed that such a thing was unlikely—every lodger in the building should have heard the sound of the rodents' passage in the walls—but Lucy forestalled me.

"Nonsense," she said. "'Tis the fault of the York. All sort of rubbish they toss in the mews, sir, from their kitchens, and the rats are drawn to it. But I'll swear they've never set foot in here."

"Has your mistress put down poison in the mews?"

Lucy shook her head wordlessly.

"This rat was certainly poisoned," Hargate said with menace, as tho' Lucy had baited them for pleasure.

I broke in, "Have you an idea, sir, what sort of poison? Might an examination reveal it?"

Dr. Hargate sighed. "I attempted to examine the stomach contents of the dog"—at this, Miss Garthwaite gasped—"for various poisons, but alas the sample was too small. I thought at first mercury might be to blame, but detected none. I then tried hydrogen sulfide in the presence of hydrochloric acid, as per Hahnemann's test for arsenic; but the results were inconclusive."[5]

"You believed the macaroons on Mrs. Smith's plate were tainted with *mercury*?" I asked, startled.

"Tea cakes had nothing to do with it," Hargate replied irritably. "It is obvious the dog ate a dead rat, and was sickened as a result. It remains only to learn from Mrs. Potter what she has set out in the mews—this stupid girl knows nothing. I shall then confirm the nature of the poison with this extinct rodent." He gestured at the *Cheltenham Chronicle* and its rigid burden.

The sound of female voices, raised in argument, drifted to our ears; and at that moment Captain Pellew thrust open the parlour door and peered into the room.

"Ah, Hargate," he said. "Would you be so kind as to glance at her ladyship? She is in a most awkward and delicate position—possessing just enough health to observe an Assembly, but not nearly enough, it seems, for sustained travel. She requires your *expert* opinion."

---

5 The more exacting Marsh Test for arsenic was not invented until 1836. Hahnemann's Test was less conclusive, and the results could not be effectively preserved as evidence.—*Editor's note.*

21

A MOST ILLUMINATING EVENING

Monday, 3rd June, 1816
Cheltenham

"**O**bserve that the pavilion is erected on a moveable platform," Mr. George Dinsdale said, "so that it may be wheeled by the attendants directly into the room, as the orchestra plays 'God Save the King!' That shall be a very pretty display, at midnight."

He was gesturing towards a composition of screens, roughly ten feet high and arranged in an octagon, that nearly filled a side chamber off the Cheltenham Assembly's ballroom. Dinsdale's earnest desire to instruct us was only a little marred by the voluminous nature of his costume. He had elected to attend the masquerade this evening in the guise of a Raven, complete with black-feathered wings. The lower half of his countenance was wreathed in smiles. The upper half was hidden by an impressive black mask, painted to resemble an inky-blue beak. Had his cherubic face not been partially visible—and his creaking corset faintly audible—we should never have known him for the benign engraver of recent acquaintance.

"The prints look very well, George." Mr. West, dashingly arrayed as a Russian Cossack in a full scarlet vest draping to his knees and a tall, fur-trimmed hat, leant over the velvet rope that divided the structure from ourselves, the better to study the coloured engravings. "You used equal parts mastic and turpentine, I assume, to achieve the transparency?"

"A full three coats," Dinsdale supplied, "requiring an entire week to dry."

I allowed my eyes to roam over the various depictions of Royal life. Closest to me was a life-sized figure of George III in buckskin leggings, with a scythe over his shoulder— George Farmer, as the common people called him, for his self-professed love of pigs. Mr. Dinsdale had managed to capture His Majesty's likeness without hinting in the least that the poor man was insane.

Cassandra, arrayed in the copper-coloured brocade of Queen Elizabeth, was fixed in contemplation of a second print—this one, of Princess Charlotte before the makeshift wedding altar in the Regent's Red Drawing Room at Carlton House. The Princess looked well enough in her gown of silver net, with Prince Leopold's diamond bracelet on her arm. Cassandra's lips moved slightly; I could almost hear the words *ten—thousand!—pounds.*

"Have you ever made transparencies, Miss Austen?" Dinsdale enquired. "It is, I know, a cherished hobby of many ladies."

"Not for me, I'm afraid. My sister is the more artistic."

"The linen paper used in these prints is quite thick, but absorbent," he explained to Cassandra. "By brushing it with a varnish of gum resin and turpentine as West describes, the particles in the paper that might otherwise reflect light are flattened and subdued, permitting for translucency—the passage of light *through* the paper. All that is required is to place a candle behind it, or in this case a mass of candles, to illuminate the image."

I had glimpsed such things before—it was a practise in London to set transparencies in the front windows of houses, and illuminate them for the delight of passers-by. But what Dinsdale attempted here was something greater. Within the structure he had built—or *pavilion*, as he called it—was erected a series of shelves. They held dozens of candles, all unlit at the moment.

"You mean to light a fuse, I gather?" West asked. I could not glimpse his brow behind his mask, but imagined it furrowed with interest.

"A series of them, indeed! I have borrowed a cunning arrangement from the masters of firework displays, in connecting the wicks of my candles. Observe, West, that there is a fuse at both ends of the pavilion—they shall each be lit by a footman, and flare simultaneously. The initial fuse, *bearing* fire, leads to a second, *taking* fire, which is connected in turn to the candlewick. The *bearing* fuse alights each of the *taking* fuses leading to the candles in swift succession! I have tested the mechanism now three times in my workrooms. At the touch of a taper from each end, the flames shall meet in the center, and the pavilion become a gigantic magic-lantern."

West emitted something between a snort of disbelief and grudging respect.

"Colouring the prints does not inhibit the effect?" I asked.

"The paint being water-colour, and thus translucent itself, it only adds to the beauty of the whole," West told me. "What you have done is commendable, George."

"I expect it will be acclaimed a triumph," Dinsdale said simply, "once the initial wonder is survived. Indeed, the spectacle this evening shall make my reputation as the foremost artist in Cheltenham—or so I hope."

"It still wants some two hours until midnight, and that triumph." West offered me his arm. "Shall we proceed to the ballroom, Jane?"

THE CHELTENHAM ASSEMBLY IS very much like any other fashionable set of publick rooms designed with a view to frivolity. The entrance foyer is ample, with a wide passage giving onto the ballroom, supper room, card rooms, and cloaks rooms, etc., at either hand. This evening, despite its being June, fires were kindled in the several hearths that lined this lofty passage, rain having descended once more upon Cheltenham with a vengeance.

The decorative stile of the place is nothing out of the ordinary way, being all plaster ornaments and pilasters, false columns and pale paint, easy on the eye and certain never to clash with a lady's gown. In short, those who have seen the Upper Rooms in Bath have seen Cheltenham. How the new Assembly to be opened in a few weeks' time shall improve upon these rooms I cannot say, other than with an increase of air and glazing on every side.

"While these rooms are pretty enough in their way,"

Dinsdale assured us, "and adequate for the present celebrations of His Majesty's Natal Day, they should in no way accommodate the crush of couples one should witness at the height of the Cheltenham Season, which I must tell you is most oppressive in July and August. The crowds then are beyond everything—so severe, indeed, that I should not vouch for your comfort and safety in such a rout, and must decline to escort you into danger."

"How many couples do you imagine we join at present?" Cassandra enquired, glancing about the room. Her brown hair, flecked with grey, was plaited into a towering headdress dotted with trumpery pearls. The starched white honeycomb of her ruff supported her chin to majestic perfection.

"Some hundred, I daresay," Mr. Dinsdale replied. "Shall I escort you to the refreshment table, Your Majesty?"

My sister inclined her head and extended her hand; the Raven held out his arm; and with the most exquisite ceremony they progressed forward together, for all the world as tho' they were players at Shakespeare.

"Jane," Raphael West murmured in my ear, "you are so ridiculously fetching in that Spanish mantilla and gown, I cannot bear to keep you from the floor any longer. May I have this dance?"

I SHOULD LIKE TO report that I was all that was staid and respectable in the quadrille, or that I acquitted myself with serene aplomb in the Long Meg; but both are, it must be said, *flirtatious* dances; and as I was unobserved by anyone with authority to censure my conduct, being surrounded almost entirely by strangers, I may have thrown caution to the winds. I may have danced with joy and energy, Mr. Dinsdale offering himself as partner once Mr. West's turn was done; and I may have so far forgot myself as to smile entirely *too much*, and persuade myself I was a decade or two younger, with a lifetime of enjoyment before me. But the third dance being called the Royal Nuptials—a fitting tribute to the celebration at hand, but sadly a figure I had not yet learnt, my mastery of country-dances being thoroughly out-of-date and only occasionally revivified from exposure to my nieces' more timely information—I was obliged to sit out. The interval provided a welcome chance to recover my breathing; repair my headdress with a judicious visit to the lady's cloakroom; and observe the rest of the couples vigorously stepping the length of the ballroom.

With a promise of my swift return to Mr. West, so that he might escort me to the supper-tables, I hastened alone down the passage from the ballroom in the direction of the ladies' retiring room. I had barely achieved half the distance when I encountered a tall and slender lady wearing a costume patterned in black and gold diamonds, and the face-paint of a French Columbine.

"Miss Austen!" she exclaimed, with one hand extended. "How very well you look, indeed! But you must let me do up your flounce—it has been torn a little in the dancing."

For the first time since I had met her, Hannah Vyvyan had left off her dowdy cap, and her glorious hair cascaded in ringlets over her right ear. Her smile was as warm as ever, but the combined effect of paint, mask, and costume was obscurely sobering. Having become used to a Mrs. Smith, I felt in a single instant that I glimpsed Miss Vyvyan's hidden power—for *here* was a woman born to beguile and command.

"How glad I am to find you here," I said warmly. "Did Mr. West procure you a ticket?"

"I am sure he would have done so, had it been necessary; but in the event, Captain Pellew was so kind as to include me in his party. I left him in the ballroom with the Viscountess and Miss Fox. Or should I say . . . Cleopatra and her Turkish page?"

"I shall know them in an instant. But do not let me be keeping you from the dancing, my dear! I may mend my own flounces; I have been doing so these twenty years at least."

We parted, she with a merry jingling of her stick of Harlequin bells, I to secure my mantilla and press a cooling cloth against my heated cheeks. The lady's retiring room was a riot of silks and finery, perfumes and pomades, with elbows jostling for a turn at the looking-glass. I found a chair in a corner with an excellent side-light and drew out the needle and thread I had secured in my reticule.

"Miss Austen, I think?" I glanced up into the kohl-eyed visage of an elegant Cleopatra, all cloth-of-gold and exotic jewels. The body of a snake, jade and gold, twined about her left forearm, and a diadem of gold bound her forehead. Her wig was black and intriguingly free, the hair sweeping to shoulder length, where it looked to have been severed abruptly by an axe. "Miss Williams! But you have left off your basket-chair!"

"*Mrs.* Williams," Cleopatra corrected, "and I do not ape my stepdaughter's weakness, I assure you."

"But . . ." I paused. There had been a rage for antiquities, of course, ever since Buonaparte took Egypt. I might discover any number of Empresses of the Nile in the present ballroom. Or perhaps Lady Portreath had rebelled against the choice of costume, and chosen another. I should find her in a moment arrayed as a Dresden shepherdess.

"How very well you look this evening!" Mrs. Williams said. "But your flounce is sadly torn."

"A testament to the vigour of my dancing."

"May I be of service?" She drew forward a chair and seated herself near me. "The tear is at the rear of your gown, and must be difficult to address."

"Thank you—I should be very grateful." I handed her my needle and thread. We had not exchanged more than salutations since our interview over tea at the York Hotel; and yet I felt I understood from others far more of the lady's history and ambition than she would wish known. "How delightful to find you at the Assembly, Mrs. Williams! I am glad to know that Lord Portreath's impatience to be gone does not preclude *all* enjoyment."

"No, indeed," she said with a smile. "Lord Portreath is of a sanguine temperament—being forced to idle in a backwater, he is determined to amuse himself. No reproach will pass his lips when he might easily be dancing, or playing at silver loo in the card rooms."

"A happy chance, then, that the masquerade is held while you are still in town!"

"Yes—I was in transports when my costume was delivered to the hotel this morning. Granville had only to see it, to be determined that we must attend—and dressed himself as Wellington, mad for the diversion!"

I found it difficult to envision the compact form of Granville Basset in the stile of Old Douro, Victor of Waterloo, the Iron Duke; but what is the point of a masquerade, if not to appear as we wish to be seen?

Mrs. Williams knotted her seam; snapped the thread between her teeth; and presented me with the needle. "There. By all means, continue dancing."

"I certainly shall. I'm grateful for your assistance."

"Pray, think nothing of it." She rose with a graceful smile and joined the throng before the mirror.

Refreshed, I made my way out of the retiring room and up the broad passage towards the ballroom. The strains of a Scotch reel drifted to my ears, and most of the couples being occupied in the dance, the passage was nearly empty. I had nearly achieved the ballroom when an arm shot out from a heavily-draped French window, and the tall figure of a Russian Cossack drew me aside. He held a finger to his lips for quiet.

"Mr. West," I whispered.

He did not reply, his attitude alert and intent. He was overlistening a conversation, I realized, taking place in the anteroom adjacent, where Dinsdale's pavilion waited behind its velvet rope. A woman was speaking *sotto voce*, but indignantly enough to be just overheard.

"—Think I yearned for a word from you? I forgot you as soon as we parted that dreadful day."

"I have not been so fortunate." The gentleman's voice rose

a trifle. "The thought of you, alone in the world, has troubled me. I wish to make amends, and to offer my support—so that you may not be dependent upon the caprice of strangers, unworthy of you."

"I need no assistance of yours." The tone of contempt was audible. "I am happy in *other friends*, more suited to my taste and temperament."

"My brother would hate to hear you say so."

"Your brother would know the value I ought to place on any promises of *yours*." I could hear that the woman was smiling, now, but it was a bitter triumph. "You think to buy my silence! I had far rather leave you in suspense—of all I could tell, did I chuse to. And now I must beg leave to return to the ballroom, sir. The reel is ending, and there will be a crush. I do not wish to be seen in your company."

There was a rustle of skirts and a light tread of footsteps—a word that might have been *Stay*, broken off—and then silence from the antechamber.

I glanced at West. He was already moving away from the French window, his gaze searching for a figure hastening ahead—but it was true: the reel had ended, and fifty people or more had surged into the main passage, intent upon the supper room, the card rooms, or a breath of air. What had drawn West's attention, I wondered, to a private interview between two strangers?

I peered searchingly through the anteroom doorway. The small space was brightly lit by wax tapers, and entirely empty but for Dinsdale's structure—and a stick of Harlequin bells, discarded on the parquet.

22

ENACTING A
CHELTENHAM TRAGEDY

Monday, 3rd June, 1816
Cheltenham, cont'd.

"The lobster patties are certainly as well-made as those Henry and Eliza were used to serve in Hans Place," Cassandra observed. "And I believe the cheese straws are superior."

"I have only sampled the ices," I replied, "but they are unobjectionable."

"May I fetch you ladies some punch?" Mr. Dinsdale enquired. "I believe it is champagne."

"We should be charmed, sir," Cassandra said.

He glanced at his pocket-watch. "We shall have just time enough for a glass before midnight! You will recollect my transparencies are to be illuminated then."

"We shall never be allowed to forget," I murmured under my breath.

As the Raven bowed and made his way through the supper room crowd, my sister leant towards me conspiratorially. "An exceedingly kind gentleman, Jane, but his cloak sheds insupportably. I have been forced to stifle a sneeze countless times this evening, for being drowned in loose feathers, and shall be glad to bid Mr. Dinsdale *adieu*."

I pressed her hand impulsively. "My poor dear. And here I thought you were enjoying yourself!"

"I am! It is the plumage I cannot abide, not the ball. The Assembly is everything that is delightful; and despite being a masquerade, is highly regular! No unpleasant scenes or drunken routs, no improper advances or masked seductions—"

"I feel your disappointment," I soothed, "but the night is, after all, still young."

"Mr. West dances very well," she ventured.

"Entirely due to his choice of partner." I meant this as a joke, but the sally fell poorly on my ears; vanity, Jane! Vanity!

"I suspect he means to ask Mrs. Smith next," Cassandra said. That was my reward for boasting—a set-down from the mouth of my sister. No one else is so casually annihilating.

She was looking across the supper room at a collection of persons disposed around a table too small for their number—always an enviable situation, implying as it does a selective crush. A Turkish page in a scarlet turban; a broad-shouldered Sylph with silver-gauze wings; a Cleopatra reclining in a litter; and a Harlequin. Standing over the latter was the Russian Cossack, his head bent as tho' listening to a charming conversation.

"Mr. West has known Mrs. Smith some years," I told my sister.

"She looks remarkably well in her costume."

"He regards her in the role of daughter. She was a school-mate to his Charlotte."

"Was she, indeed?" Behind her mask, Cassandra's eyes narrowed a little in speculation. Surely she could not be imagining West had a *tendre* for Hannah Vyvyan?

"Your servant, Miss Austen."

Mr. Dinsdale, with his champagne. Cassandra accepted her glass and I took mine from his hand with as good a grace. I was thirsty enough, and neither lemonade nor tea had satisfied me. Despite the howling storm outside, the Assembly Rooms were overheated; too much finery, too vigorous exercise, too many bodies in too confined a space.

"Are you a trifle fatigued, Jane?"

I looked at Cassandra. Behind her mask, her eyes were alert and anxious. I must have allowed my spirits to flag. "A trifle. Nothing to signify. Are *you* well, Cass?"

She sighed. "Exceedingly. It has been so remarkably pleasant to *dance* again, despite the encumbrance of Queen Elizabeth's hoops! Such a simple pleasure—but so wanting in our lives of late."

I smiled. "Then let us not waste a moment of this delicious opportunity. Who knows when it may fall in our way again?"

"Miss Austen!"

Captain Pellew, the very picture of a Sylph in his coat of plated silver, black mask, and remarkable wings. "Have you received any word of Captain Austen's Admiralty Board today?"

"None as yet, I'm afraid." Charles's ordeal had naturally

preoccupied Cassandra and me throughout the morning, but short of an Express sent direct from Edward in London with the news, we could not hope to hear the outcome before Wednesday's post.

"Pray join me, and greet your friends," Pellew urged.

The party at the other table was breaking up. The Russian Cossack and the Harlequin stood a little apart, in earnest conversation; the Turkish page was endeavouring to maneuver the basket-chair through the crush of chairs and people in order to regain the ballroom. But as Pellew and I moved towards them, a different couple intersected our path: Wellington and Cleopatra.

"Can that be *my wife?*" The Iron Duke raised a quizzing glass and surveyed the seated figure rolling towards him. "I must compliment you upon your beauty, my dear, as I know it drives you wild to be told you are in excellent looks. I fear I cannot award you a prize for originality, however—you are the second Cleopatra in the room, and the costume loses much of its *éclat* when crumpled into a basket."

"Granville," Mrs. Williams said softly.

Her ladyship snorted in laughter. "I shall return the compliment in the spirit it was meant, Portreath, and declare that your Wellington loses much in being so *short*. The finest piece of your costume is that sword; a pity you retired your own."

Lord Portreath smiled, but his eyes were cold behind his mask. He grasped the hilt at his waist and drew the blade. "You mistake the matter, my dear. This is no trumpery sword, but the light cavalry sabre I carried in the Seventh Light Dragoons, under Old Douro's command. I mastered its use from a child—and count my years in the Peninsula as among the most distinguished of my life."

For an instant, it seemed as tho' each of us held our breath, observing the light from the supper room's chandelier gild the curved steel blade. But then the Viscount said, "Enough fencing, Rose: How come you here? —I thought you were on the point of death."

"And yet you were prepared to dance." Her ladyship bared her teeth. "On my grave, no doubt."

"If you are well enough to endure an Assembly," the Viscount said, "you are well enough to travel." He looked directly at the Turkish page. "I care not whether you chuse to accompany her, Miss Fox, but her ladyship leaves Cheltenham tomorrow. My carriage departs at noon from the York stable yard; and if I must, I will put her forcibly into it."

"I had rather die first," cried the Viscountess. And indeed, arrayed as Cleopatra, with all her passion in her face, she looked every inch the tragic queen. Miss Fox reached out to calm her charge, but it was Mrs. Williams who hastened forward, already sympathy, to bend over her stepdaughter.

With a sudden clash of horns, the orchestra signaled a change—the crowd around us fell silent—and from the adjoining ballroom came the first strains of "God Save the King!"

"Midnight," I breathed, and hastened forward. I did not wish to miss the sight of Mr. Dinsdale's triumph—the lighting of his pavilion.

The supper room crowd surged with me. Captain Pellew was at my left, and Raphael West to my right. Hannah

Vyvyan was beside him. Ahead of me I glimpsed Cassandra's Elizabethan ruff. Lady Portreath's basket-chair and poor Miss Fox in her turban were caught in a surge of spectators and dragged back; Lord Portreath had not room enough even to lower his arm and sheath his sabre, but held it aloft as he staggered forward, Miss Williams clinging to his free hand.

We collected in a ragged wave at the edge of the ball-room. From each corner of the lofty space an hundred other voices broke into song in celebration of the Sovereign's birthday. As the final chorus rang out, two liveried servants rolled George Dinsdale's eight-sided structure into the center of the room.

The Raven, I observed, followed them, his glossy-feathered cape billowing with his passage; a compelling sight, impossible to ignore. Every eye was trained upon him in apprehension as he approached the pavilion, as tho' he must bring with him some momentous intelligence: a birth, a death, a revolution?

He bowed to each side of the ballroom in turn, then swept his winged arms wide. "Gentlemen, ladies, I beg your indulgence. My attendant shall light the fuse—behold, the Illuminations in Honour of King George and Princess Charlotte!"

No reference to the Royal spouse, Leopold of Saxe-Coburg Saalfeld; he was merely a necessary prop to the celebrated nuptials, much as Mad King George was to his own birthday. But Dinsdale stepped back, gesturing reverently at his transparency screens; the servant at each side of the pavilion bent forward with his taper; and the separate flames began to run towards each other, meeting in the center of the octagon and fanning out to each of the candles in a starburst of light. It was lovely! And as the beautifully-coloured transparencies glowed to life, a murmur of admiring voices rose around us.

Bang!

A bolt of flame rose skyward.

I started back, a cry on my lips.

One of the transparencies—towards the back of the octagon, invisible to those of us ranged before it—had caught fire, and the screen was rapidly being consumed!

Bang!

Another screen—adjacent to the first—shot into flame.

Dinsdale cried out, and ran towards his pavilion, beating at the fire with his feathered arms. Immediately, flames licked up his wings, and he was outlined as sharp as a bird of carrion against a red-tinged field of battle.

"No!" I gasped.

Raphael West raced up to his friend, tore at the velvet cloak he wore, and dashed it to the ballroom floor. Two other men—strangers to me—held Dinsdale back, to prevent him from burning himself further, as the illuminations flared one to another, and another.

West sped to the tall French windows that lined the ballroom and tore down a length of drapery, then hurled the heavy stuff over Dinsdale's cape where it lay burning in the middle of the room. That fire was smothered in an instant, but the pavilion—

The wooden structure was completely ablaze.

So much varnish coated the massive transparencies, formed

of turpentine and mastic resin, that the pavilion was but a massive torch.

More of the Assembly's servants dashed forward, water jugs in their hands. They tossed the contents on Dinsdale's masterpiece, but it might have been so much dew, vaporised in seconds.

Captain Pellew grasped my shoulder. "Miss Austen! We must get out, at once!" He whirled me around towards the supper room, but that room offered no outer door. I turned instead towards the main passage from the ballroom, but that was thronged with costumed figures, shrieking and jostling. Where was Cassandra?

I looked frantically in every direction. There was her towering headdress of braids, strewn with false pearls! Some five people separated us, all pushing towards the clogged passage. Some would be trampled if they did not take care.

Impossible to reach my sister; impossible to struggle through the doorway, once I did.

"Captain!" I shouted. "The French windows!"

He looked towards them, a range of eight windows parading across the back of the ballroom. There would be a terrace beyond, and from that, a flight of steps to the ground. He surged forward, heedless of his game leg, his hand clasped firmly around Hannah Vyvyan's wrist.

Well done, I thought breathlessly.

"Cassandra!" I pulled off my mantilla and twirled it over my head. "Cassandra! The windows!"

Across the crowd I found my sister's eyes, and felt more than saw her comprehension. Immediately, she picked up her skirts and turned away from the mob, heading instead straight towards the fire.

It was the obvious course to take—directly into danger, rather than away from it. We met in the space left by the hysterical crowd's retreat, and joined hands.

"Captain Pellew," I gasped. The smoke was becoming intolerable. Great clouds of it billowed around us, obscuring sight. I glanced back; I could no longer see the scrambling figures in the passage. That way was barred to us.

Dimly through the haze, I discerned that Pellew and the Harlequin had reached the set of windows farthest from ourselves. Pellew appeared to be wrestling with the bolts that secured the tall panels to the ballroom floor. Given the force of tonight's storm, they had never been unbolted, and rain no doubt had swelled the surrounding wood. I craned about wildly and saw Raphael West, his arm supporting George Dinsdale's waist, steering him to safety.

I reached out my hand. West grasped it with his free one.

The top spars of the pavilion crashed to the floor not three feet from where we stood, in a shower of sparks.

"*Damnation*," I spluttered, with an excess of nerves.

We four staggered forward, lungs seared at every breath.

Pellew had got the bolts shifted. He flung the French windows wide, and the rush of air cleared a little of the smoke. I saw that he had lost his mask in the melee, and that there was an angry weal on his left cheek—he must have been struck by a flaming scrap of screen or wood. No matter; he was accustomed to worse, by far, on any quarterdeck he had commanded in battle.

Being a Royal Navy Captain, however, he seemed determined to be the last to leave this particular ship, and stood back until all of us had hastened over the threshold.

At the last, Hannah Vyvyan grasped him by the lapel. "Enough heroics, Harry," she cried, and pulled him through the window. Together we stumbled, gasping, down the steps to the drenched lawn.

I crouched there, doubled over, my chest to my knees, drinking in the rain-wet air. Rain was on my head and on my face, and I did not care that it was soaking through my thin Spanish silk. Where had the black lace mantilla gone? Up in flames, no doubt.

A hand in the grass reached for mine, fingers twining in my own. *Not* Cassandra's delicate bones; West's strong ones.

He lifted my palm to his lips and kissed it.

"Never mind Mad George," he gasped. "God save *us*, Jane."

23

THE WEAPON IN QUESTION

Tuesday, 4th June, 1816
Cheltenham

I would like to be able to write that Cassandra and I, in the company of Raphael West, George Dinsdale, and our fellow-lodgers at Mrs. Potter's, found our paths home to boardinghouse and hotel in swiftness and peace. I was anxious to exchange my wet clothes for dry; Cassandra was heartily sick of her headdress and ruff; and poor Mr. Dinsdale had sustained shocking burns to his hands—an anxiety for any artist—that demanded the attention of a doctor.

We had no sooner collected our wits and ourselves, however, than Captain Pellew said tensely, "Hannah, did you see which direction Miss Fox and Miss Williams were gone?"

Mrs. Smith merely shook her head.

"Did anyone glimpse the basket-chair?" He looked from one to the other of us.

"I did not," I said, "but the smoke was considerable, and the crush of persons chaotic. It should be a wonder if a single pair of our friends were discernible from the whole."

Captain Pellew struggled to his feet. "Please, Hannah—get these cursed wings off my back. A fellow can't move properly with them flapping about."

From behind us came the crackle of flames, and a brilliant red glare suffused the window panes of the Assembly Rooms.

"We should move towards the street," West said. "The rest of the ball guests will be collected there, and perhaps a bucket brigade to quell the fire."

"The Assembly Rooms are insured." Dinsdale spoke for the first time. His countenance, revealed in the lurid glow of the flames, was ravaged with shock; he held his burnt hands carefully before him, lest the slightest contact cause agony. "The fire mark is prominently displayed on the building's front façade. The engine brigade will already have been summoned."[6]

He was correct, as we saw so soon as we achieved the High Street, where a large crowd of ball guests in fancy-dress vied for position on the paving with spectators of disaster from all Cheltenham. We were in time to witness the arrival of the insurers' fire brigade wagon, the hand-pump engine prominent in the body of the cart, with six men deployed to work the pumps in turn and another four carrying hoses into the Assembly.

"Come with me, West," Dinsdale said. "As the author of

---

6 Before 1824, when the first municipal fire brigade was formed in Edinburgh, Scotland, fire-fighting forces were hired by insurance companies to respond and protect only those buildings that were owned by policyholders. The first municipal force in London was not organized until 1833.—*Editor's note.*

this hideous disaster, I ought to inform those fellows how exactly the conflagration started, and where." The two men shouldered through the milling crowd and approached the pump engine cart, shouting for the foreman's attention.

I had witnessed such scenes in London, where prominent bankers and prosperous warehouse owners paid private insurance brigades to answer the threat of fire, but I had not thought the practise arrived in the spa town of Cheltenham. It was a surprising comfort to see a team of efficient fellows working the ingenious machine in the cart, while the horses stood so patiently, their eyes blinded to flames with thick, black cotton scarves. Would a similar brigade ever be formed in Alton, I wondered—or perhaps Basingstoke?

"Surely they will douse the fire soon," Cassandra cried in my ear; the noise all around us was terrific.

Captain Pellew started away. "There is Miss Fox! And Miss Williams!"

I peered after him and saw the basket-chair pulled up on the far side of the High Street, its occupant convulsed with coughing. "I wonder she was not overturned, in the effort to flee the building."

"That will be Miss Fox's care," Hannah Vyvyan said. "The woman is all that stands between Miss Williams and death. If she were ever to desert her friend—" The Harlequin hastened after Harry Pellew, her soaked skirts bunched in her hands.

"We may safely walk to the Potters', now, Jane—would not you agree?" Cassandra asked.

I craned on tiptoe over the heads of the crowd to search for Raphael West, but the numbers of interested onlookers had swelled considerably. An enterprising few of the townsfolk, with an eye to the main chance, were even risking the flames to loot the building of its parcel-gilt chairs and silk draperies, emerging through the clouds of smoke with rasping coughs and heavy bundles on their shoulders. As the Cheltenham constables served purely for the honour of their office, being appointed by St. Mary's vestry and entirely unpaid, it was unlikely the sack of the Assembly Rooms should be punished. I could make out neither West's height nor Dinsdale's rotundity in the silhouettes thrown by the greedy flames.

"Jane!" Cassandra shouted, in desperate tones—the roars of the fire were dreadful, drowning out most conversation, and punctuated now by the crash of falling timbers. I hesitated only an instant longer before turning for Cassandra, and our weary walk back to the Potters'—when West appeared, looming out of the haze before me, his errand with the fire brigade completed.

"Mr. Dinsdale should accompany us," Cassandra shrieked over the tumult. "Dr. Hargate must attend to his burns."

"Hargate is already here." West had lost his tall Cossack cap, and his dark hair was wildly disarranged. Sweat or rain ran down his face; all our masks had long since vanished. But in the reflected glare of flame and water, I could not discern the expression in his eyes. "There were a number of injured in the mad crush to escape—and the fire brigade has recovered a victim, lost in the chaos."

I lifted my brows. He read the silent question in them.

"Cleopatra," he said.

I drew a quick breath; *not* the Viscountess, who had been

saved by her assiduous friend—but her stepmother. "Louisa Williams! But how terrible! Did she stifle from the smoke?"

"I wish it were so." West glanced towards the Assembly Room doors, through which a shrouded form was being carried on a wooden plank, Hargate in attendance. "That would be simpler to explain. But I'm told her throat was cut, Jane."

"How? *When?*" I cried.

"That is what all the world will wish to find out," he said grimly.

I WOKE EARLY THIS morning to the gentle patter of rain. Would it never *cease* to fall? Was it possible to be driven mad by the sound of water slashing through gutters and pelting roof tiles?

I rose, my body aching from the exertions of last night, and donned my dressing gown. I sat down at the small writing desk in this bedchamber and drew out my journal, to set down an account of the terrible tragedy we witnessed in the Assembly Rooms, before the starkness of my impressions should fade; I had been writing a full half hour when a slight sigh caused me to turn my head, and discover Cassandra watching me from her bed. "I slept wretchedly," she said.

"I managed a few hours."

"That unfortunate woman, Jane."

"Yes," I agreed. "Hardly thirty, I should think—yet already married, widowed, dead."

"Not just *dead*—"

I did not answer her, but returned to my journal. So much had happened in such a short interval of time; only by setting it down in black and white, could I hope to understand what I had observed.

Lord Portreath had appeared at the boardinghouse door not long after we arrived home from the masked ball. He had come, of course, to impart the news of Louisa Williams's death to her stepdaughter, Rose—and I was struck that his usual appearance of indolence was entirely fled. The Viscount's looks were grim and his voice subdued, but he remained master of himself. Lady Portreath heard him out with a stricken aspect, her hand to her throat, then threw a fit of hysterics, which poor Miss Fox was hard-pressed to quell.

Mrs. Potter sent her husband out into the night in search of Dr. Hargate, who called on us all in his way home. The late Cleopatra's corpse had been carried to his surgery, he told us.

Having achieved the safety of Mrs. Potter's sitting-room fire, we were all too weary, too stunned, too redolent of smoke to move. Poor Mrs. Smith's generosity with the costumes was thus wretchedly repaid—would she be fined by the theatre for the loss? I resolved to consult West on the matter—and determined that her friends ought to recompense her, if Mr. Bowles Watson demanded a pound of flesh.

Viscount Portreath, remarkably, did not desert us for his bed at the York, but remained in suspense of the doctor's report on his wife's condition. Captain Pellew paced in his limping fashion, desperate for some call to action, while Hannah Vyvyan moved a pencil idly over Miss Fox's abandoned sketchbook, which she had found lying on the writing table. Even Raphael West remained sunk in a chair, his chin in his hands, staring broodingly at the flames that Mrs. Potter had obligingly built up for our comfort. Cassandra and I huddled on the sopha, where our damp gowns were slowly drying in the warmth of the coals. I reflected, in some abstraction, on the soothing nature of fire—and yet its extraordinarily destructive power—when Dr. Hargate emerged from the private parlour.

"She'll do," he said wearily, wiping his fingers on a handkerchief already darkened with soot and a dark crimson I assumed, shudderingly, to be Mrs. Williams's blood. "I have administered laudanum, and expect her to sleep heavily within moments. And now, sir, if you would be so good as to show me your burns—"

George Dinsdale rose from his position beside West and extended his hands. West having torn the feathered cloak from his body, the artist was dressed only in a black suit of clothes. Even his shirt had been sewn from black cloth, as tho' he had anticipated mourning. The cuffs of the sleeves were charred, and the skin of his hands an angry crimson from exposure to the flames.

"You must plunge these into a cold water bath—Mrs. Potter! A basin of cold water, if you please, as cold as may be found!" Hargate cried, in the direction of the kitchens. Then, peering back at Dinsdale, "Change the water as it warms for the next half-hour. If ice could be got . . . perhaps the York Hotel . . . but this late in the year it is, of course, too scarce . . ."

"I shall go and enquire," West said, rising immediately. "You do not advocate spirits of wine, then? Or bindings dipped in vinegar?"

"I do not. Sir James Earle is all for the application of simple cold water in such cases; and the opinion of His Majesty's surgeon is good enough for me. Refresh the water with ice, if it can be got, and then allow the skin to dry of itself. It will blister, but the blisters will heal in time."

"Thank you, sir," Dinsdale said. "West—I shall accompany you; do not incommode poor Mrs. Potter. She has enough to be getting on with. We shall order up the ice-basin at the York together, and a bottle of brandy to endure it."

"Very well. I shall be with you directly."

"A moment, doctor," Viscount Portreath said, coming forward from the bow window where he had been staring down into the darkened High Street. "I should like a word."

"If you mean to ask whether your wife may be moved to Cornwall tomorrow, the answer is emphatically *no*," Hargate snapped.

Portreath shook his head wordlessly. "Not that. I care nothing for . . . that is . . . *Mrs. Williams.* How exactly was she found?"

The physician drew himself up. "You don't know? I had thought you were her escort this evening, my lord."

"I was. We were separated when the fire broke out. The crowd in the doorway was maddened with the impulse to flee, and in the disorder and smoke I lost sight of Louisa." His eyelids flickered, but his countenance remained impassive. "I heard something—a rumour only—that she died by violence."

The physician's hard gaze roved around the company. "My lord, there are ladies present."

"And a lady is dead!" Portreath's voice resounded harshly

in the low-ceilinged room. "Enough of your squeamishness, Hargate; speak plainly, man."

"Very well. If you must know—her throat was cut. The poor creature's neck was slashed from ear to ear."

An indrawn breath from Portreath; no one spoke. Hargate's words stopped our mouths and thoughts. Even Pellew had ceased pacing. Hannah Vyvyan's pencil clattered to the desk.

"How?" Portreath managed.

Hargate stared at him, brows furrowed. "I must assume it was the sword, my lord. One was found lying by her side, the blade stained with blood."

"*Sword?*" I repeated involuntarily. "Or . . . cavalry sabre?"

Every head turned to gaze at Viscount Portreath, still in his stained and creased Wellington uniform. In all our minds at that instant, I am sure, was the memory of candlelight gilding the curved blade of the weapon as he held it aloft. What had he said? *I mastered its use from a child . . .*

Now, the sword belt and scabbard were gone.

"Where is the blade that killed her?" Portreath demanded.

"With the corpse," Hargate replied, "in my surgery. I intend to compare the throat wound to the weapon found near the body. There will be an inquest into the cause of Mrs. Williams's death. I shall be forced to appear before the coroner."

"An inquest." Portreath rubbed fretfully at his brow.

"Of course. You apprehend why it must be impossible for you or her ladyship to quit Cheltenham for Cornwall—why all travel must be suspended for the remainder of the week. The body may not be moved until the coroner has empaneled his jury and taken testimony." Hargate's voice sounded harshly in all our ears. "Not to mention, rendered judgement! And then there will be the burial to consider . . ."

Unnoticed by the doctor and the Viscount, who were wholly engrossed in their conversation, the private parlour door had opened, and Miss Fox stood on the threshold, surveying us all. She had been silent as a tomb as she overlistened the exchange; but now she voiced the one question in all our minds.

"Where is the sabre, Granville?"

He turned his head slowly to meet hers. "I cannot say. It was torn from me in the struggle to flee the building."

"Was it, indeed? How unfortunate. Had you kept it sheathed, this tragedy might not have occurred."

"*Don't.*" Portreath held up his hand, his face twisting. "Mine may not be the weapon responsible. There were any number of trumpery swords among the masqueraders tonight."

"But trumpery should hardly kill," Miss Fox persisted. "And why should anyone murder Louisa? She was a stranger to Cheltenham."

"Enough! Do you not know that I *blame myself* already?"

The last was uttered in the deepest bitterness. At the blaze of anger that suffused Portreath's countenance, I had an idea of how he must have looked before the walls of Badajoz. *Here* was a man capable of killing.

Raphael West stepped forward and grasped the Viscount's arm. "We are all overwrought at this hour of the morning, my lord. Come back with us to the York, and we will see you to your rooms."

24

THE UTILITY OF TABBIES

Tuesday, 4th June, 1816
Cheltenham, cont'd.

We offered up our prayers for the repose of Louisa Williams's soul in the peaceful silence of St. Mary's church. It was a relief to shut out the world for an interval and kneel in contemplation. The events of the past few days had been so varied and numerous, that when I closed my eyes over my folded hands, a parade of images danced before them: the basket-chair rolling towards me along the Colonnade; Thucydides lying dead on the dining parlour carpet; Mr. Dinsdale's illuminations, seconds before they burst into flame; a branch of Harlequin bells discarded on the anteroom floor; a rat dangling from Mr. Garthwaite's fingertips; and Hannah Vyvyan sketching idly with a pencil.

"I do not wish to take the waters this morning, Cass," I said as we rose from our knees. "I have not the stomach for it."

"I will *not* meet Dr. Hargate again with a falsehood on my lips," she retorted. "The good man asks perpetually whether the Montpellier's third pump is doing you good, and I have not the heart to tell him you have sampled it only once. If

242 · STEPHANIE BARRON

we hurry, we may choke down two full glasses of the hateful stuff and be returned to Mrs. Potter's in time for breakfast."

Overcome with remorse—for Cassandra should certainly have found a better use for her leisure had she not travelled with *me*—I submitted with good grace, and allowed her to lead me down St. George's Place in the direction of Montpellier Grounds. There would be fewer people there than in the Royal Well's Long Room, which should make the errand expeditious.

In the event, we found the Montpellier Well almost deserted, and were able to take our two glasses each (three remained insupportable) from the third pump without a lengthy interval between. I confess, however, that I was nearly gagging when I was done, and may have tipped the last quarter-cup of my second potation into the sad-looking urn of columbines upon exiting the pump room door.

"I suppose any number of patrons may be lying still a-bed," Cassandra said thoughtfully, "after the tragic disturbances of last evening. The report of *murder* may not yet have travelled far abroad, but certainly *arson* may keep your general run of convalescents within-doors."

"We do not know that the fire was contrived." I walked briskly, hoping the fresh air would settle my queasy stomach. The usual mist of rain that characterised this woeful spring was light as a moth's wing against my cheek. "Mr. Dinsdale's transparencies were gross invitations to flame, after all. So much turpentine. So much mastic resin."

"He had tested the fuses!" Cassandra objected. "Three times, by his own admission."

"But did he test them with the transparencies in place?" I did not pause to wonder at Cass's defence of the gentleman; they had, after all, been much together the previous evening, and no woman should like a friend to be blamed for the conflagration in the ballroom, much less for an untimely and gruesome death.

"You told me," my sister pointed out, "that you and Mr. West overheard a conversation in the anteroom where George's pavilion was held in waiting. It seems obvious that two Assembly patrons, at least, could have trifled with the fuses. Unbeknownst to us all, while the dancers and George were otherwise occupied—"

I had indeed shared my experiences of the previous evening with Cassandra as we walked to St. Mary's church. She was not to be put off in the matter of my suspicions, and the brief pause for prayer had only quickened her interest. But I had not heard a tampering with the pavilion or its fuses as I listened to the conversation in the anteroom. (Between Hannah Vyvyan? And which gentleman?) It was all gross supposition. To be sure, if the fuses *had* been meddled with, it *must* have been before the structure was rolled into the ballroom. Cassandra's idea was purest conjecture . . .

And she was calling him *George*. None knew better than I the seductive power of artists, but was it possible my sister cherished *hopes* of a man who wore corsets?

Resolutely, I set this trifling concern aside.

"To what end would a stranger meddle with Mr. Dinsdale's fuses?" It was a hard thing, I apprehended, to see so much artistry go up in smoke, but the notion of sabotage was childish.

Unless . . . "Are you suggesting that the blaze was a planned diversion, to confuse the evidence of murder?"

"The one event—*fire*—is certainly more comprehensible in light of the other—*murder*."

"I cannot conceive why Louisa Williams would be deliberately murdered," I said, "by the gentleman who gave every appearance of valuing her, whether it was his sabre that slit her throat or no."

"But, Jane," Cassandra pointed out reasonably, "if you would suggest that his lordship intended to murder his *wife*, then everything falls into place! Lord Portreath simply killed the wrong Cleopatra!"

"Mrs. Williams is no Lady Portreath, in her basket-chair," I retorted. "And there is Miss Fox to consider, that guardian angel. Neither lady, recollect, stirs without the other; and for his lordship to confuse his wife with his lover must be impossible."

"I do not begin to understand it." Cassandra raised her chin and stared at me in defiance. "I only know that George is not responsible!"

I clasped her hand in mine. "I am sure, my dear, that you are right."

THE BREAKFAST TABLE AT Mrs. Potter's was rather forlorn. Captain Pellew had already quitted the place for the Cheltenham Library, where he preferred to read his daily and weekly journals in relative peace; and Mrs. Smith, we were told, had departed barely a quarter-hour before.

"It is Tuesday, of course," Miss Garthwaite noted

contemptuously, "and that woman must be about her business at the *theatre*."

I had forgot that a performance was scheduled for this evening, and had no notion what it was to be, or which misbegotten actor Hannah Vyvyan was meant to school. From the thought of that lady's duties to consideration of her borrowed trunk of masquerade costumes, so freely shared among ourselves, was but a moment; I felt anxious to know whether the damages from singeing and smoke would be deducted from her wages. I resolved to enquire as soon as might be. At the very least, I could recompense her for my vanished mantilla.

"I apprehend from Mrs. Potter that the pursuit of dissipation last night ended as it inevitably must," Miss Garthwaite persisted, "in misery and regret. I do not think I slept a wink, for all the noise."

"Fire," Mr. Garthwaite added. *"Murder."*

The Garthwaites were our cheerless companions for tea and toast and eggs. Mrs. Potter, after an utterly broken night, was to be commended for putting even so little before us.

"I see you rose early, however, to receive a full report." I sipped at my tea, which was hearteningly scalding. "I wonder you remain in such a disordered household, ma'am. It cannot be good for your brother's nerves."

"We have paid our charges for the remainder of the week," she returned crisply, "and shall not depart an hour earlier. Tho' my conscience urges me to be gone, I respect the value of coin, Miss Austen. *I* do not spend more than I ought. *I* do not indulge in wasteful behaviour."

"Inquest," Mr. Garthwaite said, reaching long fingers towards the toast rack, "tomorrow. She means to attend."

This was news. How had the Garthwaites learnt of it before ourselves?

"The jury is to be empaneled at the Eight Bells publick house in Church Street," Miss Garthwaite confided, leaning across the table, "at two o'clock. Lord Portreath called not half an hour since to inform *his wife* that she is on no account to quit Cheltenham before the coroner's inquest. I suspect he does not like the duty of escorting the remains to Cornwall alone."

I lifted my brows. "He actually thinks the Viscountess would quit Cheltenham in the face of so much trouble?"

Miss Garthwaite shrugged. "Miss Fox is capable of anything, of course, and might spirit her friend away in the middle of the night; but I regard her ladyship as possessing a greater sensibility. Indeed, I believe her to be prostrate with grief. She has not shown her face; she keeps to her rooms, as you see."

I glanced over my sister's shoulder at the closed parlour door. Grief was possible, to be sure, given Lady Portreath's notable hysterics last evening; but I was inclined to doubt the depth of her anguish. She had shrieked just as loudly at first sight of Mrs. Williams last Thursday. To throw a fit was her ladyship's preferred manner of avoiding what she did not like. Her husband's discomposure ought to be the more genuine; but any sense of loss must be compounded by an equally-severe perception of personal danger. There was the matter of his lordship's missing light cavalry sabre—which might be the weapon held in Dr. Hargate's surgery.

Had his lordship attempted to identify it? I wondered.

"Note for you, Miss Jane," said Mrs. Potter as she bustled into the dining parlour. She placed a sealed missive next to my teacup.

I saw at a glance that it was from Raphael West. His hand was like his sketches: swift and unerring.

"Mrs. Potter," I said as she made to turn away, "would you be so kind as to answer a question?"

"Certainly, ma'am."

"Have you ever had occasion to poison a rat?"

She frowned, her lips pursing. "Lucy said as Dr. Hargate was accusing me of keeping an unclean house. There are no rats in my kitchen, ma'am, however many that nasty York Hotel may hold."

"You have not purchased any arsenic, then, or mercury, from your apothecary?"

"Not on your life, ma'am! Dangerous for my tabby—and she's an excellent mouser. Mice we *have* seen, mind you—but any household may say the same. A problem best dealt with by a decent cat, and none of the lodgers feeling anxious about the health of their victuals."

"Thank you, Mrs. Potter."

She curtseyed, casting a defiant look at Miss Garthwaite, as tho' daring her to challenge the utility of tabbies; and left us.

I broke the wax on West's note, and perused the few lines. "Cassandra, my dear, I am going for a walk."

"But it rains!" Miss Garthwaite cried, dropping her toast.

My sister leant close and said into my ear, "Pray enquire after Mr. Dinsdale's burns, Jane."

West was leaning against the outer jamb of Mrs. Potter's door, his high-crowned hat sloping above his compelling profile and a caped driving coat thrown over his shoulders, as tho' he meant to set me up in his hired curricle. But he had only just quitted the equipage, I learnt upon my greeting—having driven to George Dinsdale's villa to see how his friend did.

"His hands are blistered and sensitive to the touch," he told me, "but less ravaged than I feared last night. Hargate's advice proved correct, in this at least."

"I am glad," I said. "The loss of his transparencies must be heavy, but once his hands heal he may look forward to fashioning others."

"If his reputation survives the fire, which I earnestly doubt." He frowned. "The poor fellow hoped to make his name from that remarkable display. It will not be the first time that ambition scuttles a man's hopes."

"But not in quite so incendiary a fashion. You wish to walk along the High?"

He gestured with his umbrella. "I am happy to unfurl this and escort you wherever you like to go, Jane; but I had another purpose, I confess, in seeking you out. I have been troubled with no little anxiety for Miss Vyvyan—and I thought to enlist your sympathies."

I had not quite expected this. The memory of Cassandra's narrowed gaze as she studied West and the engaging Harlequin last evening flitted across my mind. "Of course," I said, recovering. "She is overset by the havoc done to her costumes."

"Come with me to the theatre," he said, placing his hand on my arm, "and speak to Hannah. You know that it was *she* we overlistened last night, when I drew you into the French window; she, who spoke with such contempt to an unknown man. There is a history between them—and threats and possible violence. I believe it is imperative that we learn the man's identity."

I stared at him, my heart sinking. Such vehemence! And such an obvious desire to preserve the young woman from harm. "West," I said faintly, "you are not going to meet the gentleman with pistols at dawn, I hope?"

His eyes widened, and he glanced about as tho' I had mistaken him for someone else. "Good God, Jane! Of course not! What do you take me for—Hannah's jilted lover? I am old enough to be the girl's father!"

"Fathers have defended their daughters' honour before this," I said feebly; but in fact I felt so flooded with relief that my knees might have given way.

"It is Dinsdale who put me in mind of it," he said, thrusting himself away from the Potters' door and raising his umbrella. He offered me his arm, and I slipped mine through it. Never mind that the theatre was but a few steps across the street. I felt in need of support.

"Of Mrs. Smith? But why?"

"He believes someone tampered with his fuses."

"I confess that Cassandra and I share a similar thought. Do admit, the fire was a perfect diversion from the act of murder."

"Or merely offered a chance that a murderer seized." West shrugged wearily. "It must be natural for poor George to cast about for someone to blame for the ruin of his hopes—but it is more than probable that the fuses were flawed from the beginning. I could not help but recall, however, that *deuced trumpery* structure sat waiting in the anteroom—that I had seen Hannah slip into it in the most furtive fashion—that I had tarried in the French windows from a concern for what she did there—and that we heard the unknown blackguard accuse her of *something.*"

"And she, him." I glanced sideways at West. "You saw her slip into the anteroom? I had no notion it was Mrs. Smith until I espied her Harlequin bells lying discarded on the floor."

"That is another reason for my concern," West said grimly. "Did you know that the body of Mrs. Williams was discovered in that self-same anteroom, along with the sword that killed her?"

2 5

A HISTORY OF LOSS

Tuesday, 4th June, 1816
Cheltenham, cont'd.

We found Hannah Vyvyan sorting through a vast mound of costumes, stinking, damp, and torn from the chaos of the masque, and returned by all Cheltenham to John Bowles Watson's theatre.

She had donned one of her sober, nondescript gowns, a simple muslin cap hiding her glorious hair. Her sleeves were buttoned at the wrist and her bodice at the neck; the delightful French Columbine doll of the previous night was fled, along with her face paint. I detected shadows in the hollows of her eyes, and too little colour in her countenance; a want of spirits uncharacteristic in one so resolute.

When we paused at the entrance to the backstage room in which she toiled, some slight noise startled her, and she flinched as visibly as tho' she had been struck, turning with a gasp to stare at us.

"Good morning, Hannah," Raphael West said gently. "You are abroad and at work far earlier than I would have expected, given the ordeals of last evening."

"Mr. Bowles Watson can have no notion that I was present at the masquerade," she breathed. "That is not my proper station in life, sir, as you know. I am at my post as usual this morning, lest I lose my place. There are costumes to be repaired and catalogued."

She clenched silks in her fingers as she spoke, turquoise and sapphire, brilliant as a peacock's feathers. West stepped forward and took them carefully from her hands. "Will you not sit down? Miss Austen and I would speak with you."

For an instant she hesitated, and I thought might put us off. Then the very stillness with which we regarded her seemed to calm her agitation, as it might a wild fawn. She closed her eyes and drew a shuddering breath. West grasped her elbow, concerned that she swayed.

"Here," he said, guiding her forward. "You should sit."

She sank onto the straight-backed cane chair. "Thank you, Mr. West. You are very good. Did I mention that I wrote to Charlotte on Sunday?"

"I am glad," he said simply, and drew forward a second chair. "Miss Austen?"

He meant to stand over us in our *tête-à-tête*. But no; being West, he thrust his shoulder against the doorjamb as I settled myself beside Hannah, content to observe us from a safe distance.

"You are excessively fatigued, my dear," I said.

She laughed unsteadily. "From more than lack of sleep."

"Any of us who endured the unexpected chaos of the Cheltenham Assembly must feel drained and mopish. It is not every day one escapes death."

"That is very true," she said.

How did West wish me to proceed, I wondered? His countenance offered no hint of the tactics I should employ. Then I apprehended: he trusted me to manage a young female better than he could himself. I had long been acquainted with the type; it was enough to act on my instincts.

"What is the performance to be tonight? —And whom are you expected to reform?"

She laughed again, gaining a little in confidence. "*Catherine and Petruchio*—a variation on the theme of Shakespeare."

"*The Taming of the Shrew*, in more exalted circles. I do hope Jasper is to play the male part; I have grown quite fond of his regal accents."

"I should have loved to play Catherine," Hannah mused. "It is a role exactly suited to my prickly nature. But Mr. Bowles Watson does not agree, alas."

"He regards you as meant for something higher and finer than a sharp-tongued spinster?" I suggested. "In that I am quite in accord. We all long to see you restored to your proper sphere, my dear. It is high time you left off your fancy-dress, and claimed your birthright."

Her brows drew down. "Mr. West has been talking out of turn, I see. I had not thought you so little to be trusted, sir!"

"However faulty my character, Miss Austen's is beyond reproach," he said. "I have trusted her with my life. But pray continue, Jane."

"It was Captain Pellew who first suggested, Mrs. Smith, that your past situation in life was very different from your present one," I supplied. "You and the Captain appear to hold each other in mutual affection and esteem."

"I doubt there is a truer friend than Harry in all the Kingdom—and I have been happy to call him thus from birth. Our fathers were intimate; our mothers were cousins."

"Which leads me to believe it was not Captain Pellew who earned your contempt last night, by offering you monetary support in the Assembly anteroom."

She drew a sharp breath, her gaze flying to West's face. "You overlistened my private conversation?"

"Yes," he said baldly. "I saw you slip alone into the anteroom and wondered what you were about. I merely meant to stand your protector, should a masked rake attempt a liberty. In the event, I was the more disturbed by veiled threats and subtle innuendo. Who was it, Miss Vyvyan, who threatened you?"

"I thought it was *I* who threatened *him*." She held her head high, eyes blazing at us.

"Indeed," I mused. "You interpreted his insulting offer of support as an attempt to buy your silence—and refused him."

"Why interrogate me in this fashion?" Miss Vyvyan was rigidly poised in her seat, her pallid face composed and challenging. "My affairs, past or present, are solely my concern."

West sighed. "You might have been correct—yesterday. But this morning we are confronted with a murder, one that will demand a coroner's panel in two days' time."

"That can have nothing to do with me!"

I reached for her hand; it was chill with nerves, and for an instant I thought she might snatch it away. But her manners were too good; she relaxed a trifle under my touch.

"My dear," I said. "You carried a stick of Harlequin bells with your costume last night."

"I did. I must have dropped them in the crush to reach the door—I came away without them."

"You left them behind in the anteroom," I said.

She frowned. "Did I?"

"I saw them lying there. I ought to have retrieved them, but—"

"What can it matter?"

West left the doorframe and moved slowly towards us. "Hannah, Mr. Dinsdale is convinced that someone tampered with his fuses. He had arranged and tested them carefully in the framework of the transparency screens. You must have observed the structure in the anteroom."

"It stood in readiness, behind a velvet rope."

"Did you notice anything amiss during your interview there? —Did the man you met, meddle with the fuses, perhaps?"

Her brows drew down over her deep green eyes, which had a look of calculation in them. "Not in my presence. But he was waiting in the room before I arrived. It is possible he did some mischief then."

"The body of Louisa Williams was also found in the anteroom," I said. "Alongside the sword that killed her. As well as your stick of—"

"No," Hannah whispered in horror. "Not my Harlequin bells? But it cannot signify—we all met with Mrs. Williams *after* I was in that room! We saw and spoke to her—still alive!"

"And it will be vital to inform the coroner of that much. To confirm, under sacred oath, that you left the bells on the anteroom floor *before* the body came there. You see," I concluded, "why we should like to know whom you met. He might swear to the time and place—and prove vital to your freedom."

She drew back, studying my countenance and West's in turn. "But it is absurd! I should no more have reason to kill Louisa Williams than . . ." She hesitated.

". . . Lord Portreath himself?"

A sharply indrawn breath. "I see, Miss Austen, you understand how it was."

We bade Hannah Vyvyan put on her cloak and raise the hood, to discourage the chilling rain. Then the three of us walked out into the unseasonable June day and made for the protection of the Elm Walk.

"How came you to suspect it?" she asked. "I was careful to betray no acquaintance with his lordship. Indeed, I believe even *he* was ignorant of my identity."

"Your face betrayed you, the first time he walked into Mrs. Potter's sitting-room, after *Julius Caesar* Thursday night. You went white, Miss Vyvyan."

She smiled crookedly, her eyes on the wet paving. "He affected no notice of me, however—and I suspect would have continued not to know me, had I never appeared in masquerade dress. With my hair well-arranged and figure displayed in a well-cut gown, however, I was once more recognisable as a young lady in her first Season, whom he had encountered years before. Granville never forgets a lady's figure."

West drew in his breath sharply and turned towards her. "Is he the Devil who—"

She placed her hand quellingly on his arm. "I was once affianced to Lord Portreath's elder brother," she said. "The Honourable Piers Basset. I was to have been a member of Lord Portreath's family."

"The elder brother," I sighed, "who died untimely."

"Yes. We met at Almack's some five years ago. Piers's father was then in good health, and there was no thought of succession; but my uncle—Sir Charles Markham, who was also my guardian and sponsor—thought it a good match, and promoted Piers's suit. There was the fact that in marrying Viscount Portreath's heir, I should be returning to the part of the world from whence I came. Tho' raised in Plymouth, I had often been in Cornwall as a girl, and if I did not yet know Godrevy Manor, the way of life should not be so strange to me as Derbyshire and London."

"What of Mr. Basset? Forgive me, but—aside from your uncle's blessing, did you like him for himself?"

"I did." Hannah drew an unsteady breath. "Indeed, I loved him. Do not be thinking I was *forced* to the consequences of my reckless decisions! He was an excellent young man, Miss Austen. Too volatile in spirits, perhaps; too ardent in feeling and action—but I was equally heedless, and borne along by the strength of my feeling. I will offer no other excuse for what occurred. I have repented with time, and paid in full for my indulgence."

West said, "How came he to abandon you?"

"Not by choice," she replied, with a watery smile. "He was

killed in a hunting accident, three weeks before we were to be wed."

"A broken neck? Thrown by his horse?" West asked.

"That would have been cleaner, and easier to bear—tho' he had been trained to the chase from boyhood." An elm leaf, bright green and slick with rain, drifted to our feet as we paced along the gravel path towards the Royal Well. "But Piers was not mounted. It was September—pheasant season. A discharge of shot tore into his lung. He bled to death before he could be carried home."

"How tragic!" I said. "And pointless."

"I have wondered." She threw me a swift look. "Because there was Granville to consider, you see."

"The brother who benefited from his death." West nodded once. "He was on the pheasant shoot, I take it?"

"Yes. My uncle had invited both Bassets to Grassmoor Lodge—his Derbyshire estate—for my engagement party. Granville was on a brief home-leave from the Peninsula."

"How many were the party that morning?"

"Some dozen gentlemen."

"And none claimed the stray shot?"

She shook her head. "I own that I was surprised, even in my grief. I expected the person responsible for Piers's death to admit it. For of course it was a mistake—dreadful, to be sure, but somehow worse for being unacknowledged."

"And it is for that very reason," West suggested softly, "that you suspect his brother."

"Yes." She turned to him a countenance riven with emotion, the pain of her lover's loss still sharp. "I have never been able to free my mind of suspicion. Granville had everything to gain by stepping into his brother's shoes. An honourable man, having discharged his gun by accident, would have owned it—with remorse; yet none did."

"A soldier trained in His Majesty's cavalry should certainly hit at what he aimed," West said thoughtfully.

"You have no proof of a murderous calculation, however." I slipped my hand through Hannah's arm, drawing her more fully under the protection of Mr. West's umbrella. "You suggested otherwise, in your hints last evening."

"When I rebuffed Granville's bargain?" she said contemptuously. "Do you not think it odd, Miss Austen, that he should make such an unguarded offer—having met with me for only the second time in five years?"

"It suggests a consciousness—of shame and guilt."

"Tho' I imagine," West countered, "that if challenged on his words, his lordship would have solely the welfare of his brother's betrothed at heart. He is the head of his family, now, recollect; his pride may demand that he appear generous."

"Did the two brothers like each other?" I asked.

"They were very different," Miss Vyvyan said. "Piers was sent to Eton and Oxford; Granville was educated privately at home, and excelled in everything to do with sport and horses. Old Lord Portreath bought his commission in the Queen's Seventh when he was but nineteen, and from then on the two brothers saw little of each other. After Piers's death, of course, Granville sold out—as Portreath's heir, his duty was in England."

"You describe divergent circumstances and lives," I pointed out. "But I asked if they cared for each other."

Hannah's footsteps slowed. We had nearly reached the pump house of the well, and a knot of patrons were collected at the entrance, regardless of the rain. Her words must be for ourselves alone; we halted to hear them in privacy at one side of the walk. "I cannot say. I knew them too briefly as brothers. They shared a common dash and spirit. Both ready to laugh, ready to wager a fortune on a whim. But Piers had the backing to do it—and Granville lived by his wits. Had Piers acceded to his father's title, he should with time have settled into his responsibilities. He loved Godrevy, and would have managed its welfare."

"Granville has *not* done so?"

"Money runs through his fingers," she said simply. "I have heard, from an old acquaintance, how he has stripped the estate of its revenues since coming into his inheritance. He must have the same object for Lady Portreath's fortune—he is always in want of funds."

"You believe he married Miss Williams for her money?" I asked.

"I assumed so. I could not blame him. Granville was wed already a full year before I met Piers—younger sons, after all, require *something* to live on. Their habits of expence do not allow them to marry where they like."

"And so he found a fortune *and* rank, within the same year," West murmured. "Quite a successful campaign on the officer's part. I underestimated Lord Portreath. His appearance of indolence is deceiving."

26

DISCOVERY OF A DISH OF MILK

Tuesday, 4th June, 1816
Cheltenham, cont'd.

We treated Hannah Vyvyan to tea and Queen cakes at Gunton's confectionery in St. George's Place, then returned her to the theatre, somewhat restored in spirits. West assured her that he believed Viscount Portreath *must* appear before the coroner's panel—if only to bear witness to the last time he saw alive, the lady whom he had escorted to the ball.

"I expect he may be asked to examine the sword that killed her," I added, "and if it proves to be his own . . . any number of questions will follow. I am ready to swear that I noticed your stick of bells discarded on the anteroom floor well before Mrs. Williams's body was discovered there. I may also attest, with others, that his lordship's sabre was on his person before midnight when the fire broke out. If it proves necessary, I shall not hesitate to give evidence before the coroner."

"I shall have to put my trust in the probity of the Law," Hannah said simply.

"And in your friends." West bowed. "You have many more than you credit, my dear."

"How well I know it," she told him, and stood on tiptoe to kiss his cheek.

"There is one friend I could wish she acknowledged more fully," I observed as West and I left the theatre by its side-passage door.

"Harry Pellew?"

I nodded. "I suspect the Captain is all admiration for Mrs. Smith, despite Lady Portreath's efforts to attach him—but there is a certain puzzle I cannot explain. Have you plans for the balance of your morning, West, or will you accompany me to the Cheltenham Library?"

West did *not*, and most certainly *would*; the rain had subsided for the moment; and so, invigorated by all we had learnt, we furled his umbrella and walked together to the Reading Room.

WE DISCOVERED CAPTAIN PELLEW perusing the final pages of the *Plymouth and Dock Telegraph*, one of the Reading Room's vast collection of newspapers. He was seated in a comfortable armchair near one of the coal braziers set at intervals along the outer wall, his feet warming near the coals. It had been some days since I had glimpsed a newssheet of any kind, and the homely sight of Pellew's absorption and the ink smudging his fingers inspired me to wonder what intelligence the London journals had to report. From thence it was but an instant to the thought of my brother Charles—whose panel verdict had yet to reach us. How swiftly all anxieties of a personal nature were sped once *murder* demanded its share of notice.

"Miss Austen!" Pellew tossed aside the *Telegraph* and made as if to rise from his chair in greeting, but West held out his hand.

"Stay." He drew forward a straight-backed chair for me and one for himself, setting them companionably near the Captain's so that we should not disturb other readers with our conversation—or be overheard. "You look surprizingly fit for one who suffered such a wretched night."

"Parts of the evening were excellent," Pellew retorted with humour. "I may say that you, Miss Austen, weathered the Assembly's trials with aplomb!"

I inclined my head. "I intend to take a well-deserved rest this afternoon, Captain. I would not wish to be yawning during the inquest tomorrow."

"Has one been scheduled, by Jove?" He looked at West in surprize. "That is quick work."

"I imagine Dr. Hargate has been in communication with the coroner at Gloucester, as the corpse is in his surgery," West said.

"I have no notion of whether that fellow has any right to take charge of poor Mrs. Williams's remains," Pellew mused, "but presumably the Cheltenham parish constable offered him no argument."

"The parish constable being appointed by the St. Mary's vestry," I said, "argument should be unlikely. Dr. Hargate does much good among the parish poor, I am told—and it is possible the constable, tho' unpaid, serves in part at his pleasure."

"The jury is to be empaneled tomorrow at two o'clock, at the Eight Bells," West told him. "Miss Austen and I mean to be there."

"I have never witnessed an inquest." Pellew clasped his hands and leant towards us. "Do you think it entirely respectable, Miss Austen, for a lady to attend?"

"Mrs. Smith will bear me company," I said tranquilly. "I hope to provide some evidence of her innocence to the coroner—and respectable or no, I should never shirk what I regard as my duty."

"Her innocence!" Pellew cried. "What absurdity is this! Hannah no more had anything to do with Mrs. Williams's murder than I! Indeed, we were together—" He stopped short, glancing from my face to West's. "You are joking, surely?"

"A part of Mrs. Smith's costume was discarded in the same room as the body," I told him, "and the sword that killed her."

"Nonsense!" Pellew looked all his consternation. "You met her in my company last night, Miss Austen, in the supper room. We moved together to the edge of the ballroom to observe Dinsdale's illuminations. From that moment forward, she was never out of our sight."

"As I intend to inform the coroner. I may also testify to the fact that her bells were discarded long before Mrs. Williams was killed in the anteroom, under cover of fire, smoke, and a generalized chaos among the Assembly's patrons. But I am sure Mrs. Smith would be happy in your support at the inquest. Do you mean to go?"

The Captain hesitated, and his gaze fell to his hands. "I should like to be attend, of course. But there is Lady Portreath to consider."

"Lady Portreath?" I repeated in all innocence. "How is she concerned in the affair?"

"She will demand support as well—having lost her step-mother in such vile circumstances, and being too weak to observe the proceedings. She has not appeared outside her rooms today, I collect?"

"She has not." I persisted in staring at him so steadily that I believe I *willed* Pellew to lift his eyes and meet my gaze. "Captain, something I have twice witnessed in recent days has puzzled me exceedingly. If I do not deceive myself, you harbour a deep admiration for Mrs. Smith—Hannah Vyvyan, as I believe we may agree to call her, among ourselves. Is that not true?"

The ready colour rushed to his cheeks, and he ran his fingers restlessly through his red hair. "You are a witch, Miss Austen! Never tell me that Hannah has revealed her name to you!"

"I owe the intelligence, and the lady's revelation, to Mr. West."

Pellew's bright blue gaze moved in challenge to my friend. "West! Why should *you* be privy to Miss Vyvyan's secrets?"

"Hannah and I are old friends, Pellew. I regard her in some wise as another daughter. I certainly never learnt of any marriage between Miss Vyvyan and a Smith; and when taxed with my reproaches, at having missed her wedding, she imparted the truth."

"I see," he said heavily. "I am glad to know that the secret is no longer mine alone."

"Is it possible, Captain Pellew," I said softly, "that you are come into Gloucestershire with no other object than to find Miss Vyvyan, restore her confidence in your early regard, and persuade her to entertain your addresses?"

With a quirk of his brow, he leant towards me intimately. "What else should I be doing in this curst watering-place, Miss Austen, if not dangling after a captivating young lady? I had no sooner been turned ashore six months ago than I went in search of Hannah—and discovered from her old nursemaid, whom I have known this age and more, that she was gone into Gloucestershire. Old Nancy tried her best to keep confidences, and dropped only hints of Hannah's trouble, but I daresay I'm older than seven. I collected soon enough there'd been a scrape of some sort and Hannah's fine relations had cast her off. I won't scald your ears with my opinion of *them*. I persuaded Nan to give over the direction of Hannah's lodgings—wrote to Mrs. Potter to secure a room—and descended on *Mrs. Smith* with all the force of a broadside!"

"She'd be a fool to refuse you," West said.

But apparently, I thought, *she had.*

"What *was* the lady's reaction?" I asked.

Pellew expelled a heavy sigh. "All manner of codswallop! She insists that she should dishonour my name—thwart my advancement up the ranks. I have assured her that is impossible—I am content enough with my prizes, my fortune, and my game leg, and mean to be satisfied with life on shore, in my own home in Plymouth. All such a life wants, for perfect happiness, is Hannah."

"In fact, she refused you," I concluded, "and by way of return, you attempted to make her jealous by remaining tiresomely underfoot at Potter's, and turning your obvious attentions to Lady Portreath. Or Miss Fox. Or both. It is the usual way with gentlemen who have been spurned; they may even believe, for a time, that their hearts are easily thrown to another."

Pellew's mouth opened, then shut firmly on whatever retort he had meant to lash me with. "You are correct, of course," he admitted ruefully. "I have been every sort of fool. But there is no one to equal Hannah, as surely you have seen yourself, Miss Austen. I will remain in Cheltenham until I succeed in engaging her."

"Good man." West slapped Pellew on the shoulder.

"Perhaps you could explain, then, what has been puzzling me," I persisted.

Both male heads turned to regard my countenance.

"On two occasions—the early hours of both Saturday and Sunday, between two and three o'clock in the morning—I was awakened by the slightest of noises in the passage outside my bedchamber door. Upon investigation, I saw Lady Portreath *walking*, under her own power, in the direction of your rooms. I saw her clearly as she passed under the oil lamp suspended at the turning in the passage; her blond hair is unmistakable."

"Good God!" Pellew cried.

"Jane," West said at the same moment. "Are you *certain*?"

I drew a deep breath. "One such spectral visitation I might have dismissed as a dream, brought on by the dubious effects of the Montpellier Well. But two—"

"And she was walking towards *my* bedchamber?" Pellew's brows drew down.

"I assumed so. You are, after all, her favoured friend, as Mr. Garthwaite is not. But her perambulation was brief; within a moment, or less, she was returned along the passage and descending the stairs to her own quarters. I merely wondered, Captain, *why*."

He looked abashed, his blue gaze shifting from West's face to mine. "You are aware that her ladyship is addicted to poetic composition?"

"Of course."

He pursed his lips in distaste. "She has dedicated a number of her works to *me*."

"She thrusts *poems* over your threshold? In the dead of night?" Raphael West looked as if he might give way to laughter, but mastered the impulse.

"To be frank, I had thought Miss Fox the emissary—she is Lady Portreath's scribe and amanuensis. I never thought the lady herself . . ."

"Naturally not," I said. "Were they love poems, sir?"

"Love poems! I hardly know! A fellow in my line is no judge of such sick stuff!" Pellew cast about for his stick. "I must go to her, and tax her for the meaning of this bizarre behaviour. A lady in her condition—so feeble and ill-supported—ought not to be venturing from her bed in the dead of night. She might have fainted. She might simply have fallen, anywhere between her rooms and mine, and done herself the gravest injury."

West said brusquely, "Captain."

"What is it?"

"Say nothing to her as yet, I beg of you."

He grasped his stick and forced himself upright, out of his chair. "But I desire an explanation. Devil take it, West—she has *lied* to us!"

"So she has. But she is also in distress at present." West rose from his chair and held Pellew's gaze. "Consider of her delicate health! She is hardly mistress of herself. She cannot be expected to answer you collectedly. Indeed, any sort of interrogation from you might overset her entirely. Better to school your patience until the inquest is done—and judgement rendered for Mrs. Williams's death."

2 7

A DISCOURSE ON POISON

Tuesday, 4th June, 1816
Cheltenham, cont'd.

"I fear you are fatigued, Jane," West said as we quitted the library. "Shall I escort you back to your lodgings, or have you energy enough to accompany me on one more errand?"

Last night's unhealthy excitement and the extraordinarily late hour at which I retired were indeed telling upon my strength; but my spirits and curiosity were high. "Where do you mean to go next?"

West glanced along the High Street's paving; the rain had lessened a bit, and there were any number of people going about their business: fashionables promenading, butcher-boys hurrying along with brown paper parcels, an orange-girl strolling with her basket. A stray dog lifted its leg against a hitching post and trotted on, nose to the gutter. "To Dr. Hargate's. He will no doubt judge me impertinent, and declare that I meddle in questions that are not my province, but a trifling uneasiness on Miss Vyvyan's account urges me to persist. I should like to know whether he has identified the owner of the weapon found near Mrs. Williams's body."

"Hargate is unlikely to answer you in my presence," I said. "He may be examining the *corpse* of a murdered woman, but recollect he considers the subject unsuitable for a woman's *ears*."

"I'm not ready to part with you, Jane."

West's dark eyes were on my own, warm and probing; I quelled the familiar surge of excitement his attention always inspired and said, "I long to discuss Mrs. Potter's rats with the good doctor; so I shall put on my most brazen face, and force him to answer my questions as well as yours."

"Her *what?*" West's brow quirked.

"*Rattus norvegicus.* —Or rather, the poison she employs to kill them. They are said to emigrate from the York Hotel, whose premises are far less clean than ours."

He laughed. "Explain yourself."

"You recall the poisoned pug?"

"Miss Garthwaite's animal. It ate the macaroons . . . from Miss Vyvyan's plate."

"And the assumption was that those were somehow unwholesome. They also, I must point out, came from the York kitchens—a gift on the part of Lord Portreath, to tempt his wife's appetite."

"What appetite? It is impossible to tempt, by any means."

"Exactly."

West held out his arm. I slipped mine through it, feeling the strength of him through the wool of his sleeve. How I should miss these intimate moments! "Are you suggesting," he asked, "that the Viscount meant all along to poison *Hannah*? But she insists he failed to recognise her until last night."

I shook my head. "I do not think Mrs. Smith was the intended victim."

"How do the rats come into this?"

"Through no fault of their own, poor things."

We turned down Back Street; a few paces further, and we achieved Dr. Hargate's establishment. It was a respectable-looking, tho' plain redbrick edifice, its front stoop diligently scrubbed. We rang the bell, and were informed by the equally plain-faced maid who answered it that the physician could be found in his surgery—accessible by the side passage.

"I don't know as he's at home to patients," she said, eyeing us doubtfully, "on account of he's anatomising the corpus; but if you like to leave a note, I'll make certain he sees it, and calls round later."

West declined the offer, and as soon as the shining black door was closed, drew me around the side passage to the surgery. He proceeded to pound on its portal with a gloved fist, and call Hargate's name with some urgency, which caused the doctor to fling back his surgery door and confront us with querulous ill-humour.

"Yes! Yes! You will not raise the dead even with so much noise," he sputtered. He wore no coat, and his shirtsleeves were rolled back nearly to his elbows. He continued to dry his hands on a linen towel as he stared at us. "What is this about? How may I serve you?"

He, too, had been abroad much of the night, and harassed by multiple claims on his time and attention; it was hardly surprising that he should be uncivil.

"We wished to speak with you," West said, "regarding murder."

"Speak to the coroner tomorrow, if you must," he returned, and attempted to close the door.

"We mean to do so." West placed his booted foot across the threshold. "But by sharing what we know in advance of that proceeding, we might prevent further violence. May we come in, Hargate?"

He glanced over his shoulder, then back at us. "Miss Austen, as well?"

"Particularly Miss Austen."

The physician sighed in exasperation. "One moment."

West withdrew his foot and Hargate closed the door. When he reopened it half a moment later, he had donned his coat and discarded his square of linen. With a gesture, he invited us to enter the low-ceilinged room—in another life, it had served as household offices, I suspected—and offered us chairs near the fire.

Of Mrs. Williams's body there was no hint. A closed door to an adjoining room—the former scullery, per-haps?—suggested where it might lie, and I detected a faintly animal odour of blood in the close air. I nearly asked Hargate to leave the outer door ajar, so that we might bring some freshness into the room; but I forced down the threat of sickness with resolution. Now was no time for missish airs.

"Your time is valuable, so we shall be brief." West held out my chair, and I sank into it. "Miss Austen has a question regarding poison."

"Poison?" Hargate stared at me as tho' I were mad. "The woman's head was nearly cut off!"

"Not Mrs. Williams," I interjected. "Recollect Thucydides, and the rats."

Dr. Hargate threw up his hands. "Are you still mourning the foolish pug? He did what all dogs will do—hunted and devoured vermin—and the sad truth is that a sickened rat did not agree with him."

"I will not trouble you overmuch," I said gently. "Pray believe that my enquiries tend in a useful direction. Answer only two of them, and I will be satisfied."

His grizzled brows lowered. "Very well. Make haste."

"Did you fully anatomise the dog? Or the dead rat Mr. Garthwaite presented to you?"

Hargate snorted in contempt. "The dog died because it ate a poisoned rat!"

"Did you discover the remains of one in Thucydides's stomach, sir?"

He stared at me, arrested by my words. "I . . . did not."

I lifted my brows and studied his countenance.

Flustered, Hargate shifted his gaze to Raphael West. "I have had rather more on my mind of late than rats! What does she mean by this?"

"It is obvious," West replied. "If the rat did not poison the dog, then something else did. Which would suggest that our original supposition of poisoned macaroons is correct. Lord Portreath brought those macaroons as a gift to Potter's, and offered them to his wife. If he first dusted them with white arsenic, the better to be rid of his domestic infelicity, he should not dare to protest when she sent his proffered cakes into the dining room."

"What you describe is reckless in the extreme," Hargate protested. He looked rather white about the mouth.

"Indeed. But if the Viscount's treatment of his wife was deliberately brutal, in an effort to make her swoon—and send Pellew to disturb the breakfast table—he might prevent an accidental poisoning."

"His lordship may be a soldier, and yet know little of poison," I suggested. "He may have thought his powder would only sicken those who sampled it. One macaroon or two is not very much, after all—we might all have suffered a wretched indisposition, and nothing more. But poor Thucydides was such a mite—"

I stopped short. The pug had, after all, been a dear little dog.

"You have not the slightest justification for such rank suspicion of the Viscount," Hargate said. "This is conjecture only."

I would have spoken, but West placed his hand on my wrist and leant earnestly towards the doctor.

"You do know that he cannot touch a penny of her fortune—it is held in trust—until such time as she produces an heir . . . or dies?"

"How should I possibly be in possession of such privileged intelligence?" Hargate cried.

"Well . . . you might have listened to the lady, as we did ourselves," West said. "She has been free enough with her private affairs. Miss Fox told you outright that her ladyship's life is in danger. But no matter. The point is this: Lady Portreath means to separate from her lord and set up her own establishment with Miss Fox in London. For that, she requires control of her fortune.

"Outrageous!" Hargate spluttered. "Where do these women absorb their radical ideas?"

"The writings of Mary Wollstonecraft," I supplied. "They are most consoling to those of us with untried wombs."

West shot me a puzzled look. "Have you compared the wound in Mrs. Williams's neck with the sword found by her body, Hargate?"

"I have." The doctor's chin rose pugnaciously. "And is that weapon Lord Portreath's cavalry sabre?"

"But this is absurd!" Hargate declared. "Lord Portreath should never kill his own . . . *relation*. He gave every appearance of valuing Mrs. Williams highly."

"Recollect that Mrs. Williams was attired as Cleopatra," I said. "As was Portreath's wife."

"If you would suggest the Viscount meant to murder her ladyship . . ." Hargate paused, his countenance choleric. "But he should never confuse the two. The Viscountess is confined to a basket-chair!"

I glanced at West, who nodded slightly. "As to that, Dr. Hargate, I fear I must enlighten you. When she chuses, Lady Portreath is quite able to walk . . ."

28

A DISH OF MILK, AND OF TEA

Tuesday, 4th June, 1816
Cheltenham, cont'd.

West escorted me to Mrs. Potter's, but of course he was merely bent upon his own rooms at the same time—the York Hotel being directly adjacent. I stood a moment on the paving before the boardinghouse as he bent over my hand, and said: "Is there a way to access the stable yard, West—or even the mews—from your hotel?"

His eyes narrowed speculatively. I apprehended that half his interest in me lay in my power to surprize him. "Without walking around the building, you would mean? Of course. Through the coffee room."

"Come with me," I said.

He stood back to allow me entrance to the York's lobby, then offered his arm. I slipped my hand through it, and was ushered into the hotel with all the pomp of a wife or mistress. If I found this amusing, I betrayed no hint of inner mirth, but held it close for later appraisal. West swept me into the coffee room and raised his hand to the manservant.

"Tea for the lady," he said, "and some Naples biscuit. I must just step into the yard and see that my horse is comfortably stabled."

"Of course, sir." The fellow bowed and left the room.

"You have no horse," I whispered to West. He had hired one along with his curricle.

"No more I do. What do you want with the mews, Jane?"

I drew a breath. "Rats. I intended to look for dead ones. And a possible agent of their demise."

"I doubt the ostlers leave dead vermin strewn about the yard. The York is not a coaching inn—but any number of private coaches arrive here, and the ladies within them cannot be handed down into—"

"Yes, yes," I said impatiently. "I intended to *speak* to someone about the rats. But this was all very much of a plan formulated on the fly, West, and I have not fully arrived at the details—"

"Drink your tea," he advised. "A woman interrogating the ostlers will provoke comment. In the case of poison, comment is ill-advised."

He exited the coffee room by a side door just as the serving-man reappeared with a tray of tea, two cups, a waste vessel, sugar, and a pitcher of cream. "We have no Naples biscuit," he advised, "but the cheese straws are excellent."

I thanked him, and waited for the tea to steep.

I had just lifted the pot to pour out my cup, when the door to the stable yard opened, and West slipped inside.

"Pellew was correct; you are a witch," he said as he settled into his chair. "A clairvoyant. A reader of runes."

I leant towards him. "Tell me."

"Of late the ostlers have found a number of dead rats lying

each morning in the mews. They have also discovered a dish of milk, set out not far from Mrs. Potter's back door and only a few yards from the perimeter of the stables. A dead rat being noticed beside it again this morning, the ostlers assume the milk is bait—and poisoned."

I glanced surreptitiously over my shoulder, but at this hour the coffee room was deserted, and no one overlistened our conversation. "Where is the milk now?"

"The ostlers left it. They believe it to belong to Mrs. Potter, and thought it none of their concern. Have you reason to doubt their judgement?"

"Yes." I handed West his empty tea cup. "We require a sample of that poisoned milk. I should be infinitely obliged if you could fetch it, West, and take it immediately to Dr. Hargate."

WHEN I ENCOUNTERED GRANVILLE, Viscount Portreath, upon my return to Mrs. Potter's, I could not help but regard him as altered from the bored nobleman he had formerly appeared to be. It was possible that Louisa Williams's brutal murder had shattered his complacency, and that the loss to his self-possession was writ on his face; or that from knowing more of his past, and how he had come into his title, I discerned a leashed violence in his looks and manner that I had previously set down to the careless privilege of aristocracy. Certainly in my own coolness upon greeting him there was nothing of the sympathy I had originally felt for his loss. I suspected him of too much, to be entirely susceptible to his air of suppressed grief.

He was seated, to my surprize, before the common sitting-room's writing desk, penning a note he might just as easily have written in his rooms at the York Hotel, or at one of the admirable little tables that establishment scattered about the saloon where Cassandra and I had taken tea with Mrs. Williams but a few days before. More surprising still was the fact that Miss Fox and Lady Portreath were seated near the sitting-room fire, companionably sharing a tea tray. I had not known them to abandon their private parlour for such a publick display before.

"Good morning," I murmured politely as I drew off my gloves. "My lord, my lady. Miss Fox."

Apparently, my appearance startled the party, because the Viscountess jerked a little in her basket-chair, and her tea spilled over her cup. She had been in the act of raising it to her lips, and held the saucer in her left hand; the hot liquid splashed the silk of her gown, and she cried out a little, before biting her lip.

Lord Portreath turned to glance at her. "What have you done, Rose?"

She set the cup in its saucer with a shaking hand, sloshing more of it still, then replaced both on the tea tray. "Scalded myself, of course. My nerves are torn to shreds. Sarah, look how I have ruined this silk! Fetch something to blot it, quickly!"

An ugly damp stain marred the deep pink cloth over her knees. Miss Fox rose immediately and hastened into the private parlour adjacent, while her ladyship picked at the sodden silk with an expression of distaste.

"Allow me." The Viscount rose from the writing table and drew a handkerchief from his coat.

Lady Portreath grasped it without a glance or word of thanks, and pressed it against her knees. Then, with a sharply-indrawn breath, she hissed, "How foolish. The flesh beneath is sensitive to the touch, and I have only caused it to pain me further. Miss Austen, would you wheel me into my rooms? I must change this gown for another, or be *completely* wretched."

"I shall do it," the Viscount said, with an edge of impatience, but his lady raised her hand.

"You have your letter to finish. Do I not know that it regards *her* death? You cannot conclude it soon enough! Miss Austen—"

I had no real desire to waste my flagging strength on shifting the basket-chair, but as hysterics threatened, and I disliked such scenes far more than personal weariness, I steered her ladyship into the private parlour. There was a little jostling over the threshold, and she hissed in discomfort, but forbore to rain vituperation on my head. Miss Fox appearing from the bedchamber, cloth in hand, I explained what was wanted. An expression of concern immediately suffused her countenance.

"Poor Rose. I hope the burn is not *too* severe," she said with sympathy, and took command of my charge.

I reemerged to find Lord Portreath pouring out his own tea. With a level look, he enquired if I should like a cup. An invitation to take tea with a viscount! And one, moreover, whom I suspected of murder!

"Very much," I told him cordially. "I shall just step upstairs and remove my cloak."

The gentleman was still standing when I reappeared in the sitting-room, and waited politely until I had seated myself opposite the two ladies' empty chairs. A fresh cup of tea steamed before each of their places.

"I ought to pour out for *you*, my lord."

"You regard it as beneath my dignity to take up a teapot?" he returned, as he selected a clean cup. "I have been used to drinking wretched coffee boiled over an open fire, from a tin flask, and sleeping in my saddle-roll. Do not be thinking me too elegant for the necessary tasks of life, Miss Austen. Every civilized being is at base a savage. Do you take sugar? Cream?"

"Neither. You remind me, sir, of my brothers in the Royal Navy. However polished their manners when forced into Society, they are equally capable of standing watch at the wheel in the midst of a hurricane. Indeed, I suspect they prefer it."

"Exactly so." He handed me the cup of black Bohea. "Our Captain Pellew is just such another, I do not doubt."

I watched the Viscount pour himself some tea; smiled benignly at him as he added a trifling quantity of milk; and only after he raised the cup to his lips and I observed him to actually *swallow*, did I consent to sip my own Bohea in turn. One must be on one's guard when sitting down with a potential poisoner. The Viscount being little inclined to conversation and the tea scalding, I was content to pass a silent interval allowing it to cool, while her ladyship changed her dress. Miss Fox being accustomed to assist in this exercise several times each day, the two ladies were soon returning.

"What is that you say, Granville? Of what are you speaking to Miss Austen? Do not pretend to admire the Captain; I know him for your enemy."

Lady Portreath rolled up to the tea-table with Miss Fox. Her expression was stormy, her pink gown discarded for one of pale blue. "Do not pretend you have not taken Pellew in the deepest dislike!"

The Viscount looked surprized. "I can name no reason for hating the man." He handed his wife her tea.

"There is every reason in the world!" Her ladyship's blue eyes flashed with anger, and her teeth were bared unbecomingly, like a cat about to spit. "He has stood in your path at every turn, and thwarted your attempts to master me! He is my champion when you would see me into my grave!"

"Nonsense."

She reached for the sugar bowl and added a spoonful. "Sarah knows it to be true. But for Captain Pellew, I should have been bundled back to Cornwall days ago."

"I would to God you had," Portreath muttered. "Then we should never have attempted that senseless masquerade, and Louisa might still be living."

"Aye!" Colour flamed up in her ladyship's cheeks. "You may well be tortured by what might have been. Was it you, Granville, who told her to ape my costume? —So that she might display to advantage before all the world, and take the shine out of your wife? Did you think I should suffer a humiliation, *folded into my chair,* as you put it, while you danced with the *first Cleopatra?* It must have been a shock when you murdered the wrong woman!"

With a clatter, Miss Fox dropped her cup from nerveless fingers. The pottery smashed on the table before us.

"Lord, Sarah, how can you be so *stupid?*" her ladyship cried. A puddle of tea welled across the table.

With a flurry, the Viscount, Miss Fox and I hastened to avert catastrophe. Miss Fox carried the tea tray to the writing desk; the Viscount mopped with his handkerchief at the spilled tea; I carefully collected the fragments of Staffordshire china.

Miss Fox's countenance was remarkably pale, and for an instant I wondered at it—before recollecting that Lady Portreath had actually accused her husband of murder. However little Sarah Fox admired the Viscount, such vehement words—uttered without the slightest apparent provocation— could not help but shock the most hardened listener. I turned back to the table and saw that Lord Portreath had abandoned it to stand, as was his habit, in the bow window and gaze down upon the rainy High Street. His compact form was rigid with suppressed outrage.

Abruptly, he turned and tossed his sodden square of linen in the midst of the spoiled tea tray. "I have changed my mind, Rose," he said. "I no longer wish for your company on my return to Cornwall. Indeed, I do not wish for your company ever again. Go your own way to London with such friends as you still possess. I take my leave of you—and hope never to see you again."

He bowed into the stunned silence, and quitted the room.

Miss Fox sank down into her chair and heaved an uneven sigh.

"Sarah," the Viscountess said. "You look utterly spent. You have taken nothing all day. Have my tea—I do not want it, I assure you."

Miss Fox took a sip of the proffered cup and grimaced.

"Poor lamb." Her ladyship pressed a hand to her mouth and laughed a little. "I forgot that it was sugared. I know how much you hate it!"

MUCH LATER—AFTER A WALK with Cassandra to the post office in hope of some news of our brother Charles, only to be disappointed; after Mrs. Potter's dinner of rabbit pie, without either Hannah Vyvyan or Captain Pellew to distract us from the Garthwaites' dispiriting conversation; after Cassandra's reading of *Guy Mannering* and the noise of the Captain's return from the theatre, whither he had gone alone to enjoy *Catherine and Petruchio*—I lay wakeful in bed, listening to the bells of St. Mary's toll the hours. The pain in my back had returned to plague me, and I felt an unwelcome touch of fever; nothing very extraordinary after the tumult of the past two days, but unpleasant all the same.

The bells had tolled two, and I was listening for the quarter-chime from Mrs. Potter's mantel-clock, when a blood-curdling scream sent me bolt upright in my bed.

"Jane!" Beside me, I caught the dim outline of Cassandra raised up on her elbows. I reached for my bed-candle and moved hurriedly to the hearth, where a few coals still glowed red. Reaching for a taper, I lit it in the fire and then in turn lit the candle. Raising it aloft, I stood listening.

The scream had turned to a wretched sobbing.

I unlatched our bedchamber door and peered out.

At the far end of the passage, Captain Pellew limped into view. Across the hall, Miss Garthwaite's door creaked open.

Hannah Vyvan stepped into the hallway, her candle raised. "Harry! What can it be?" she cried.

"The Viscountess," he said, and limped past her.

We turned as one, and followed him, a party of women in hastily-donned dressing gowns.

As I reached the bottom of the stairs, I saw the door to the private parlour flung open and light spilling into the darkened sitting-room. Captain Pellew's outline was black against the opening.

"Oh, God, Pellew," a voice cried. "Help me—*help me!*"

"What is it, my lady?"

"Sarah," said Rose Williams, more frantic than I had ever heard her. "She is dead, Pellew—*dead.*"

29

THE VISCOUNT'S AFFAIRS

Wednesday, 5th June, 1816
Cheltenham

An inquest over the body of Louisa Williams, widow of Aloysius Williams of Penzance, was held at two o'clock before William Trigg, Gentleman Coroner of this county of Gloucester, at the Eight Bells in Church Street.[7]

A jury of twelve men—solid Cheltenham tradesmen and prosperous farmers, by their dress and looks—was empaneled at Mr. Trigg's direction. Those of us determined to witness the proceedings were ranged closely upon hard wooden benches—Raphael West and Dinsdale to my right, Captain Pellew and Hannah Vyvyan on my left.

My sister Cassandra had elected to remain behind at Mrs. Potter's and tend Lady Portreath. Doctor Hargate had administered laudanum to the Viscountess, and in her weakened

---

7 William Trigg, Gentleman Coroner, appears repeatedly in reports of inquests printed during this period in the *Gloucester Journal*. He was appointed by and in the employ of the Gloucester courts, which governed the prosecution of crime through Gloucestershire, including Cheltenham. He frequently used the Eight Bells in Cheltenham for inquests.—*Editor's note.*

physical condition, the dose had taken strong effect. She had subsided into a state of insensibility, tucked up in her bed, with only my sister's vigilance against the evil that had struck down her intimates.

"All rise!" bellowed a florid young man in a dark green worsted suit—the coroner's clerk, I presumed.

With a creaking and shuffling of benches, we submitted—a crowd of a few dozen persons concerned in the lady's death. Lord Portreath, I observed, was at the front of the room with a manservant in attendance. He appeared pale but composed, and irreproachably the mourner in a suit of densest black. His sanguine air surprized me; but I supposed he had been schooled from birth to betray neither anguish nor fear.

Mr. Trigg making his entrance, he held aloft a testament and administered the jury's oath. Duly sworn, the unfortunate fellows were ushered into the publican's coffee room, where all that remained of Louisa Williams was shrouded upon a pair of trestles. An intervening door prevented the rest of us from viewing the body, thank Heaven; the countenances of the panel members were sickly enough as they reassembled near the coroner's desk.

Doctor Hargate was also established on the front bench. I studied his ravaged countenance with sympathy; he deserves a period of rest and reflection after all he has endured—in Bath, perhaps.

Mr. Potter had grossly disturbed the poor man's sleep last night, as I well knew, at half-past two o'clock in the morning. The physician had materialised in our sitting-room a quarter-hour later, and examined the body of Sarah Fox—which in its

death throes was not discernibly different from Thucydides
the pug. She had been repeatedly and vilely ill, Lady Portreath explained, a little after midnight. Her ladyship had
rung for Lucy, who was already abed and appeared in her
night-rail, with her hair down her back. The Viscountess
demanded weak tea for the sufferer, and some Naples biscuit.
She had not thought it necessary to send for the doctor—and
for a time, Miss Fox's stomach troubles subsided, tho' she
remained in a feverish state. She took a few sips of tea from
a spoon—administered by Lucy, who also carried away the
chamber-pot—and appeared a little quieter. It was possible,
Lady Portreath admitted, that she herself had dozed.

She was awakened an hour or so later by Miss Fox's violent
dying. The scene had reduced the Viscountess to a pitiable
state.

At his arrival, Doctor Hargate first attended to her ladyship—dosing her with tincture of laudanum and seeing her
returned to her bed under Mrs. Potter's eye. He had then
made a cursory examination of Miss Fox's corpse, saw it lifted
onto the empty bed in that young woman's chamber, and
covered it with one of Mrs. Potter's sheets.

I was tempted to enquire whether Hargate believed Miss
Fox, like Thucydides, to have hunted down and devoured a
poisoned rat—but with a murderer in our midst, it seemed
unwise to reveal the trend of my thoughts. For his part,
Hargate shared nothing of his conclusions with those of us
assembled anxiously in the sitting-room, but his looks were
grim.

"I shall send a carter to convey the body to my surgery as

soon as it is light," he told Mrs. Potter as he handed her the tincture of laudanum. "See that her ladyship is dosed with another five drops when she awakes. You may wish to hire a professional nurse for her care—but that, of course, is a decision for her husband. I will leave word for him at the York of what has occurred."

Tho' Cassandra and I returned to our room once the disturbance was at an end, I do not think either of us slept. I was too busy revolving events in my mind, while Cass was engaged in planning our immediate removal from Mrs. Potter's house.

"The *Cheltenham Guide* informs me there are over a hundred such lodging-places in the town," she observed. "I cannot believe that people expire in *all* of them."

At first light I penned a brief note for Raphael West, with the news of Sarah Fox's death, and begged Lucy to convey it to the York. He returned a reply that he should be happy to escort Cassandra and me to the Royal Well after breakfast—and would wait on us at ten o'clock.

I was happy to take his arm for the interval of the Elm Walk, but declined to drink the waters.

"There have been enough inadvertent poisonings of late," I told him, as Cassandra grimaced over her glass.

"Sarah Fox was hardly murdered by a well," he replied.

"Nor by Mrs. Potter's rabbit pie, which each of us consumed. I cannot believe she drank from a dish of arsenic milk, left as bait for a rat. She appears," I added, "to have died just as Thucydides did—from a treat intended for another."

"Rose Williams?" West asked.

I nodded. "In this case, tea. Granville Basset poured it out for his wife. But Sarah Fox drank it."

Now, in the Eight Bells, a member of the private fire brigade was sworn in and duly told William Trigg, Gentleman Coroner, how he was summoned to the Assembly Rooms Monday night—or rather, in the first hour of Tuesday morning—to douse the ballroom flames. He had paused in working the hoses to collect himself, coughing against clouds of smoke—"and in looking down, your worship, I saw the water at my feet run red."

He had put down his hose and followed the blood to its source: "A lady on the floor in fancy dress, appearing like an 'eathen, and her head near cut off."

Mr. Trigg demanding if a weapon was found, the brigade-man assented. "A sword there was, on the floor beside her, and its blade dripping with blood."

Gasps and murmurs from the attentive crowd.

"Was the hilt in her hand?"

The brigade-man: "No, your worship. It lay a bit away from the lady. Off her port bow."

"The brigade-man," Captain Pellew whispered, "appears to have served in the Royal Navy."

"What did you then?" Trigg demanded.

"Told my brigade-chief as I'd found a dead 'un."

Trigg thanked the man, who stood down. Dr. Hargate was then summoned, and sworn to his oath.

I had witnessed a number of inquests, and knew how such proceedings unfolded. Hargate must speak to his examination of the body, and the nature of Louisa Williams's wound—whether the flesh was yet warm, and the blood still flowing.

"Do you consider it likely Deceased inflicted grievous harm upon herself, in an instant of insanity?" Trigg demanded.

"I should consider it impossible," the doctor replied. "The wound is a single slashing cut from ear-to-ear, such as a cavalry officer might deliver in mid-charge; nothing like the injury a woman should deal herself. Moreover, from callouses on the fingers, I should adjudge Deceased to have been right-handed, and the sword was flung down on the left side of the body."

He had only to attest that the blow was delivered not long before the body's discovery—in the very midst of the fire's chaos—to be done with the coroner.

No one had made mention of Miss Vyvyan's bells. It was possible, I thought, that the brigade-man had regarded them as part of the "heathen" costume, and being unlikely to cause a vicious wound, had dismissed them from his testimony. I glanced over at the lady seated beyond Pellew, and saw that her gloved hand was firmly clasped in his.

Granville, Viscount Portreath, was next summoned.

He swore his oath with an air of gravity, his gaze unwavering. He described Louisa Williams as his wife's relation, a dependent in his household, and concerned for the welfare of his wife, who had lately been taking a course of waters for her health in Cheltenham.

"You have recently taken rooms at Sheldon's York Hotel?"

"So recently as Saturday last."

"But your lady wife is lodged at an adjacent boardinghouse, while Mrs. Williams was also at the York?"

There were murmurs among the spectators.

"She is. Viscountess Portreath arrived in Cheltenham in advance of ourselves, in the company of her acquaintance."

Trigg stared narrowly at the quarto volume in which he inscribed his notations. "The acquaintance being one Sarah Fox, spinster, of Portreath?"

"That is correct."

"—Who expired in the small hours of this morning, from grievous bodily illness?"

"That is also correct," the Viscount replied.

"My lord," Trigg enquired, with an air of suppressed triumph, "did you attend the masquerade ball mounted at Cheltenham Assembly Rooms on the Monday instant?"

"I did."

"And was Deceased also in attendance?"

"She was. I escorted her to the ball that evening."

"My lord, in what character did you appear?"

Portreath hesitated, but then said, with a lift of his chin, "As the Duke of Wellington."

Trigg displayed a sword with delicate fingertips. "Do you recognise this weapon, my lord?"

"I do. It is my cavalry sabre, which I carried during my campaigns in the Peninsula with the Seventh Light Dragoons."

"Why is it not at present in your possession, sir?"

"It was lost during the confusion of the fire at the Assembly Rooms on Monday."

Trigg frowned. "Lost?"

"I wore the sabre as part of my masquerade dress."

"Was it not hanging in its scabbard, on your sword-belt?"

"It was. I drew the weapon to exhibit it to my acquaintance."

"Your acquaintance? —I believe you are a stranger to Cheltenham, sir?"

"Yes—I displayed the blade to a few couples, friends of Viscountess Portreath."

"And was Deceased among the party?"

"She was." The Viscount's voice faltered a trifle, then resumed. "Some few moments later, the crowd pressing close upon me as it surged towards the ballroom to witness the illumination exhibition, I was jostled so severely that I dropped the sabre. The same crowd prevented me from turning back to retrieve it."

"You *dropped* your sabre, sir?" Trigg's voice was disbelieving. "How many years did you serve under Wellington?"

"Four."

"And was it not commonplace to be jostled in the midst of a cavalry charge?"

"Of course. But I was generally mounted—"

"Did you ever drop your weapon in combat?"

Portreath's lips tightened and a muscle pulsed on the right side of his jaw; but if he was offended by the question, he kept a stiff rein on his temper. "The cases are not the same. One does not go to war in a ballroom."

"Indeed," Trigg said. "But for the fact that on Monday instant, someone did. Could you relate for the benefit of this panel, my lord, your sentiments towards Deceased?"

"Sentiments?"

"Your opinion—your degree of regard—your animosity, if such applies?"

"I felt no animosity towards Mrs. Williams. Quite the reverse. We were on the greatest terms of intimacy and admiration."

"—Tho' you are married to another, sir, and had come into Cheltenham to join her?"

Portreath, stiffly: "My domestic affairs are none of your concern, sir."

"On the contrary," Trigg retorted, "at present they are my concern above anyone else's in the Kingdom, sir."

It remained only for the coroner to recall Dr. Hargate, to hear his sworn testimony—that Louisa Williams's throat gave every appearance of having been cut by his lordship's sabre—for the inquest to be done.

Within a quarter of an hour, Trigg's panel returned their verdict: Willful Murder, against Granville Basset.

30

A WINNING BEDSIDE MANNER

Wednesday, 5th June, 1816
Cheltenham, cont'd.

"**B**ut what of Sarah Fox?" Hannah Vyvyan demanded, as we walked together with Pellew and West back towards Mrs. Potter's. "Will an inquest be held over her body as well?"

"Tomorrow, I should imagine," West told her. "Hargate will have requested time to examine the remains. If, as Miss Austen believes, her tea was poisoned . . ."

Miss Vyvyan exclaiming a little, I related what I had witnessed yesterday in the sitting-room.

"Lady Portreath spilled her tea on her gown. Miss Fox quitted the party for her rooms in search of a blotting-cloth, but her ladyship feeling the need for a change of dress, asked that I push her basket-chair into her bedchamber. I was gone but a moment from the sitting-room, but upon my return, discovered that Lord Portreath had poured out two fresh cups of tea, and placed them before the ladies' respective chairs."

"You think he poisoned Miss Fox's?" Pellew demanded. "But why?"

"I suspect it was his wife's tea he meant to spoil," I said. "There was, however, an unexpected turn to the conversation—and Miss Fox being startled and dismayed, she dropped her cup, smashing it. When we had done tidying the mess, her ladyship offered Miss Fox *her* tea as consolation. Miss Fox drank it."

"I have rarely known Miss Fox clumsy," Hannah Vyvyan mused. Her quick wits, I perceived, kept pace with my own. "What startled her so?"

"Lady Portreath." I gave a small sigh. "She had just accused her husband of killing the wrong Cleopatra."

"But why should that disturb her?" Miss Vyvyan stopped short on the paving. "It is what Miss Fox has been asserting for days—that Lord Portreath wished to be rid of his wife, and that her life was in danger. Why should she be so amazed at the idea of murder, as to drop her teacup?"

I halted beside Miss Vyvyan, and stood an instant in thought. As I listened to Lady Portreath yesterday, I assumed that one part of her conversation was more startling than all the rest. But what if Sarah Fox heard the conversation differently? I forced my mind to retreat to the scene in the sitting-room, and review what had been said; and suddenly, I understood it all.

"Hannah," I said, "did Louisa Williams obtain her Cleopatra dress from your theatre stores?"

"She did not—I should never assign the same character to a pair of women so likely to encounter each other! I suspect Mrs. Williams devised the costume herself, and consulted a milliner in town."

"But *why* should Mrs. Williams ape her stepdaughter's character? Lady Portreath accused her husband of urging it, on purpose to embarrass her—as he certainly attempted to do, when they met in the Assembly supper room. And yet . . ."

"He appeared entirely surprized when he saw Lady Portreath Monday night," Hannah said.

I gripped her arm. "Thank you, Hannah. You have roused my faculties wonderfully."

My sister Cassandra emerged from her ladyship's room as our party disposed ourselves around the sitting-room fire. The Garthwaites having come up with us on the paving outside the boardinghouse, having also attended the inquest, the sopha and chairs were as full as they could hold. It being Wednesday, and the theatre dark, Miss Vyvyan was not required at her duties, and Captain Pellew seemed more than content to remain in her company. Mr. West was similarly disinclined to part with mine.

"How are you, Cass?" I enquired of my sister, who appeared fatigued. "And how is your charge?"

"She is awake," she returned in a lowered tone. "I do not know what I am to do, Jane—whether more laudanum is to be administered. Is Dr. Hargate likely to call?"

"I cannot say," I told her. "He is grossly encumbered with corpses at the moment. Is Lady Portreath sensible? Or is she still prone to hysterics?"

"At present she is calm. But I am not a nurse, and cannot feel easy in my judgement of circumstances."

"No, indeed." Dr. Hargate had advised the hiring of a

nurse, but had said the decision was Lord Portreath's—but all decision was beyond that gentleman's power at present. "The Viscount is under charge of murder."

Cass gasped, and glanced involuntarily over her shoulder at her ladyship's closed door. "How dreadful! Poor Lady Portreath has had the narrowest of escapes!"

Mrs. Potter appeared in the sitting-room doorway, her countenance wearier and more oppressed than I had ever seen it. "I've set out a nuncheon in the dining parlour. Cold ham and cheese, and bread and porter, if you've an appetite— although I daresay as none of you will wish to touch a bite from my kitchen, what with Miss Fox lying cold."

Miss Garthwaite's voice overpowered my own. "You will be pleased to know, Mrs. Potter, that my brother and I are happy to sit down to your table. We intend to remain your lodgers. We are not to change our rooms after all. You behold us reassured by the course of justice. Viscount Portreath is even now in the hands of constables, and will be conveyed to the gaol at Gloucester, to await the Quarter Sessions in August."

Her words were loud enough to penetrate to the private parlour and the bedchamber beyond.

"What is that you say?" a faint voice cried. "What has happened to my husband? Pellew—I wish to come out!"

The Captain reached for his stick, and would have got to his feet, but I held out my hand.

"Let me," I said. "I should like to speak with her ladyship."

I ENTERED THE PRIVATE parlour and found it as my sister had left it: an oil lamp burning low against the grey light of the sodden June day, and the basket-chair abandoned near the coals of a small fire. Cassandra had been reading: *Guy Mannering* sat on the chair she must have occupied all morning, with a length of red embroidery silk trailing from the pages as a bookmark.

The door to the adjoining bedchamber was ajar. A single lit candle on the side table cast a warm glow over Rose Williams's countenance. She turned her head on the pillow to glare at me as I stood in the doorway.

"I don't want you. Where's Pellew?"

"Otherwise engaged. You require some assistance, I collect?"

She raised herself slightly against the bed-cushions. For the first time since we met, her golden curls were loose and frowsy, her appearance unkempt. Her eyes glittered feverishly—several doses of laudanum on an empty stomach will inflame the senses. "What has happened to Portreath?"

"He has been charged with the murder of your stepmother, and taken to Gloucester Gaol."

"Divine intercession," she whispered.

"I hardly think so."

She frowned, and her fingers plucked irritably at the coverlet. "I wish to get up."

"Pray, do! Nothing prevents you."

"That is a vicious taunt, to one as ill as I."

"But no more than the truth. I am resolved to say nothing that might be construed as fiction, your ladyship, for the remainder of our acquaintance—however short it may be. Item the first: I have twice seen you walk past my doorstep in the dead of night, tho' you are never glimpsed on your feet in daytime."

"That is a lie."

"Item the second: You quitted your bed and your chair in order to leave love poems under Captain Pellew's door—purely as an excuse, in the event you were discovered in your *true* errand: discarding dead rats outside Mr. Garthwaite's room."

She uttered a faint bark of laughter. "Absurd! Why should I?"

"Because you hoped he would bring them to our general attention—where another guest might simply have reported the vermin to Mrs. Potter. Garthwaite, being of a melancholy disposition and inclined to read doom in the slightest portent, was ideally suited for a sinister interpretation. You hoped to deepen your fellow-lodgers' fear of a murderous evil at work."

"You are mad," her ladyship said flatly. "Where should I find dead rats?"

"In the area behind Sheldon's York Hotel, immediately adjacent. You left a dish of milk there, tainted with some of the arsenic you brought from Cornwall. Mr. Garthwaite informs me that arsenic is one of the metals mined in your late father's pits, everywhere available in your home country. Our housemaid Lucy believed Mrs. Potter baited the rats; but the good woman denied doing so. Her apothecary agrees."

She smiled at me disdainfully, completely unmoved by my words. "Even supposing I could walk—why do such a ludicrous thing?"

"To test the strength of your poison. You planned to take

a little yourself, in order to throw suspicion on your husband; but you did not wish to *die*, after all."

"I have never been sickened," she retorted, "because I take little food or drink. That is a glaring fault in your lies."

"—A fact you turned to advantage. Arsenic is most often ingested. Your refusal to eat provided a convenient blind: others should suffer from poison intended for *you*. Dusting white arsenic on the Viscount's macaroons—then sending them to us at breakfast—was your first attempt. Had we eaten one, we should have been slightly sickened. Poor Thucydides, however, was mortally affected. That was when you decided to calibrate your dose on the rats."

There was a slight sound behind my back, as of a snort indignantly stifled; but Rose Williams did not hear it. *Miss Garthwaite*, I thought; and hurriedly continued.

"Your plan was to throw suspicion on Lord Portreath, to strengthen your claim for legal control of your fortune once you had separated from your husband. But Thucydides's death gave you another—and far more devilish—idea. *What if the Viscount were actually charged with murder?* It need not be *your* murder, after all, but someone he was presumed to have mistaken for yourself."

"As he did." Her ladyship had thrust herself upright again, her weight resting on her bent arms. Her bright blue gaze bore into mine. "You know Portreath should never have killed Louisa on purpose; it was *I* whose throat he believed he slashed, in the confusion of the fire."

It was the first hint that the Viscountess closely followed my reasoning. Encouraged, I went on.

"Louisa was critical to your plan, was she not? To rid yourself of Portreath was merely half the problem; for the entire control of your fortune and complete freedom, Louisa must also be dispatched. How ingenious, then, to have Portreath hang for her murder!"

There was an instant's silence. Then Lady Portreath lifted her voice and cried, "Pellew! Come at once! There is a madwoman here, spouting nonsense—and I will not be disturbed any longer!"

"You might have succeeded in your object," I said, "had you stopped there, Lady Portreath. Had you planned a trifle more wisely or acted less rashly. But opportunity was afforded you—and you seized it. I speak, of course, of the Assembly fire."

I felt someone move near the door behind me. All the lodgers were collecting there—Miss Garthwaite, her brother, Cassandra, and Pellew. Miss Vyvyan no doubt, and Raphael West with Mrs. Potter behind. I did not betray that I was aware of their presence; it was vital to keep the half-feverish Rose suspended in her daydream.

"As the masquerade revelers surged from the supper room to the ballroom at midnight to view the illuminations," I said calmly, "the Viscount's sabre was raised high above their heads. I saw it myself. Your basket-chair, pushed by Miss Fox, was well behind me. I suspect she rammed your chair into his lordship, perhaps by accident or the force of the crowd. He stumbled and nearly pitched headlong, dropping his weapon. I imagine you snatched it up as you moved forward . . . until the fire and smoke and general disorder provided a *different* opportunity."

She continued to stare at me wordlessly, as tho' I were nothing but the voice of conscience, repeating its charges in her mind; but her fingers were clenched on her coverlet. I slowly approached her bed and sat down on the edge, deliberately intimate.

"In the chaos that followed the fire, Miss Fox—being at the rear of the crowd—pulled your chair into the anteroom where the pavilion had stood, to prevent your being trampled. I think then she went in search of aid—a gentleman, perhaps, to carry the chair hastily from the building. She may have sent your stepmother to you—or perhaps Louisa Williams discovered you herself, and stayed by you in the anteroom until the crowd should disperse. In the dense cloud of smoke you seized your moment. You slashed her throat and dropped the sabre by her side."

Rose Williams laughed harshly, a noise with no joy in it. "I should have been covered in blood," she cried.

"If you were facing her, and seated in your chair, no doubt you would have been. But we have established that you are perfectly able to rise and stand. If Mrs. Williams was before you, her back turned, the thing is easily done. Reach around with a protective movement, as one woman should do to another in crisis—and strike."

Her eyes widened with false incredulity. Her teeth, I noticed, were small and pearly as a child's; milk teeth. In a grown woman they were jarring, and I suppressed a shudder. "But Sarah would have known!"

"Not at first. I imagine you pushed the chair a little out of the room as tho' desperate for rescue—and when Sarah returned, the smoke was so dense behind you she never thought to examine the place. You told her immediately that Louisa was gone—had abandoned you to the fire—had saved herself and left an invalid behind to die. Naturally, Sarah believed you. Until our tea party yesterday, when you betrayed yourself."

Her lips moved slowly, as tho' I held her in a trance. "What do you mean?"

"You startled Sarah, and she dropped and broke her cup. At first I believed it was your accusation of murder—you charged Lord Portreath with killing the wrong woman. But later, when I reconsidered your words, I perceived what disturbed your friend so. You demanded whether his lordship deliberately told Louisa to dress as Cleopatra—to humiliate you, by comparison, in the masquerade. I suspect Sarah knew that to be false. I suspect *you* ordered the costume—as a supposed kindness to Louisa, a stranger in Cheltenham—and had Sarah deliver it to the hotel. You *meant* to be confused for Louisa. That was the only way you could kill your stepmother and throw suspicion on the Viscount."

I leant closer and raised my voice. "That is why Sarah is dead. You put white arsenic in the sugar bowl and dosed your own tea before handing it to her. The rest of us, as you observed yourself, did not take sugar in ours."

For an instant she hesitated, and I feared I had misjudged. But then her hands darted out and clutched my throat in a furious grasp, so that my vision went black and gunpowder exploded in my mind. My constricted throat seared with pain, and I heard myself, dimly, choking, before strong hands clutched at her wrists and tore them from their hold.

I fell over on the bedclothes, gasping for air, my hands on my neck.

Beside me, West fought with Rose Williams, who bucked and surged beneath the bedclothes. He had one knee propped on her body and her arms forced back beside her head, but she screamed into his face with an animal ferocity.

"Good God! What is this?" Dr. Hargate said, shouldering between West and me, on his appointed rounds.

"Your murderer," West said grimly. "For the love of God, Hargate, summon a constable—and Pellew, fetch a rope!"

31

A PARTING OF THE WAYS

Monday, 10th June, 1816
Cheltenham

For the first and no doubt last time in my life, I received a mark of gratitude from a viscount.

Lord Portreath, on his release from Gloucester Gaol, took the trouble to return to Cheltenham before once more turning south into Cornwall, a far more solitary figure than he first appeared. His first act was to stride across the sitting-room to where I sat with my volume of *Belinda*, and to bend low over my hand.

"I am in your debt, ma'am," he said without preamble, "in a fashion I cannot hope to repay for the rest of my life. Consider me your servant—and name any reward in my power."

I studied him an instant in surprize, and then said, "There is nothing I require from you, sir, I assure you. But if you would like to perform some gesture of thanks—pray use your power on Miss Vyvyan's behalf. A word from you to her estranged guardian should do much to further her solicitors' suit, and wrest several years' unpaid allowance from that disgruntled gentleman."

"Consider it done," he replied, "tho' I cannot believe Hannah will welcome my interference in her affairs."

"You may find her softened," I said. "She is in love, and on the verge of a happy betrothal, and such circumstances alter everything. If I may press you one instant further, my lord— she remains in doubt of the author of your brother's death. Do you know who fired the errant shot that killed him?"

Granville Basset's eyes widened in surprize. "By what right do you ask that question, ma'am?"

"None at all," I said affably. "I merely thought that the sudden restoration of your hopes and future might encourage you to unburden yourself of a weight you have carried for half a decade."

"You are correct." He raised his head and gazed over me, at some faded memory. "It was my father, the previous viscount, who discharged his gun in error on the hunting field that day. The accident to his elder son—the loss of his heir—was impossible to publickly admit. But his private grief destroyed him. He died but a few months after, and I found myself the sole male survivor of a family devastated by misfortune."

I had suspected as much, once my understanding of Lady Portreath's motives for murder became clear. The sudden and surprising elevation of her husband to his title—her own enforced position as viscountess and prospective mother of sons—had precipitated her dangerous withdrawal from life, obsession with self-control, and mad determination to win her freedom at any cost. The death at the pheasant-shoot had cost any number of lives, it seemed, and no doubt encouraged Granville Basset to pursue a career of heedless dissipation for a time. I could hope that the loss of Louisa Williams—whom no doubt he had held dear—and the brutal reckoning that awaited his wife, might prove salutary to his future. A second attachment, perhaps—the happiness of a family—and the worthier effort of restoring Godrevy Manor to prosperity, are all the good fortune I could wish for him. He has been granted a reprieve—and must order his future life far differently.

The Viscount's ostensible reason for calling at Mrs. Potter's on Saturday was to order his wife's clothes to be packed up and conveyed to her prison cell, where she awaits the judgement of the August Quarter Sessions. Knowing her penchant for self-mortification, as well as her fierce desire for absolute freedom, I do not expect her to survive so long. I suspect she will refuse all sustenance, and swiftly cheat the hangman.

Miss Fox's effects his lordship presented to Mrs. Potter for her use and that of the maidservant Lucy; anything they do not need, they will pass on to the Society of Friends, for distribution among the poor.

Cassandra and I spent our remaining interval in Cheltenham happily enough, in taking the waters, trying the ices at Gunton's, escaping the rain over newsprint in comfortable chairs by the Reading Room fire. We heard, at long last, from my brother Charles in London—whose Admiralty Board acquitted him of negligence in *Phoenix's* foundering, to our profoundest relief and celebration. Cassandra and I gave thanks at St. Mary's, lighting a candle in memory of Charles's late Fanny, and looked forward to carrying the news to all our dear family on our return to Hampshire.

Saturday brought a second invitation to dine at the York Hotel, before the theatre Saturday night, in the company of Mr. West and Mr. Dinsdale (whose hands are healing admirably). Captain Pellew and Miss Vyvyan joined us in the private dining parlour—for Hannah is no longer to earn her wages in the theatre wings, schooling wayward misses in the management of their vowels.

I welcomed the diversion of so much joyous company, for I had been treated to my own disconcerting interview earlier that day—with Dr. Lionel Hargate.

He had sent round a note to Mrs. Potter's, delivered at Saturday morning's breakfast, and requested that I pay him the honour of a visit to his consulting room in Back Street. It would be as well if I came alone, he cautioned me. Cassandra being engrossed in a pattern of knitting intended for our brother Frank's latest infant, she paid me no attention when I told her I meant to take a brief airing.

I did not bother to ring the bell at Hargate's front entrance, but went directly to the surgery door off the side-passage. He opened at the first knock, his wig firmly in place and his attire correct, and gestured me to a seat. He took the one opposite.

"I will not trifle with your understanding, Miss Austen, which I have learnt to value and respect; nor will I stoop to the sort of deception so often visited upon females, out of deference for their sensibilities. You deserve to be treated to the truth—for it is obvious that you have pursued it with vigour throughout the course of your life."

"Thank you, sir. I am grateful for plain-speaking."

He eyed my countenance a moment. "You have been taking the waters, as I instructed."

"I have—tho' I admit they border on unpalatable."

"I suspect most of the dishes you have sampled of late have tasted like ashes."

I knit my brows. "You are correct. I have had little appetite in recent weeks."

"Does your back ache?"

Involuntarily, I placed my hands at the lower rear edge of my corset. "I may perhaps lace too tightly. But yes—"

"I note, also, that your skin appears increasingly tanned."

"No miraculous consequence of travelling in summer," I suggested

" But for the fact that there has been no sun. It has rained continuously, ma'am, and yet your complexion has sallowed and darkened, even in the brief period we have known each other."

I waited, wordlessly, for his pronouncement.

"I will not trifle with you. I judge that you are experiencing jaundice—a failing of the liver and kidneys—from the insidious working of disease in your blood. I suspect, moreover, that it is irreversible. I have no treatment to offer you, ma'am."

No attempt to soften the blow, or to cajole me into good humour with false hope. Hargate merely gazed at me with a faint spark of sympathy, his mouth set.

"How long?" I said.

"Six months—a year, perhaps."

For an instant, I could not draw breath. For an instant,

it was as tho' my heart had stopped. I closed my eyes, and a voice within me cried, *So little?*

I rose and offered the physician my hand. "You do me the honour, sir, of telling me the unvarnished truth; and for that, I am immeasurably grateful. I know now that I must cherish every day, and use each as wisely as I am allowed."

"The honour is mine, ma'am." He bowed, and showed me to the door.

I related nothing of the interview to Cassandra, but carried the knowledge like a stone beneath my heart.

THE EVENING AT THE theatre was everything that was delightful, and I could have flattered myself that a new spring of hope and promise would be offered me, from the clear enjoyment Raphael West appeared to gain from my company, and the tenderness with which he listened to my every word. As he parted from me on the threshold of the boardinghouse—Cassandra being engrossed in her farewells to Mr. Dinsdale—he said in a lowered tone, "Walk with me tomorrow, Jane, after morning service?"

"I should be happy," I said. And was restless for the remainder of the night, as Cassandra slept deep and dreamlessly in her neighbouring bed, in composing what I knew must be said.

I dressed with care once morning came. A gown that West had seen on several occasions before, but that hardly mattered. I looked at myself squarely in the glass of Mrs. Potter's bedroom, and saw what Hargate had seen. My visage was sallow. In places, it was darkened with unaccountable shadows and spots. Even the whites of my eyes appeared tea-stained, like an old dog's. The lower region of my back—directly over my kidneys—ached, tho' I had deliberately loosened my stays.

Cass and I walked through the cold rain to St. Mary's, and listened to Mr. Jervis's call for repentance on our knees; and as we quitted the ancient stone building, there was West standing a few yards from the entrance, his umbrella raised.

"My dear," I said to my sister, "go ahead without me. I should like an interval with my friend."

She inclined her head, smiled at West, and walked briskly towards the High without a backwards glance. I wondered what she expected: that I should return with intelligence of my betrothal? That she must feign a degree of joy, at a loss that should make her miserable? Cass has never lacked for delicacy or courage.

West held out his arm. "I could wish the Heavens had seen fit to provide a more suitable day, Jane, but it is immaterial. Where would you wish to promenade? The Elm Walk, or Montpellier Grounds?"

Anywhere will suffice, I thought, *so long as we breathe the same air for a time.* "Let it be the Elm Walk," I said; and as he led me in that direction, I went on: "Have you received any word from your daughter, sir?"

"I have," he said. "Charlotte is increasingly well, and found such news as I could convey of Miss Vyvyan, deeply engaging. She means to invite Hannah to visit her in Bath, and I am confident that the two ladies will renew their bonds of affection and mutual esteem. Of all the little matters you and I have undertaken during our time in Cheltenham, Miss Vyvyan's is the most satisfying."

"No more than Captain Pellew's," I added.

"A forthright man, who always knew his errand, and was confident in the outcome." West slowed to a halt, and turned towards me. "Jane, I am equally convinced of my purpose. You have long been the object of my hopes and wishes."

Had I, indeed? Had I owned West's heart these many months? Such exquisite felicity in the knowledge—and yet, how late it had come to me!

"You must know how ardently I admire and love you," he continued, his voice deepening with emotion. "Do I presume too much—or may I hope for a return of feeling? Will you do me the honour of becoming my wife?"

I released his arm, and grasped his gloved hand, my eyes filling with tears. "Too good, too earnest soul! You are deserving of every possible affection—and must know that you have owned my heart entirely these many months."

A smile suffused his countenance, and he let go of my hand to grasp my shoulder. "Jane—you make me the happiest of men."

I drew a deep breath, and felt my tears slip down my cheek. "But I cannot marry you, Raphael. I cannot consent to bring you a grief I now know to be inevitable. You have endured too much already, in seeing *one* wife laid in the grave. I will not force such a loss upon you, a second time."

His hand fell to his side. He stood as if stunned.

The rain pattered on the umbrella over our heads,

unceasing, relentless. Our breath steamed in the chilled air between us.

"What are you talking of?" he demanded, low and broken.

"I have seen Hargate—and he has seen me." I smiled at him faintly. "He gives me half a year. Perhaps twelve months."

"Impossible!" West cried. "You are—*young*—"

"I am not," I said with a tearful smile, the pain and the love too entwined for bearing, "and I am dying."

"No. I will not believe it." He suddenly strode on in the direction of the well, leaving me rooted on the gravel walk, staring after him. Then he wheeled abruptly and returned. "Hargate is a fool. It cannot be . . . Is it *true*, Jane?"

I nodded wordlessly.

"Oh, my darling." He dropped his umbrella at our feet, enfolded me in his arms, and kissed me.

I have never been kissed, to be sure, as West kissed me; and the flare of light and warmth that shot through my being might almost have given me hope. But when at last he released me, only to hold me close against his heart, I summoned the strength to say what had to be said.

"No," I told him, "I will *not* consent to spend what little time I have remaining in the world with you, so pray do not ask it of me. I will *not* consent to make your happiness into a death-bed vigil, for the sake of a few weeks of shared joy. Neither will I deprive my dearest sister of the office she will wish to perform—in guiding me out of this life, as she once led me into it."

"Jane—"

I stepped back resolutely, and looked candidly into his beautiful, dark eyes.

"I must return to Chawton, Raphael, and my family. But I will carry the knowledge of your love in my heart. It is the greatest gift anyone has ever bestowed."

His countenance set into rigid lines, the better to accept the blow. "It is your right, of course, to determine in what manner you wish to spend your remaining hours. But know this, Jane—if ever you change your mind—a word from you at any hour will suffice to summon me. My wishes and hopes will not alter."

He kissed the back of my gloved hand, tucked it into his arm, and conveyed me back to Mrs. Potter's in silence.

I SAID NOTHING OF all that passed to Cassandra; my heart was too full. She did not press me to reveal the substance of my conversation with West, or explain why we did not see each other again on Monday morning, as our trunk was taken by Potter's carter to the yard of the Eight Bells, to be strapped onto the back of our coach. I told her nothing of Dr. Hargate's judgement of my health; that should become obvious to her with time, and I saw no purpose in an early burden of grief.

The rain abated slightly as we bid farewell to Mrs. Potter, Hannah Vyvyan, and Captain Pellew—whose delight in the judgement of Charles's Admiralty Board was all that was sincere and heartfelt—and set off down the paving towards the Eight Bells.

"Only think how much we shall have to tell, when we have reached James and Mary in Steventon!" Cassandra observed.

And how much I shall have to conceal, I thought.

We passed the Assembly Rooms, where the odour of burnt

wood, soaked with rainwater, permeated the atmosphere. "How fortunate that the new Rooms are to be opened," my sister said, "and how much I should like to view them! Perhaps we might return, Jane, for an interval of rest in September— now that the anxiety of Charles's future is decided."

"You ought to consider inviting Mary," I suggested. "I do not think the waters entirely agree with me; but Mary is a glutton for them."

Cassandra sighed. "I do not think they agree with me, either. But I should not be averse to attending the theatre with Mr. Dinsdale again. Is everything in order between yourself and Mr. West, Jane?"

"Perfectly," I said. "He will live in my memory as the most amiable gentleman I have ever known, and the most worthy of esteem and affection."

"Is that *all?*" Cassandra demanded.

I smiled at her as I stepped up into the travelling-coach. "For now, my dear—it must be enough."

AFTERWORD

The Year Without a Summer, 1816, has echoed through the two centuries since as a period of abrupt climate change, crop failure, and global famine. It brought us one great work of literature at least—Mary Shelley's *Frankenstein*, written during this horrid season when she travelled through a sodden Europe with George, Lord Byron, and her future husband, Percy Bysshe Shelley, at the age of eighteen. It was also the period when Jane Austen spent a fortnight at Cheltenham Spa, in an effort to improve her health.

Little is known of Jane's time in Gloucestershire because her usual correspondent and recipient of her vivid descriptions—Cassandra—accompanied her to the spa. A few possible details emerge from a letter Jane later wrote to her sister in Cheltenham in September, 1816, when Cassandra returned to take the waters with her sister-in-law, Mary, and lodged at Mrs. Potter's boardinghouse in the High Street. (Letter No. 145, dated Sept. 8–9, 1816, in *Jane Austen's Letters*,

Deirdre Le Faye, editor: Oxford, Oxford University Press, 1995.)

An excellent study of English spa culture in the Regency era is *The English Spa, 1560–1815: A Social History*, by Phyllis Hembry. Most useful for my purposes as editor of this volume of Jane's reminiscences, however, was Carolyn S. Greet's article in the Jane Austen Society's Report for 2003, "Jane and Cassandra in Cheltenham" (*Collected Reports, 2001–2005*, Jane Austen Society, Hampshire, 2001). In addition to providing an excellent period map showing the location of the old Assembly Rooms, Potter's boardinghouse, Sheldon's York Hotel, and St. Mary's, Ms. Greet provides a summary of theatrical performances and their dates during Jane's stay, as well as a mention of the June 3, 1816, masquerade ball in honor of His Majesty's Birthday and Princess Charlotte's Late Nuptials. She made no mention, however, of an inconvenient conflagration or suspicious death of a Cleopatra.

The medical theory that the majority of a woman's health issues developed as a result of the influence of the "humours" of her uterus was prevalent at this time. As outlined in Janet Oppenheim's *Shattered Nerves: Doctors, Patients, and Depression in Victorian England* (New York: Oxford University Press, 1991), which also covers the earlier Regency period, an occasional female response to male governance of women's education, property, and reproductive lives was anorexia. Extreme self-control over diet was one method of denying control to others, particularly as anorexia resulted frequently in the cessation of menstrual cycles and the inability to conceive a child.

Addison's disease—also known as primary autoimmune adrenal insufficiency—was not recognized at the time of Jane's illness. It has been suggested by medical analysts as one possible diagnosis from the symptoms she outlined from 1816–17 in letters to her various family members. Pancreatic or liver cancer are also suggested. As I worked on this volume and researched Addison's, however, I became intrigued by the apparent sudden onset of the disease in Jane's case. A 2002 study by researchers at the National Institute of Child Health and Human Development (NICHD) found that women who experience early-onset menopause, or premature ovarian failure (POF), are *three hundred times* more likely than women in the general population to develop autoimmune destruction of the adrenal glands—or Addison's disease. Early-onset menopause is defined as occurring before the age of forty (https://www.nichd.nih.gov/newsroom/releases/ ovarian_failure, accessed 11/15/2020).

As always at the conclusion of a bout of fevered novel-writing, I am profoundly grateful to those who turn these pages into an actual book. Juliet Grames, my extraordinarily gifted editor at Soho Crime, has my deepest thanks; so, too, do the patient and exacting Rachel Kowal, copyeditor Rachel Field, and publicists Paul Oliver and Erica Loberg. Jane and I are indebted to you all. A final thanks to Rafe Sagalyn, who knows I owe him my writing life.

Stephanie Barron
Denver, Colorado